under the
blood red moon

under the
blood red moon

MINA HEPSEN

AVON

An Imprint of HarperCollins*Publishers*

HarperCollins books may be purchased for educational, business, or sales promotional use. For information please write: Special Markets Department, HarperCollins Publishers, 10 East 53rd Street, New York, NY 10022.

FIRST EDITION

Designed by Diahann Sturge

Library of Congress Cataloging-In-Publication Data
Hepsen, Mina, 1983–.
    Under the blood red moon / Mina Hepsen.—1st ed.
        p. cm.
    ISBN 978-0-06-137325-1
    1. Vampires—England—Fiction.   I. Title.
    PR9570.T873H478   2008
    823'.92—dc22   2008006889

08 09 10 11 12   OV/RRD   10 9 8 7 6 5 4 3 2 1

For Mom and Dad

acknowledgments

A great big thank you to Alexis Hurley, my friendagent (okay, I made up that word, but it's accurate). You believed in me when all I had was a manuscript in shambles and a crazy idea. *Mwah!*

A pretty *merci beaucoup* to my editor, May Chen, for tearing my work apart with the sweetest tongue and making it oh-so-much better, and to Carrie Feron, for having the foresight to make this happen.

A bagpipe-playing–kilt-wearing thank you to Emir, Blythe, Iain, Aileen, and Sara: the special people in Scotland who helped me celebrate when I found out this book was being published!

A humongous purple-and-pink-striped thank you to my family: my humanitarian sister, Sho (for warm chocolate-chip cakes and big-time editing help); my sneaky sister, Shmefy (the soon-to-be criminologist who gives me the greatest advice on how to kill off characters in my stories); my coffee buddy/cousin, Dido (the only person in the world that joins me in dancing like a fool to King Louis singing "I Wanna Be Like You"!); my artist cousin, Omer (for those big smiles and for being so damn talented—check out annanne.com); my cuddly cousin, Kerimi (for giving the hugest hugs and reminding me to "chill"); my uncle Amco (for a bottomless positive attitude); my aunt Gulgun Teyze (for sticking by me even when she knows I'm lost—hey we found the monument in the end, right?); my grandpa Dede Man (for that wonderfully infectious laugh); my beautiful mom (for holding my hand through everything—thanks for still coming with me when I need to get a vaccination; I really hate needles!); and my dad—il Babo—(for making me watch vampire movies when I was little and loving teddy bears as much as I do!). Thanks to all of you for believing in me and making life oh-so-interesting.

Last but not least, a polka-dotted thank you to Acelya, Ali, and Dodo (aka musketeers who don't carry weapons and aren't really dressed like musketeers), who laugh with me, laugh at me (but always to my face), and generally warm my heart.

prologue

The history keeper scratched his head with the end of the wooden quill before dipping it into the pot of ink. There wasn't much light in the basement of the monastery, but that did not bother his vampire eyes.

Leaning over the fragile papers before him, he wet his lips with his tongue then began to write.

The 24th day of the seventh month of the year AD1678

> *Amidst a human war between the Ottoman Empire and Imperial Russia, vampire slayers attacked a castle where one-hundred-twenty vampire children and forty adult vampires waited to be taken out of Eastern Clan territories.*
>
> *Slayer assassins were also dispatched to the Ottoman and Russian camps along the Tyasmyn River to*

kill two well known vampires: Grand Vizier Ismail and Prince Alexander Kourakin.

The prince was in Ismail's tent at the time of the attack and the assassins that came to the Ottoman camp were killed.

Prince Alexander's sister, Helena, was in her brother's tent and died in his stead.

Upon finding Helena's body, the two vampires made their way to the castle to rescue any survivors. They found only eight-year-old Kiril and five-year-old Joanna. The children were taken to safety by Ismail.

Prince Alexander stayed behind to fight the slayers who were still in the castle.

Sixty-seven slayers were killed.

Unused to being at a loss for words, the history keeper hesitated, his quill frozen above the parchment. Only hours had passed since the slaughter of the vampire children, only minutes since Alexander Kourakin walked into the castle, his sword drawn.

For a hundred years, vampires were hunted and killed by slayers and only seconds ago it had all come to an end. A hunt for the last slayers had been called by the clan leaders.

The history keeper breathed deeply. He had been writing about the deaths of vampires each day for the last century and this day would be the last such day.

He bent his wrist forward and wrote.

Prince Alexander Kourakin of the Eastern Clan ended the Age of Vampire Slayers.

Chapter 1

*G*rooms as far as the eye could see. Men with blond hair, brown hair, black hair, auburn hair . . . was that green hair? Angelica stood amidst thousands of white-gloved hands holding dozens of multicolored flowers all belonging to equally smiley faces.

"Marry me!" one of them called out. He was old, quite old, Angelica realized, and reminded her a little bit of a drawing she had seen of the philosopher Plato.

"No! Marry me!" others sang. Sang? Yes, they were quite literally singing! Oh God, this had to be a dream. A really bad dream . . .

"Come on Angelica, you know you want to marry me!"

"Prince Albert?" Angelica asked with some shock. "But you

died ten years ago from typhoid! Queen Victoria mourns you still!"

Albert wiggled his brows at her lecherously and had Angelica stepping back.

"Now, just wait a minute. I don't really want to marry, and if I must, I could hardly pick from all of you!"

Silence followed her frustrated declaration and had her glancing about warily. The smiles were fading quickly, and Angelica watched as several bright flowers dropped to the ground.

"Gentlemen?"

"Freak!" The word came from somewhere in the distance and echoed eerily. The eyes that had looked upon her with devotion only a moment ago were accusing.

"Freak!"

"Monster!"

"Wait, let me explain!" Angelica raised her voice so that she might be heard over the growing chanting, but to no avail. The anxiety that had begun to flutter in her stomach was quickly turning to dread.

"Kill the monster!" It was Albert. He pointed his royal finger at her and repeated, "Kill the monster!"

The men closest to her seized her, and try as she might Angelica could not shake them loose.

"Wait. Please, I am no monster. I'm innocent! Pease, I did not ask for this curse. No! Someone, help!"

Angelica woke with a start to find her brother watching her, a wry smile etched on his boyish face.

"Did someone fail to tell you that it is bad manners to sleep at the breakfast table? Supper or dinner maybe, but breakfast, it is a definite faux pas my dear."

It took her a moment to get her bearings. Her eyes darted across the table to ensure that none of the men in her dreams were here in their sunny breakfast room. They were not. Of course they were not, she thought with a hefty dose of relief.

Mikhail was looking at her with a slightly quizzical expression that served to pull her out of her thoughts. Straightening her hair with an expert hand, Angelica pushed aside the remnants of her dream and smiled for her brother's benefit.

"At least I am *at* the breakfast table. If you had gotten as little sleep as I did last night, you would have skipped it altogether."

Mikhail ignored the truth of her declaration and continued with his jibing, laughing at his sister over a warm cup of tea. "I really do not know what is more scandalous. Falling asleep at the breakfast table or burning away the candles reading all night."

"Well, if you did not insist on dragging me to late dinners and balls each night of the week, I would hardly have to be up till all hours, now would I?"

Rolling his eyes, Mikhail sighed in frustration. "You cannot still be mad about your debut, Angelica. You had to be introduced to society formally sooner or later, and in this instance it was definitely later!"

Angelica made no response. There was no use in telling her brother that she would wholeheartedly prefer to be living in their country home, where no such fancy debuts would have ever been necessary to begin with! No, she definitely could not tell her brother of that desire, not when she had to stay in London to keep an eye on him.

Receiving no answer other than a frustrated exhalation of

breath, Mikhail shrugged good-naturedly. "So, what do you have planned for today?"

"Oh this and that, though first I will have to change my dress, since we took Rotten Row today. I swear that path must be the sandiest track on this side of the globe."

Mikhail tried valiantly to hide his smile. "I can see that our rides in Hyde Park before breakfast take a rather large toll on you, dear sister. You can always take Ladies' Mile next time."

Angelica did not bother to make a response in the face of that piece of rubbish. Ladies who rode for the sake of showing off their new riding habits and elaborate coiffures rode Ladies' Mile. Anyone out to ride for the sake of riding would not even consider it. Then again, anyone out for the sake of riding would probably not find themselves in Hyde Park, where the fashionable members of the ton could invariably be located in the mornings.

"As I was saying, I will have to change," Angelica said quickly. She picked up the paper she had been reading before she had fallen asleep and continued, "After that, I honestly haven't a clue. What can a lady in London do during these hours of the day? She can shop, for which I am in no mood for, pay bills, which I have already done, or pay house calls, which I cannot do."

Mikhail laid down his own paper to regard his sister with puzzled eyes.

"And why, may I ask, can you not visit with friends? I saw you speaking avidly with the Spanish ambassador's wife just last night. And what about that German chit . . ."

Angelica thought back to her brief conversation with

Felipa the ambassador's wife, and barely managed not to sigh. The woman had seemed pleasant enough, but Angelica had not been able to concentrate on a single thing she had said. She had been too busy wishing herself at home with a good book.

"I hardly spoke a full five minutes with the ambassador's wife. In either case, a *well-bred person never calls on a casual acquaintance during the morning.*" Angelica mimicked the high-pitched voice of her aunt with a mockingly serious expression. Aunt Dewberry was their only living relation and took great pleasure in her monthly visits, during which she lectured Angelica on everything from ladylike behavior to catching a husband. The poor woman could not seem to understand why her charge did not act more like a normal lady. Angelica thought she might have had a better chance at acting the part of a normal lady if it were not for the tiny setback caused by her tendency to hear other people's thoughts.

Mikhail laughed as he lifted his paper once more. "I see. So I suppose, since you are such a stickler for convention, you will be keeping yourself busy in other ladylike fashions as you have been doing since my arrival in London?"

At Angelica's pointed silence Mikhail turned the page of the paper with much ado and asked, "Did I see you reading *The Principles of Moral and Political Philosophy* the other day?"

Angelica swirled her spoon through her tea sheepishly. "I am almost finished. William Paley has some interesting ideas by the by; I think you'll enjoy his contemplations."

"I am sure I will." Smiling now with secret enjoyment, Mikhail looked over his teacup at his sister, who was once more busily reading the papers. "If you had your way, this town house would be overflowing with books, wouldn't it?"

"A room without books is like a body without a soul," Angelica quoted seriously, and then smiled up at her brother. "Cicero said it, not I. If you will not take seriously the words of a mere woman, I am sure you will his."

Mikhail did not take her words to heart. His sister knew well that he respected her mind.

"Did you read this piece on the Blood Stealer? This must be his fifth victim at least!" Setting down her spoon before she sloshed more of the tea on the tablecloth, Angelica's brows furrowed as she read on with interest.

"Angel."

"*Hmm?*"

"Angelica!"

The frustration in Mikhail's voice had her instantly alert and looking up from her paper.

"What is the matter?"

Sighing, Mikhail tried to pick up the trail of their previous conversation. "You know I would be concerned if it were not for the rumors that have been flying about."

"Oh?" Knowing firsthand that rumors had little to do with truth, Angelica was only vaguely interested and tried to finish the article without appearing to do so.

"Yes," Mikhail said as he watched his sister's eyes rush across the black-and-white pages of the *Times*. "People are all atwitter about a certain Russian princess who seems to have stolen every eligible bachelor's heart. Some are certain that by the looks of it she will soon be landing herself a marquis, whereas others swear that she can hardly shake the attentions of a certain viscount."

Angelica barely took her eyes off the page, she had given up pretending. "My, what a fortunate princess."

"You simply can not be that nonchalant!" Mikhail said with some frustration. "Are none of those chaps to your liking, Angel?"

Angelica looked over her paper at her brother and smiled. She did not want to disappoint Mikhail, who had gotten it into his head, ever since he returned home from his studies at Cambridge, that it was his duty to see his sister married. She definitely did not want him to know how difficult she was finding getting to know people, and men in particular. Hearing people's thoughts had so many disadvantages, and being privy to men's carnal fantasies was only one of them.

She had tried to assure herself that to have such thoughts, initially at least, was simply part of a man's nature, but it didn't seem that they had any other kinds of thoughts—at least not in her presence. Many of them let her speak merely to humor her! So far, she had met only three men whose company she could tolerate: the viscount the gossip mill was obviously blowing about, a foreign ambassador, and a nice man who seemed to have no sexual feelings about her whatsoever.

No, she really did not want to disappoint her brother, but she had no intention of finding herself a husband, not if she could help it, not when most of them wanted her as an accessory and child bearer.

"I just find it difficult to speak to most of the men I am introduced to, that is all," she said at length.

"You cannot be serious!" Mikhail's eyes rounded in comic amazement. "I have been trying, valiantly I might add, to get you to stop speaking since, well frankly, since I could speak! And now you tell me you find it difficult to converse with these men? Who are they! Give me their names so I might shower them with gold in exchange for their secrets!"

Angelica arched a brow at her brother's dry wit and crossed her arms over her chest in a very unladylike stance. "I suppose, dear *little* brother, that you would have a ready line of conversation for a man who has just finished contemplating how well your breasts might fit his—"

"Angelica!" All humor fled from his face as Mikhail stammered in shock.

"Oh, come," Angelica said, and smiled, "I was only teasing."

Her brother did not join her laughter as he regarded her seriously. "This is no matter for jesting, Angelica. I would have to shoot the man if it were true."

Angelica schooled her features to look remorseful. There was no use telling her brother that he could not very well call anyone out for merely thinking.

"I am sorry, it will not happen again."

Mikhail lifted his brow, his arms crossing in the same stance that Angelica had assumed only minutes before.

"Do you think to manage me, with such pitiful displays of false remorse?"

Angelica could not help grinning.

"Well you are certainly right, I am not sorry, for I have a brother who would slay all my dragons!"

Mikhail shook his head sadly. "I fear, dear sister, that after you finish *talking* at your dragons, there will be nothing left for me to do."

"Lout!"

Mikhail grinned. "Our parents were unjust, Angel. They should have named you Kate."

Angelica smiled. "So you say, dear brother, so you say." Mikhail had said that many a time over the years, referring always to the Kate in Shakespeare's *Taming of the Shrew*, the play she had read to him many a night when they were younger and afraid of the dark. The dark had brought the thunder and lightning and the creepy sounds from the wooden staircases . . . The dark had brought the news of their parents' deaths.

"Has the moping ended then?" Mikhail asked hopefully as he folded his paper.

"I have not been moping! I do not mope," Angelica said indignantly. Looking at the paper in her hand she grinned. "I brood. It is far more 'bluestocking-ish,' would you not say?"

"Yes, well, Miss Bluestocking, I'm off to the club to meet some friends. I will be back for dinner at six." Mikhail winked at her as he pushed out of his seat and made his way out of the room. "Do behave."

Angelica laughed after her brother's departure, admiring the way Mikhail had launched himself onto society. After the carriage accident had taken their parents, they had been left with only one female relation who could hardly take Mikhail to the right clubs and introduce him to the right people. He had managed all by himself.

It was only four months ago that he returned from Cambridge, but in that short while Mikhail had made more friends than she could count. She supposed it was no great wonder. Her brother had learned at a very young age not to take things seriously when several incidents showed him to have a weak heart. Angelica still worried for him constantly, but Mikhail took his condition with a grain of salt and had adopted a veneer that made him singularly likable.

Her brother could charm a rattle snake if he put his mind to it.

"Princess Belanov?"

Angelica looked up to see their butler open the door.

"Yes, Herrings?"

"A message for you." He bowed, holding a silver tray with a folded piece of white paper.

"Thank you, Herrings." Angelica smiled as she took the missive and read silently.

"What?" the word came out of her mouth unbidden and she lifted her head quickly to make sure she was alone. Once she was certain, she stood from her seat at the breakfast table and moved to the large window overlooking Park Lane.

Standing in a ray of sunlight she read the letter once more, as if the light might make the contents change.

Princess Belanov,

It is my sad duty to notify you of the disappearance of the ships Reina, Mikhail, *and* Katya. *Much of the Belanov funds were tied into the cargo that was to be delivered. . . .*

Angelica put the letter down, her head spinning with the significance of what her father's solicitor had written. Five months. He said that he would only be able to send her the funds she requested monthly for five more months, and then they will have run out!

There had to be some kind of mistake! How could three

ships go missing at once? Was that even a possibility? What could they do now?

She had to tell Mikhail. Maybe he would know . . . She stopped her train of thought. She could not tell Mikhail, his heart would suffer for certain under the strain of such news. He might even have one of those attacks he got every so often when they were younger. God no, she could not tell him under any circumstances. She had to solve this mess somehow, without his knowledge, but how?

Jewels! Her mother had left her the Belanov diamonds and some rubies too. She could sell them. She would sell them if she had to. But they belonged to her family—her mother—and how long would that really tide them over?

Angelica's mouth tightened as she allowed the inevitable conclusion to pass her lips.

"Marriage."

Angelica Shelton Belanov, the only member of the aristocracy who wanted to live out her days in the peace and solitude of a country house with a large library and a good piano, needed a husband. A rich husband. Immediately!

Chapter 2

"James?"

Margaret waited while her husband shifted in their bed until he was facing her. His eyes searched her expression before dropping to her slightly rounded stomach.

"What is the matter?"

"Absolutely nothing is the matter with our son, so you can take those concerned eyes off of my midsection, thank you very much!"

James Murray, Duke of Atholl and leader of the Northern Clan of Vampires rolled his no-longer-concerned eyes before sighing.

"Margaret, there are times—"

Margaret reached out and touched the light brown stubble on his cheek. "When you wonder how it is that you love me so dearly, yes I know."

James could only laugh as he waited for his wife to tell him what had kept her awake.

"I was just thinking about our son's future and . . . James, how will he find a life mate? Our race is dying out; each century there are fewer and fewer of us left."

When her husband made no comment, Margaret lay back down, her eyes searching the ornate ceiling for answers that could not be found.

"Where are the blessed? When will they arrive? We need them, James. Our son needs them. I do not want him to end up like most of our kind: falling into darkness, unwilling to live."

Touching her red curls lovingly, James sighed.

"The blessed might just be a legend, Margaret, but you have no cause to worry; we will find a way to go on, we always have."

"It cannot be legend! The book of history speaks of them. The only human line that can procreate with vampires; if we found them, we would evolve. We would not have the thirst anymore, James, imagine. Imagine our children's children not needing blood to survive . . . It has to be true. The book of history never lies, James!"

James threw the covers aside, the leader in him needing to put distance between him and his emotional wife. His feet touched the ground. He wanted to think logically, as a clan leader should.

Margaret watched the broad back of the man she loved. She watched him bow his head and sigh. Then he was beside her once more, pulling her to him and stroking her hair.

"Have no fear, my love, all will be well."

Margaret nodded into his chest, her voice muffled as she spoke.

"I'm usually not such a baby, you know. It is this pregnancy; it plays tricks on me."

James chuckled. "You need not fear I will forget how ferocious you really are, sweetheart. I recall a particular battlefield in France where men cowered at the mere sight of you."

"And you." Margaret smiled.

A peaceful quiet settled over them, the clock on the wall counting away the seconds.

"What of Sergey?" Margaret asked at long last.

James's instinct was to let his wife go. He held her tighter instead.

"Are we turning this into a worry session?"

Margaret trailed her fingers along his arm as she voiced her thoughts. "He wreaked havoc in Western Clan territory. Ten of our kind were killed and twice as many humans. They have not been able to stop him, and now he is here in England. At the rate Sergey is going, he will alert the humans to our existence and bring about another age of vampire slayers! They call him the Blood Stealer in the papers; think about it, for all we know—"

"Hush now." James knew that what Margaret suggested might just happen. It was what Sergey wanted. For years he had spoken out against the vampire laws, taking every gathering as an opportunity to try and win supporters amongst the loyal subjects of the clans. Sergey wanted vampires to reign over humans, and after being banished he had obviously decided to take the decision out of the leaders' hands. If he managed to bring their existence to the attention of humans, war would break out as it had before.

Sergey *was* a threat to their race, but James would not allow Margaret to work herself up in this manner, not when it might affect his baby boy.

"He will be stopped, love. I received a communication from Isabelle just last evening, she has sent for Alexander."

Margaret's brows rose as she pulled back to look at James's face.

"Alexander is on his way?" She had not seen her old friend for a long time . . . too long. He had withdrawn after Helena's death, closed himself off from everyone who cared for him. Margaret had tried hard to pull him back from the darkness he had chosen, but failed. Nevertheless, Alexander was the strongest of all of them, a born executor of vampire law.

"Yes."

Margaret sighed as she snuggled closer into James's chest and closed her eyes. If Alexander was on his way, then Sergey would not cause problems for them much longer.

"Good then. Let us go to sleep."

Alexander watched the frothy liquid in his glass and cursed under his breath. He did not want the watered-down pint. He wanted blood.

The trip from Moscow had been lengthy, and for the first time in as long as he could remember he felt edgy.

"The man in the corner will soon approach us, Prince."

Alexander's gaze traveled across the space of the small pub. The tables were chipped, the chairs barely standing, and the occupants in even worse shape. He was sitting in the middle of a den of thieves and, by the looks of it, for no good reason.

Although the last of Sergey's victims was found right around the street corner just that morning, there was no trace of the vampire on any of these men's minds; though rape and murder was definitely present.

He shifted his body in the rickety chair, turning his back fully on the large sewer rat in the corner. That one had been entertaining fantasies of slitting Alexander's throat since the moment he entered the shady establishment several hours past and for no other reason than sport.

"Anything?" Alexander asked, ignoring Kiril's previous comment.

"No, Prince," Kiril replied, not taking his eyes from the rat for even a moment. Alexander was amused by the vampire's protective gesture. A man, no matter his size, was no match for him even in his weakened state.

Drumming his fingers on the table, Alexander caught the eye of a passing wench. The girl grinned, jerking on her gaudy corset so that her overflowing breasts pushed against her frail bones.

"What'll you be havin' then?" she asked, cocking her hip and eyeing first Alexander and then Kiril. Though her hiked skirt and pout suggested that she would not mind him havin' *her*, Alexander did not look twice at her exposed body.

"Another," he said, and gestured at his glass. The girl nodded, her disappointment obvious as she swayed back toward the dirty bar at the end of the small room.

Kiril cleared his throat and ran a hand through his tousled hair. They had both dressed down for their roaming, but even in their plain shirts and pants, they could not be mistaken for anything other than gents.

"Perhaps I should take care of him before he causes trouble?" he asked hesitantly.

Alexander looked across the table at the younger man.

Kiril had come to him forty years ago, proclaiming that he had come to pay his debt. It had taken Alexander a moment to recognize the man as the boy he had saved almost two centuries before. Kiril's hair had darkened, he had grown a beard, but his eyes had remained the same. The man had been by his side since that day. His loyal servant.

"There is no need; we are going to leave soon."

Looking around him, Kiril shook his head in disgust. Alexander understood the inclination. The men crowded around the tables were thieves at best. The balding male with streaks of dirt on his scalp sitting two tables away, had just returned from beating an old man for his money. The bastard had only found a few measly coins in the man's pocket, but he had thoroughly enjoyed the sight of the blood that had gotten all over his hands.

"The rat will come our way soon," Kiril warned as he continued to watch the big guy twirling a knife in the corner of the pub. Alexander had read the man's mind and knew that he was in a different league altogether.

He took a swig of Kiril's tasteless pint to wash away the bitter taste in his mouth as he recalled the thoughts he had turned off as quickly as he could. The man was a rapist and murderer and was contemplating paying a visit to an orange-colored house later this evening, where he had seen a little girl of about five that had particularly pretty blond hair.

"Here ya go, sir." The waitress placed the beer on the imbalanced table and smiled, apparently still hopeful that the gentlemen might change their minds.

"Thank you." Alexander nodded, and handed her enough coins to cover his drink and keep her well fed for several weeks to come.

"Oh, sir . . ." the woman stammered to a halt. "I . . . I thank ya from the bottom of my heart, I do!"

Alexander saw Kiril tense and knew the night was about to get more irritating than it had been thus far.

"Now what have we 'ere, Molly? Is this fella insultin' ya?" The rat approached the table and grabbed the coins from the dismayed waitress's palm.

"Please, John!" Molly protested feebly.

Eyes narrowed, Alexander watched the exchange. *John* was apparently a regular customer to this hell and felt he could hassle a newcomer without qualms from the owner. Alexander was a man of few words, but in the interest of the woman, he spoke softly.

"Give her the coins and leave."

John grunted. "I dunna think I will. You insulted our Molly 'ere and you'll be havin' to pay for it."

Kiril made to stand, but Alexander halted him. Obviously John trusted his height and thick arms to intimidate them. Too bad he had a thick head to go with the rest of him. Alexander was not looking forward to teaching him a lesson.

"I will only tell you once more. Give her the coins and go back to your corner."

Laughter filled the room as John nodded to several of his cronies. They smiled as they stood, moving closer to the table, their intent written across their faces.

"Please, John, leave 'im be!" Molly cried out for John to be reasonable just as Alexander pushed back his chair, the wood scraping against the floor with enough volume to wake the guests sleeping above stairs.

Alexander's mind wandered while he waited for the ruffians to attack. Why was he bothering with the filth? It was not his habit to interfere in human dealings. Yes, leaving the bastards unharmed this evening would likely mean that the little girl on John's mind would not live to see tomorrow and many others would get hurt, but that was not his concern. He was the protector of his people, the vampires, and had enough on his hands without feeling responsible for the lives of millions more.

There had been so many innocents . . . he had seen so many innocents die in his lifetime. Women, children, and old people he could not save.

But he could save the girl. Hell and damnation, what a nuisance!

The men looked from one to another, and then focused their attentions on Alexander.

Clan law stated no human was to be harmed unless a vampire was attacked first. He devoted his life to upholding clan law, and so Alexander waited. One, two, three, four, . . . he counted the seconds; at ten they would be upon him, and the lesson would begin.

"Take Molly out of here."

Kiril nodded. He never gainsaid Alexander, but his reluctance to leave him to fight alone was obvious in the vampire's face.

"Well, well, what have we here?"

Standing motionless, Alexander watched as the small bald one moved forward with a leer. There were three of them, a disappointing number. The ugly villain who was losing his hair, a thin one with a nose that leaned toward the left, and the big brute called John. He would have liked a bit of exercise, and this pitiful lot was not likely to give him any.

"Be a good lad and empty those pockets now." Ugly took out

his rusty blade as he moved toward him. Alexander merely watched and frowned. The smell of their excitement revolted him while the scent of their blood made him hungry.

"Hurry up then," he said simply, his eyes narrowing on the rusty blade. Ugly took exception to his attitude and lunged for his side. Customers ran for the door as Alexander side-stepped the attack easily and sent the man sprawling into several tables on the other side of the room.

The one with the crooked nose came next, his blade raised high as he charged. Alexander lifted a hand and held the man's wrist in a viselike grip, breaking several of his bones. John took a step back as his comrade fell to the ground, screaming in pain.

Alexander looked to where the two men lay and followed the third as he ran for the door. He grabbed John by his collar as the last of the customers ran from the building. The villain swung backward with his blade and scraped him across his chest. With a low growl, Alexander threw him to the ground and stepped on his leg with enough force to hear the bones crunch.

"Now even little girls will outrun you," he said as he ran his finger across the cut in his shirt. The bleeding had stopped only a moment after the cut had been delivered, but the shirt needed mending. Better yet, he would burn the damn thing.

John was not moving, having passed out from the pain. Alexander felt no satisfaction in the violence he had dished out; instead he felt vaguely sickened.

Turning from the crumpled body, he made his way out of the building. Kiril was leaning against the wall, his ankles and arms crossed.

"Did you take care of the woman?"

Kiril nodded. "She will not have to work again unless she chooses to."

"Good." Alexander began walking without another word.

Though it would take humans a good half hour at least, it took the two vampires only a few minutes to reach the three-story residence on Park Lane.

"Notify the leader of the Northern Clan of our arrival," Alexander said as he walked into his study and shut the door. It was dark, with a sole candle burning on the table that occupied the middle of the room. The dust that had accumulated on the heavy curtains had formed black designs on the green material and the burgundy wallpaper was tattered on edges; he had not been here for over a decade.

"Prince." Kiril entered the room only moments later.

"Yes?"

"A messenger from the duke just arrived with a missive."

Alexander took the letter. "Thank you, Kiril. Now get some rest."

Kiril nodded and disappeared down the hallway, while Alexander finished reading.

Apparently, the night was far from over.

Chapter 3

The large ballroom was overflowing with flounces, ruffles, and white gloves of different lengths. Ball gowns of silk and velvet with short, tight-fitting bodices were à la mode, the bustles worn high on the waist. Though Angelica fit in perfectly with her off-the-shoulder blue silk ball gown, soft kidskin gloves and her grandmother's diamond earrings, she watched the crowd and shuddered.

The heat and noise was crowding in on her, threatening to drive her mad and her head spun from dancing with the viscount. Upon reconsideration, she was simply not going to be able to keep him on her list of potential suitors. The man's sadistic thoughts had leaped out at her unbidden and left her shaken.

Her eyes searched the faces in the crowd anxiously, but could not find her brother. She was getting more nervous by the minute, and for that precise reason the thoughts of those around her were about to overwhelm her. Where in God's name was he?

Where in God's name is Henry?

A glass of port; yes, that is what I need.

Will it rain tomorrow?

Bitch, I will show her!

Tired. So damn tired.

Angelica started to raise her fingers to her ears, but stopped midway. She could not stop the voices, not by covering her ears. Her head was beginning to spin; she needed air.

"Angelica, my dear, what are you doing here all by yourself?" The hushed reprimand from her aunt could not have been more welcome. Angelica needed to find her equilibrium, and Lady Dewberry was a neat distraction.

"Mikhail should be right back, Aunt," she reassured. Lady Dewberry did not smile back, her brow puckering with concern instead. With her protruding cheekbones, long aristocratic nose, and well-kept figure, her aunt looked the part of an intimidating woman; but Angelica wasn't worried. Lady Dewberry rarely had a bad thought and had been around for her brother and herself since her parents' deaths. Granted, she had not taken them in exactly, but Angelica could not fault her aunt for that. She knew Lady Dewberry was a reserved woman who loved living alone and did not particularly like children. So it was only natural that the few times a year they saw their aunt, the lady wanted to be a positive influence.

"Nevertheless, it does not do for a young unmarried woman to stand by herself this way. It makes you look like a wallflower, my dear, and though I know you are no such thing having seen you dancing with five different partners in the last hour, others just might!"

Angelica knew it was better to give in than to protest. Otherwise, her aunt was liable to turn this into another discussion on ladylike behavior.

"Of course, Aunt, I will be more careful next time."

"Good, good." Lady Dewberry finally raised her voice to a perfectly ladylike pitch. "You were always a good girl, my dear."

Angelica barely contained her laughter as her aunt's eyes wandered around the ballroom. She knew very well that the elder lady thought of her as a hopeless case and that she had had several episodes of "illness" due to what she had called "Angelica's unwillingness to love the society that loved her."

"Ah, there you are, Lady Elisabeth!"

Angelica turned toward the lady her aunt addressed in her most formal tones.

"Princess Belanov, may I introduce Lady Elisabeth Barrows."

Angelica had succeeded in drowning out the loud thoughts of the people around her to a dull, unintelligible roar, but the beautiful Lady Elisabeth's thoughts were as clear as a summer sky.

Breathtaking, indeed! She is not half as beautiful as everyone keeps whispering. Her nose is too small for one, and her eyes, far too dark a blue to be fashionable! Without those gorgeous earrings she is nothing at all.

"It is an honor to meet you, Princess Belanov, or should I say Lady Shelton?" Elisabeth arched a brow as she regarded the woman she considered an adversary with contempt. "It does get so confusing, does it not, when one is of *mixed* background?"

Angelica did not need to be able to read the lady's mind to know that she considered being mixed in any way degrading.

"My father was a Russian prince, my mother an English lady. It is really quite simple, but you need not distress yourself with the confusion two titles can so easily cause, Lady Elisabeth, you may call me Princess Belanov." Angelica smiled and nodded at the woman who faltered halfway through the curtsey she was delivering.

Did she insult me? The Russian whore!

Angelica's fingers curled at that capricious thought, but what could she do? Call the woman out on something she had never said, only thought?

She bit back her frustration, as she had had to do countless times in her life. All she *could* do was hope that the *lady* would move on quickly. Damn it, she had to gain control of her emotions, stop being nervous. . . . It was the only way she would stop hearing!

"Angelica?" Mikhail's voice had her looking over Lady Elisabeth's shoulder to find her brother's concerned eyes on hers as he approached.

Lady Elisabeth, who had caught sight of Mikhail, was almost beside herself with excitement at the imminent arrival of *Prince* Belanov. The woman could not seem to stop herself from smiling foolishly, just as so many others did when Mikhail was around. Disgusted, Angelica looked from her brother to the lady for him to comprehend the source of her headache.

Mikhail understood, and though to everyone else the gaze he leveled on the woman may have seemed pleasant, Angelica knew better. The tenseness in his shoulders and the rigidity of his strong jaw were marked signs of contained anger.

Having reached the little group, Mikhail addressed Lady Dewberry.

"Aunt, will you do me the honor?"

Frowning at the impropriety of Mikhail's behavior, Lady Dewberry made the introductions: "Prince Belanov, this is Lady Elisabeth Barrows. Lady Barrows, Prince Mikhail Belanov."

While Mikhail sketched an elegant bow, Lady Elisabeth's thoughts shot off in Angelica's head like cannonballs.

God, he is the most exciting man in the room. Those sinful blue eyes and that strong jaw . . . oh, and the incredible form of his body. I bet all the women here want him. I do not care what I have to do to get him. He will be mine.

Angelica did not know whether or not to be shocked at the aggressive nature of the woman's thoughts, but she found it prudent to warn her brother of her intentions. She did not want him to be forced into a compromising situation by the capricious *lady!*

"Avoid dark corners and empty rooms, will you Mikhail?" Angelica said in Russian, while the Lady Elisabeth looked on with undisguised hostility.

Her brother nodded before dragging Elisabeth to the dance floor without further ado.

"I hate to say so, my dear, but speaking in a tongue others do not understand is quite rude," Lady Dewberry admonished gently.

"I do apologize, Aunt. It is an ingrained habit, which I am trying to overcome. I did not mean to be rude."

"That is quite all right, dear." The lady smiled as she patted Angelica's gloved hand. "Oh! I have seen a good friend of mine, but I fear that leaving you alone is out of the question. All the men who have been circling us while trying to think of clever ways to introduce themselves would surely pounce!" Lady Dewberry laughed, secretly delighted that her protégée was doing so incredibly well.

Angelica grabbed at the opportunity to have a few moments alone.

"Oh, please do not worry yourself, Aunt. I was just going to ask you if you would join me while I go to the powder room. Why do you not visit with your dear friend instead, whilst I take care of that? I will be right back, I assure you."

Looking a tad uncertain, her aunt agreed, "All right, my dear, but do not stay overlong. It is not seemly for you to be unchaperoned even for a short period of time."

"Do not worry yourself, Aunt. I will see you shortly."

As soon as Lady Dewberry turned away, Angelica headed for a large potted plant she had spotted earlier. All she wanted to do was stand behind the colossal leaves and hide. God, what a ridiculous thought!

Moving as quickly as decorum would allow, which was not quickly at all, she made her way across the ballroom.

The faces around her blurred as did their chatter and their thoughts; it was so incredibly loud, she felt as if her eardrums would burst at any moment. She tried to concentrate on something, anything, so that she could drown out the voices, but she was simply too tired.

Avoiding admiring gazes, her eyes shifted until they came to rest on a man standing close to her plant. She would have laughed at herself for thinking of the plant as her own if she had not been too busy staring.

He was magnetic. Standing almost a foot above all those

around him, the man clad in black formal wear held Angelica's attention as no man had done before. The voices of those around her dimmed, but she did not notice. All she saw was him.

Angelica noticed several other women looking his way, some with obvious interest and others with a touch of fear. She understood the latter reaction because she felt his power even from a distance. He did not belong in the glittery ballroom where dancers were painfully walking through the tedious steps of the quadrille and society matrons were searching hungrily for the next piece of gossip. Who was he?

Dark gray eyes in a strong angular face with hair as dark as night, he looked dangerous, like an avenger on a mission. Where had that thought come from?

It took her a moment to realize she was almost within reaching distance of the object of her admiration. How could she have gotten so carried away? It was lucky that he did not notice her, or perhaps it was not. It was vaguely disconcerting to realize that she wanted him to notice her.

She had met good-looking men before, but none had made her feel like this. So disoriented and completely addle-brained. She must be feeling worse than she had originally thought for a mere face to affect her thus.

Trying not to think too much of it, Angelica reached her plant and moved behind it quickly. She took deep breaths, her heart rate slowing with each exhalation, the sounds pounding at her losing their frequency. After staring at the big green leaves for what must have been a good five minutes, Angelica's nerves felt steady.

"It is a good spot. I should have thought of it myself." The deep voice infused with humor had her blushing to the roots of her hair and closing her eyes in mortification.

"I would not mind so much if you absented yourself so that I might pretend I have no reason to be as embarrassed as I am."

The stranger ignored her plea and instead laughed softly.

"They speak of you in hushed tones in drawing rooms, but none had warned me of your sense of humor."

Angelica's eyes snapped open and turned to see who had discovered her. Odd sensations traveled her spine as she noticed his eyes first. They were a mellow brown and smiling at her with genuine humor. They were not a steely gray, and it was disconcerting to realize she had been hoping they might be.

"I apologize sincerely, my manners escape me. Lord Nicholas Adler, at your service."

Tall, square chin, kind eyes, and beautiful hands; Angelica realized Lord Nicholas Adler may have been the most handsome man she had ever seen . . . had it not been for her mysterious man.

Her mysterious man, indeed! She had to be going daft. Irritated more with herself than with the man beside her, she spoke.

"My sense of humor is indeed intact, Lord Adler, though I daresay I find the prospect of being whispered about in drawing rooms not in the least humorous. Still I fail to see how it is you recognize me and mark me as the target of such discussions when I have yet to give you my name."

"In possession of intelligence and a sense of humor, I daresay I must tread carefully." When Lord Adler noticed Angelica's raised brow he laughed once more. "Did it take long for you to master that move? Not many can perform it with a straight face."

Angelica gave in and smiled; his laughter was truly contagious.

"Now that is much better, is it not?"

"Yes, as a matter of fact it is. Smiling does feel good when it is not forced."

"And at such dull affairs one finds oneself little amused and constantly smiling." He nodded as he looked out toward the dancers in the midst of the ballroom.

Considering his expression, Angelica recognized a kindred spirit. "What are you doing here, Lord Adler?"

"Nicholas, please, as I intend to call you Angelica."

Angelica laughed, then put a hand over her mouth lest they be discovered. "What are you doing here, Nicholas, and how on earth do you know who I am?"

Nicholas shrugged nonchalantly. "You never did ask what they say about you in the drawing room. No other woman can possibly possess that black hair and those turbulent eyes, just as no other woman left me breathless before. Since you possess all three qualities, there was not a doubt in my mind that you are indeed she."

"You are a rake," Angelica decreed.

"Hardly, though I do need to leave this safe haven and brave the crowds now, or my uncle will find us together and will not cease his prattling until I have married you."

Laughing yet again, Angelica allowed him to take her hand. "Then you had best leave, or my aunt may just join your uncle, and then you will never be able to escape."

Placing a kiss on the thin material covering her palm,

Nicholas's eyes turned serious, giving Angelica the impression of a totally different man.

"I am not so sure I would wish to escape. Till next time, Angelica."

Angelica held her hand staunchly at her side, all her mistrust rising from the pits of her belly as she watched him leave. Charming, funny, a little unorthodox but all around amiable, Lord Nicholas Adler seemed perfect. Things were rarely as they seemed.

Keeping her breathing level, she admonished herself for getting carried away. She had just met a potential husband. All she had to do now was confirm that Nicholas was rich, which by the look of his impeccable clothing he was, and he would become a solid possibility.

Damn if that did not sound cold and so utterly calculating, but what choice did she have? How else was a woman to marry in five short months?

The thoughts of marriage made the nerves resurface and before she knew it her moment of peace was gone, replaced by the jaded thoughts of the ton. *Calm yourself, and the voices will stop; just calm yourself*, she told herself over and over.

"I have to get out of here," she muttered as she pushed out from behind the plant. Her aunt would likely still be conversing with her friend, unaware of the precious moments Angelica had stolen for herself, but Mikhail may very well be looking for her.

Her steps slowed as she saw *him* a few feet away. *Dangerous!* Her mind screamed. *Just walk on and do not look in his direction.*

Another dead end! Damn it, we have to find him before he kills again.

She faltered as the words entered her mind. Before he kills again? Who was thinking such a thing?

Who are you?

The abrupt, almost angry voice in Angelica's head had her jerking in reaction. A cold shiver ran down her spine as she turned slowly to face her mysterious man.

He was looking straight at her, those hard eyes taking in every inch of her flushed face. The power of him was almost tangible.

She stood completely still, unable to take a step forward or backward. It could not be. He could not have just spoken to her. Through thoughts. Intentionally.

His eyes held hers for a moment more before they left her, and he continued looking around. She felt more alone in that moment than she had ever felt. As if that one instant when he had been a part of her world she had been whole, and now . . . now she was not.

She was just extremely confused, that was all. He had not been speaking to her. Of course not, she was a fool to have thought it possible. As for the bizarre thoughts, she must have misheard. It had happened often enough before. Angelica walked on and smiled at a recent acquaintance as Shakespeare's speculation popped into her head.

"Our doubts are traitors and make us lose the good we oft might win by fearing to attempt," she whispered the words softly.

What if Shakespeare was right? What if there was someone else like her? What if she was not mistaken?

No, it could not be. She was just confused; this ball was simply too crowded. She always felt disoriented in crowds. Edgy and disoriented; she had to leave.

As the quadrille came to an end, the orchestra struck up the first waltz of the evening. Couples dressed in elegance and perfume moved onto the dance floor, their conversations ending as they whirled on the polished floors. Angelica caught sight of a woman with bright red hair walking by with a young fop at her heels. Their thoughts intruded.

Is he following me around the ballroom?

Blimey! She has got the smallest feet I've ever seen!

There was much to be said for comic relief. The pair made Angelica laugh behind a gloved hand and the remaining tension drained out of her. God, that was truly new! Most men of her acquaintance looked at a woman's bosom, ankles, or even waist, but she had never heard a man make a comment such as that one, even if only in his mind.

You must have been sheltered if you never heard of a foot fetish.

Angelica held her breath as the voice she had heard before played once more in her head. Deep and husky, it almost scared her senseless. There *was* someone speaking to her through thoughts!

Her fingers went numb with cold as she looked around at the dozens of faces that surrounded her.

Who are you? She thought frantically. *Please, tell me who you are!*

Chapter 4

Alexander could not imagine what had come over him. What was he doing paying attention to the woman?

She read his mind, was obviously a vampire, but he had not been informed of her presence. James had supplied him with a list of all the members of the Northern Clan, which cities they resided in and which of them were currently in other clan territories. This vampire had to be a visitor.

Damn it! A murderer was on the lose intent on starting a new age of vampire slayers, he did not have time for new acquaintances . . . even if they did come in the form of the black-haired beauty.

Looking around the crowded ballroom, Alexander frowned. The informants he met had left several minutes ago, and their information had been less than adequate. There were near to no leads, though the London police were asking more questions than ever.

Tomorrow he would meet with the clans' connection to the London police. Alexander expected little help from human detectives, was rather more concerned that none of the people from Scotland Yard started getting strange ideas about the serial killer they were pursuing.

It was time to leave the ball. Sergey had to know he was being tracked, especially since he had done away with two vampires the Northern Clan sent out to bring him in several weeks ago. Reason said he would hardly present himself at any social functions, so there was no point in being at this nuisance of an affair.

Rolling the facts over in his mind once more, Alexander considered as he made his way around guests and hangers-on.

The victims were all female, most of them among the ton. Sergey took his victims into dodgy neighborhoods or the woodlands surrounding London, and then left them there in plain sight. And lastly, a necklace of red garnets was found around each of their necks.

Alexander was hoping the last would be Sergey's downfall. Unless the vampire had planned far in advance, which Alexander doubted very much, it would have to be relatively easy to find the store or stores from which the vampire did his shopping.

How many stores in and around London could possibly sell garnet necklaces?

"Prince Kourakin?"

Alexander looked at the human who had approached him with impatience. The blonde wore a look that he had seen a million times, a look that incited only boredom.

"Do I know you, madame?"

The woman smiled, her eyes glittering with invitation. "How did you know I was French, Your Grace?"

Alexander read her mind quickly. She was a vicious bitch who enjoyed taking pain almost as much as she liked inflicting it. She had no memories of Sergey.

"Call it intuition, madame."

"Call me Delphine, please."

Alexander knew she expected him to give her use of his given name. He knew she wanted to end up in his bed. He knew she had never been turned down before. He did not care one bit.

"Madame, I am not interested in what you have to offer."

Delphine bristled like a cat, her eyes becoming mere slits as she regarded him with unmasked hostility. She seemed ready to deliver some sort of put-down when her gaze became speculative.

"You 'ave no interest in a woman."

It was not a question; Delphine had reached the only possible reason in her mind that could lead to a rejection. She was right in a way, Alexander realized, for a woman had not tempted him for a very, very long time.

That was of course, until he saw the black-haired witch.

His eyes returned to the corner of the ballroom, where she stood with her back to him. Delphine must have been watching him closely for she cursed vividly.

"It is always 'er, zat bitch! Every man in ze room seems to run to 'er like good little doggies. I should rip 'er eyes out!"

Alexander turned toward Delphine.

"You will do no such thing; you will not even get close to her. You like her."

His eyes glowed a dark shade of red as a dazed Delphine nodded in agreement.

"Now leave, and forget we ever spoke."

Alexander's eyes returned to their normal color as Delphine walked away slowly. *She would cause no more trouble*, he thought with some satisfaction. He wondered for a moment why he had used his mental powers on the woman with such little provocation, but he reasoned that he was protecting his people from harm. He would have done the same for any vampire . . . wouldn't he?

Angry that he was being dragged away from the issue at hand by thoughts of the woman once again, Alexander scanned the ballroom for the twentieth time that night and zeroed in on Kiril. The man was conversing with a redhead in a silver gown, Lady Joanna. That had to be the female vampire James and he had found along with Kiril in that castle long ago. The two vampires would have a lot to say to each other . . . or perhaps not. Alexander decided to give Kiril a few moments.

Preparing to wait, an exercise he was decidedly bad at, he sighed. A brunette with artfully arranged ringlets about her ears shot him a heated look. Alexander ignored the blatant invitation.

Damnation! He had hoped for a little more information, but the night was turning out to be completely fruitless. He should be outside, roaming the streets, not stuck in this stuffy ballroom.

His thoughts gravitated toward the woman in blue once more. He had met only two vampires who could read minds with the ease he could, and they were both elders. She could hardly be an elder. He knew all the elders in Europe and she resembled neither an Asian nor an African native.

"My dear Prince Kourakin!"

At the sound of the familiar voice, Alexander blocked all thoughts from his mind and turned to face the pompous little man who was bowing extravagantly.

Recalling his receding hairline, Lord Jeffery Higgins straightened hastily and pushed a few errant strands back over his gleaming bald spot. His chubby hands shook slightly as he stiffened his back and went back to smiling like a fool, the gap in his two front teeth all the more apparent due to the brown chocolate residue across his gums.

"It is an honor indeed that you have graced our ball, Prince Alexander. My wife is overly pleased, yes yes yes, she is. And when she is overly pleased, oh my, do we get delectable dishes for . . ." The man's eyes looked positively glazed with pleasure as he trailed off. His pudgy fingers, decked with rings glittering with diamonds, twitched by his side as if playing on invisible keys.

Alexander felt distinctly uncomfortable with the amount of smiling that was being directed his way. What was the man so deliriously happy about? He did not have to wait long to find out.

"Pastries and tarts and exotic fruits, yes! yes! yes!" With each exclamation, Lord Higgins's voice climbed an octave, prompting several of the dancing couples to falter and stop to watch the spectacle the man was making of himself.

Oblivious, the lord swung his gloved hand in the air and uttered a sound that may have resembled a laugh had it been less deafening, "Two Russian princes in one affair, my wife will make me cakes, yes! yes! yes! she will. And chocolate!

My God, she will have the most delicious chocolates brought forth." Immediately after finishing his sentence, the man lapsed into a reverent silence, his eyes slowly losing their vacant stare.

Apparently shocked at having found his hand in midair Lord Higgins promptly brought it down to rest against his very round belly.

Alexander could not fathom what type of response the man expected. He hardly had time for all of the foolish prattle he was being subjected to, really, but dismissing the lord hosting the ball was hardly something he could do. For one moment, he considered the possibility of pushing a thought into the man's mind to make him leave, but Alexander was worried that Lord Higgins was not a very stable man to begin with. Doing damage, or rather, further damage, to the man's mind was not something he wanted to risk.

"Another Russian prince, you say?" Alexander feigned interest. "I think I will excuse myself now and go find him." Extracting himself from the man's presence, Alexander had taken only two steps when Lord Higgins's voice stopped him in midstride.

"Wait, there he is now." Positively exuding nervous energy, the ball of a man rushed into the crowd of faces as Alexander stood with barely restrained irritation.

Closing his eyes briefly, he pinched the bridge of his nose. This was turning out to be a damnably long evening.

"My dear Prince, this is Prince Mikhail Belanov." Lord Higgins came toward him, dragging a harassed-looking young man in his wake. "Prince Belanov, Prince Kourakin," he finished with a flourish and then departed much to the relief of the two men.

"It is quite incredible how much trouble a man of his stature can cause," Mikhail grumbled as he looked after the lord who flapped his ruffled sleeves while he spoke animatedly with several of the guests.

Alexander quickly scanned Mikhail's mind for a memory of Sergey then nodded in full agreement. "He should be satisfied now that he got us to meet. His wife will no doubt give him many chocolates for the deed." The dry comment that came out of his mouth surprised Alexander, though outwardly he looked straight-faced. When was the last time he had made a joke?

Mikhail offered his hand and smiled. "Yes yes yes, many chocolates."

Alexander found the corner of his mouth quirking upward into the beginnings of a smile as he shook hands with the Russian. It had not occurred to him to notice before that moment, but it had been years since he had smiled. It was hard to believe that his humor was restored, but why not? He was *feeling* almost everything else.

Unlike the lust he had felt at encountering the black-haired woman, this rediscovery of humor did not bother Alexander. In fact, he seemed to have forgotten how pleasant a sensation it was to find something funny.

Realizing that he had been quiet for a good time, Alexander refocused his attention on the prince. "I do not believe we have met, but your last name is familiar."

Mikhail inclined his head at a passing acquaintance. "You might have heard of my father, Dimitri Belanov."

"Ah yes," Alexander recalled the family name and the tragedy attached to it. He remembered the czar speaking of Dimitri Belanov during one of Alexander's regular visits to the palace. "Your father's work to improve relations between England and Russia and your mother's grace was the talk of Saint Petersburg for many years. Their passing was a loss to us all."

Mikhail nodded.

"I take it you spend a lot of time in England?" Alexander asked to fill the silence.

"Yes, my father's work kept him busy in London. . . . Good evening, Ambrose." Mikhail smiled at a man in an elegant green jacket who seemed to be trying to catch his attention. Alexander assessed the man named Ambrose, scanned his mind quickly and found him a good sort.

"Mikhail, do make some time for me later on; there is a matter of some import I wish to discuss."

"Of course." Mikhail smiled, then turned back toward Alexander with some apology in his eyes. "Please excuse the interruption. Where was I? Oh yes, my father's work kept him here and my mother was an English lady who liked staying close to her home." Regarding the man before him Mikhail asked curiously, "Have you just recently arrived in London?"

"Only a few days ago, yes."

"You must allow me to show you around at the club. There are some fairly pleasant pastimes in London if one knows where to go."

Alexander considered the unexpected offer of hospitality. From what he had derived through the constant smiles and greetings Mikhail Belanov received, he was a popular man, which would give him entry into all sorts of functions and parties. James was enough of an entry into London society, but being escorted by Prince Belanov might very well prove productive in his search.

"I would like that, Prince Belanov."

Mikhail grinned engagingly. "You must call me Mikhail if we are going to spend any amount of time together. All the 'Princes' are going to my head, and my sister will tell you that my self-image is as inflated as it need be."

Alexander nodded. Mikhail had a good sense of humor, and he found he appreciated the young man's outspokenness. Of course a look into his thoughts and he knew that one of the reasons the man wanted his friendship was his sister. By what misguided notion Mikhail had become a matchmaker, he had no idea, but Alexander did not consider it important either way.

"Then I suppose you should call me Alexander, although I have to say, I enjoy all the 'Princing.'"

Mikhail laughed. "I had better get going. A few friends and I are going to Whites tomorrow. It is a gambler's heaven, and the most exclusive gentlemen's club in town, so some of the more irritating members of the ton are kept out. I should be able to procure you a guest pass. How about we meet on Saint James Street at noon?"

"Agreed." Alexander nodded at his companion, who promptly took his leave.

"Prince?"

Alexander heard the uncomfortable edge in Kiril's words as he turned to face the man and Lady Joanna beside him.

"Yes?"

"A message just came from Lady Joanna's house. One of their contacts from the police force sent word of yet another murder. The police noticed that the victim was bled dry, but curiously enough they could not find any of her blood."

Alexander's eyes narrowed as he contemplated the news. Sergey had just made his biggest mistake.

"Where was the body found?"

It was Lady Joanna that revealed the answer.

"Here in London."

"Lady Joanna, I want all the vampires in London in my residence tonight, can you manage it?"

"Yes, Prince Kourakin, it will be done."

Mikhail reached for his sister's hand when he saw the tension on her face. He had been afraid that this particular function might be too crowded for her *condition*. Damn, but he should have listened to his intuition and kept her out of the larger gatherings.

"Are you all right, Angel?"

Angelica's attempt at a smile fell flat, and she looked toward Lady Dewberry with distress. She let out a pent-up breath when she noticed how deep in conversation the robust lady was with her gossiping friends. The last thing Angelica wanted was to have Lady Dewberry fretting for her.

"Mikhail, I believe I might very well have gone insane," Angelica said in a low voice.

Mikhail laughed, although his eyes remained serious as he regarded his sister. "I doubt that sincerely, my sweet sister. You would not allow for such a thing to occur, not when you think so highly of your mind."

Shaking just a little, Angelica tried to adopt a jovial veneer. "Well then, here is a little piece of news for you, love. I thought I saw someone who was like me."

Her brother's smile faded quickly upon that revelation. He

looked around the ballroom as if he would be able to spot someone with Angelica's abilities, then closed his eyes firmly for a moment.

"Who? Where? Are you sure?"

Angelica shook her head with regret.

"Yes, I am sure, and then again, how one can be sure about something like this I would like to know."

Before Mikhail could reply to that dry question, Lady Dewberry tapped him on his shoulder with a fan.

"Prince Belanov, I believe it is time to go home now."

Mikhail looked to Angelica before nodding curtly. "Of course, my dear Lady Dewberry. I believe I was beginning to suffer from a severe case of ennui as it is."

After everyone had gone to bed, Angelica left her room and tiptoed down the staircase in bare feet. Sleep was elusive to those who had something on their minds, and Angelica had a lot on hers.

Turning right at the bottom of the stairs, she crept toward the back of the house and to the room with the grand piano. If she had been at their country home, she would have ridden until her mind cleared. She longed desperately for her horse, for the open lands surrounding Polchester Hall. In London, a simple walk was even out of the question when the sky turned black.

"You are in London, for better or worse, and you had better get used to it."

Angelica's voice echoed in the large music room. Her bare feet carried her across the room, where she sat on the large windowsill, all the while giving silent thanks for the Turkish carpet that offered a semblance of warmth.

Her mind went back to the man in the ballroom once more. Was he the one who had spoken to her? Could he hear others' thoughts? Had he heard hers?

There were so many questions to ask, and yet, the possibility of getting responses scared her almost more than it excited her.

Most of all, she wanted to know why she had not suspected something like this was possible before now. Why had she not believed it possible for others like her to exist?

Her mind was dazed at such a notion, and yet how was she to find such a person? He or she could be anywhere in the world. What if she had walked past them and had never known it?

The endless possibilities whirled in her head and left her feeling more desolate than ever. She had to stop these crazy thoughts before she worked herself into a true frenzy. She had always been proud of her realistic nature, had she not? Now, more than ever, she needed to cling to that realism. She could not afford to dream with her eyes open. Let dreams be for sleep.

"Angelica?"

Angelica looked up to find Mikhail, still in his formal wear, looking at her questioningly. She must have been truly deep in thought not to have heard the front door open.

"Pleasant evening?" she asked tongue in cheek. It always amused her that her brother found it impossible to talk to her about things of a sexual nature. They both knew where he had been, and yet he would never admit it.

Clearing his throat, Mikhail walked across the dark room to sit beside her on the window ledge. "Pleasant, yes. What are you doing here?"

Angelica was almost sure that had there been light, she would have been able to see a pink tint to Mikhail's coloring.

Shrugging, she recited from one of her favorite Charlotte Brontë poems.

"I love the silent hour of night, for blissful dreams may then arise, revealing to my charmed sight, what may not bless my waking eyes."

Worry creased Mikhail's brow. "I believe Brontë referred to the beautiful dreams you might see in sleep, dear sister," he said as he stood from the ledge and offered her his hand. "Come, I'll take you to your room."

Angelica stood and tipped her face up to her brother. "I should let it go, should I?"

Mikhail thought for a moment, before he pulled her into his arms for a hug. "It would be for the best, Angel."

Chapter 5

Alexander nodded for Kiril to close the door to the large drawing room. Eighteen pairs of eyes trained intently on him as he walked toward the fireplace that was now ablaze with light. He had always had an affinity for fire. Large flames of yellow, red, and blue had an oddly calming effect on his ever-tense body.

"Alexander?"

Sitting in the armchair close by, James, Duke of Atholl, looked for all intents and purposes like a king. His evening wear impeccably cut, his necktie just so, and his light brown hair scraping his collar, he was the very picture of dignity.

James rose regally and stepped toward the fireplace. Though his body looked not a day over forty, his eyes held the experience of several centuries.

"It has been a long time, Alexander."

"So it has, James. You look well."

"And you. Thank you for coming upon such short notice. I am embarrassed to say that we could not handle this on our own."

Understanding the burden, Alexander put his hand on the shoulder of the man who had been his companion through several wars. The surprise that crossed James's face was not lost on him, and he realized how uncharacteristic his action had been. He pulled his hand away; he was not a man who touched or liked being touched, after all.

"Let us begin."

James nodded as he turned toward the other members of the clan. For a moment he had been reminded of the old Alexander, his friend who had laughed freely without qualms. Those had been good years, carefree years. But Helena's passing had changed all that. A different man stood beside him now, one that had closed his heart to all.

"For those of you who have not had the honor, let me introduce Alexander Borissovich, Prince Kourakin, leader of the East Clan."

All was silent and James continued.

"Alexander is here upon our request, to help bring Sergey Petrovalich to justice. We are all aware of the power of this vampire. He has killed many in the last few months."

Alexander looked around the room as the duke spoke. James was a soft-spoken man, a compassionate man, and yet he was the perfect candidate for the leader of the Northern Clan. His people regarded him now with respect and rapt attention.

Alexander was fairly certain of the loyalty of these members, but it was not in him to leave things to chance.

Leaning back against the wall, he began to scan the minds of those sitting around him. Their thoughts were much alike. Sergey had evoked much loathing in this group of vampires. And much fear.

He had almost reached the last member when he encountered a block. Most of them had not even realized his intrusion, and the two that had did not put up any resistance. This *hero* was trying to prove a point, though what that might be Alexander did not know. He regarded the vampire with curiosity. Brown hair, brown eyes, all of his features were of average size . . . there was nothing that stood out about him. When James ended his characteristically long speech, Alexander would make a point of finding out more about that one. For now, however, he had no time for games.

With a tiny push, Alexander breached the barrier and began to probe into errant thoughts.

The man's eyes shot from James to him. It was not anger, but shock, that Alexander saw in the expression. It took only a moment more for him to discover that the man was testing him for worthiness . . . that was something Alexander could understand.

I commend you. Your block is stronger than most.

How did you do that? Nobody has managed to breach my mind before!

I am not "nobody."

My apologies, Prince. Sergey killed my wife. I have only my son, who has not reached his majority. I need to be sure that this expedition that will take me away from him will be fruitful. I see now that it will indeed be. I am at your service.

We will bring him to justice.

With that, Alexander left the man's mind to move onto the next.

". . . Prince Kourakin will be leading the search for Sergey." James finished his allocution and resumed his seat by the fire.

Alexander was not a man prone to long speeches like his friend. In his usual direct way, he began without preamble.

"Sergey is stronger than most of you, if not all. He is also more adept at killing than you are. His mind is stronger than yours and his survival instinct keener."

He stopped to let his words sink in. There was a lot of shifting around in the room. Several men stood from where they had been sitting, sensing danger, their natural instinct was to move.

"I am telling you this because it is essential that you recognize your biggest strength lies in your numbers. Sergey is alone, and though he is stronger than every one of you individually, he cannot stand against you collectively. It will be your duty, from this moment on, never to find yourselves alone against him.

Two vampires were dispatched from this very clan. Two very able vampires who together could have brought Sergey in, but alone had no chance."

Looking into every face in the silent room, Alexander spoke slowly. "No more vampires will die, and mistakes will not be tolerated. Is this clear?"

The word *yes* echoed all around the chamber.

"Good then. Ladies, gentlemen. Sergey is in London, and it is up to us to find him. I want you all to be very social during these upcoming days. Keep your eyes and ears open. James will be holding a ball three days from now. It will be a crushing affair, and if Sergey is as cocky as his last action leads me to believe, he may very well make an appearance. I expect you all to attend."

As the vampires filed out of his house, Alexander's eyes narrowed in speculation. The lady in blue had not come. There were three members missing, yes, but they were unable to attend at short notice because they were in Western Clan territory. She had no such excuse.

Bringing his fingers together he looked into the fire that was slowly dying out. She had been on his mind since he saw her earlier that evening. There was just something about her . . .

"You are *the* Prince Kourakin, who single-handedly extinguished the Rebellion of 1678?"

Alexander turned and regarded the young boy standing behind the settee closest to him with a frown.

The man whom he had earlier conversed with moved quickly and put his arm around the whelp. "Forgive my son; he is young and does not know better."

A young vampire could cause more trouble than good in Alexander's book. Without another word, he crossed to where the boy now stood as quiet as a church mouse, his eyes wide with fear, and laid his palm across the boy's forehead.

What is he doing?
He will kill me.

The house is larger than ours.

I must smile so Father does not worry.

Mother, I miss you.

Removing his hand from the now sweaty brow of the boy, Alexander spoke softly.

"It was not single-handed; I had a lot of help. What is your name, boy?"

"Christopher Langton," came the timid reply.

"And how old are you, Christopher?"

"Thirteen."

Vampire children were a rarity, and it had been a very long time since he met one so young. The boy would have just recently started experiencing bloodlust, a very painful feeling for most vampires.

Alexander remembered when his growth had come upon him. His senses had been out of control. He had walked around for weeks, wanting to bite everyone that came too close, having to hide his glowing eyes and extended fangs throughout the day.

Though Alexander did not see the wildness in the boy's eyes, he knew it would be upon him soon. Before that happened, Christopher would need to be initiated into his clan and its laws.

Walking back toward the fireplace, Alexander addressed Christopher's father.

"His initiation will be soon."

Though it was not a question, Henry Langton responded. "Yes, Prince Kourakin. Because of the happenings the duke decided it would go on without the traditional three-day ceremony, but the initiation itself will have to happen soon. Christopher's pains have begun."

Alexander agreed with James's decree. The initiation would teach the boy to control his urges before they controlled him, and so it could not be postponed.

"Good. I will take care of the details."

Henry swallowed thickly. His wife's passing was still too fresh in his mind, taking a toll on his reasoning. He had not even considered that he would now have to find someone to take his Kristina's place during Christopher's initiation. It was usually up to the mother to find the baby that would be used, how had he forgotten?

"We would be grateful." Henry spoke sincerely and then put pressure on his son's shoulder to get the boy moving.

"Bye, Prince Kourakin," the boy said, and smiled.

Alexander watched as the pair made their way out of the room. He had not given much thought to children, although he supposed that he must. Few vampires lived to an age where they could procreate, and Alexander's time had come. It was his duty to the vampire race to sire a child, but it would have to wait until after his work in London was finished.

"How about a good stiff drink?"

James came from across the room and handed him a glass. The ruby liquid felt good as it traveled down his throat.

"Will you be staying the night, James?"

"No, I will be leaving soon. Margaret is pregnant with our first child, and I am finding it hard to leave her even for the shortest amount of time."

Alexander's brows rose in surprise. "Congratulations! I should have guessed only such a reason could have kept Margaret away. She was never one who could sit still."

James ran a hand through his hair and laughed. "Actually, I have to admit that I was the one who kept her from coming.

If it was up to her, she would be out the door looking for Sergey herself."

Shaking his head in amusement, Alexander poured himself another drink. The blood burned a path down his throat and settled into his stomach.

"How on earth did you manage it? I remember how difficult it was to get that girl to bring one a cup of tea, never mind sit at home when she does not want to."

James put his glass down and straightened his jacket. Talking about his wife had made his need to see her all the more imperative.

"My status of clan leader has its benefits, Alexander. She is honor bound to obey me without question, like all the others. And now, with your permission, I am going home to my irritated wife."

Alexander escorted his friend down the hallway and to the door when *she* popped into his mind again.

"Before I forget, do you have a visiting vampire here in London?"

"Not that I am aware of." James frowned. "Why do you ask?"

"I saw an unfamiliar vampire tonight at the ball I attended. She must have just come in and will report her arrival tomorrow," Alexander reasoned aloud.

James nodded in agreement. "When she does report in, I will be sure to notify her of what has been going on." Looking out into the darkened streets, James tipped his head to Alexander a last time before walking away.

Alexander returned to the drawing room and stood, silently watching the coals burn to ashes. They reminded him of himself somehow, the red glow dying in each log, bit by bit.

In his earlier years, Alexander had found great pleasure in life. A woman could always be found in his bed, and when the sexual pleasures failed to impress, he had fought in wars and dabbled in the arts. At one point, he had mastered the art of the paintbrush, and when he painted, he felt his soul light on fire.

Now it seemed the fire had died out and he was like the logs in the fireplace before him, desperately trying to hold on to that red glow of heat inside, waiting for a wind to set the fire to a roar once more.

The smoke in the grate lifted and twirled, dancing itself into a lithe form. . . . Helena.

His mind wandered to a time long gone, a time when his sister had danced around him merrily. . . .

"Oh come, just one dance, Alexander." Helena circled him, her hair dancing behind her, her smile like sunshine.

"I do not have time for dances, Helena, we are at war if you did not notice."

Helena stopped in front of him, hands on hips and admonished: "Alexander Kourakin, I hardly think that counts as an excuse when you are always at one war or another! Now come on and indulge me. What better way to see the joy in life, than to become a part of it? When you dance you become joy itself, you know."

Alexander shook his head and tucked an errant strand of his sister's hair behind her ear.

"What would I ever do without you, sweetling? Who would remind me to smile, or get cross with me because I frown too often, or persuade me to dance the eve before a battle?"

"Why, you needn't worry about things like that. I have the fiercest brother in the world, you know. He would never allow any harm to come to me, so I intend to be around for a good long time." Her expression going serious, her light gray eyes glowing with love, Helena held up her hands, "Now dance with me, before the Turks spoil all our fun."

Stomach clenching at the onslaught of regret, Alexander slammed his fist against the wall. By the time the crumpled pieces of stone found their way to the floor, the feeling was gone.

Sadness was not an emotion Alexander knew well. He was too sure of himself, too proud perhaps, to give in to the dark clutches of depression like so many had before him. But guilt was his constant companion, and it released him rarely.

Chapter 6

He licked his dry lips, his tongue scraping against the sharp points of his incisors. He was hungry again. It seemed he was always hungry.

It had been several days since his last meal, and the effects of the thirst were taking their toll on his senses. His eyes hurt from the sunlight out on the busy London street, and his insides clenched every time a human passed him by, unaware of the sweet smells they exuded.

He was tempted to reach out and grab any one of the little brown-haired boys that kept offering to shine his boots. It would be easy to grab a small wrist and sink his teeth into the pulsing veins that beckoned him so sweetly.

But, he had no desire for little boys, or even men for that matter. Women, human women, were softer, more giving.

His eyes scanned the street hurriedly. He needed to feel alive, and quickly. Later, much later, he would call the man to his side and give him a few more bits of information. Then the human would be ready at last to wreak havoc and begin the bloodiest war in all ages.

"Wait for me here, Richard, I will be back shortly."

He turned at the voice and watched the woman who had dismissed her driver enter a ribbon shop. She wore a pale rose day gown, its skirts adorned with flounces and ruffles more suitable for a ballroom. An overly long nose, round cheeks, and highly arched eyebrows, no one would deem her beautiful, but her round curves and sweet-smelling blood made her perfect.

He smiled a sharp-toothed smile as he made his way toward the shop, fingering the garnets in his pocket. They would look perfect, lying across her pale skin. He loved that about the English. They wore hats, gloves, and creams, everything to retain their pale color.

What are you doing? a voice inside his head questioned, but he pushed it away forcefully. He knew precisely what he was doing. He was getting dinner and adding yet another chip to the tower that would soon topple, he would see to it.

A bell jingled as the woman came out of the shop. She walked with small steps toward her waiting carriage, signaling with a single finger for her driver to get her packages. The man nodded and rushed toward the shop after having helped her into the carriage.

Sergey waited for the driver to enter the shop, then opened the carriage door and got in beside her.

"What in the name of—"

Shut up. He held her mind in a firm grip, reveling at that fear in her eyes. He knew she was trying to scream, trying to move, but she could not. She could not, because he was too powerful, he was her master now!

Racing footsteps coming toward the carriage alerted him to the arrival of the driver.

Tell him to keep the package with him and to drive you around for a while.

The woman leaned forward and pushed the yellow curtains covering the small window on the carriage door aside to speak to her driver.

"Keep the bags with you, Richard. I wish to be driven around for a while. And Rich—"

He stopped her midsentence, causing a ripple of pain to spread across her mind. She tried to scream but could not make a sound.

"Yes, my lady." Richard bowed as he climbed to the driver's seat.

He pulled the curtain so that it covered the window and smiled. She sat staring at him, paralyzed with fear. He knew there was nothing she could do, and it pleased him.

Regarding her high-necked dress, he realized that though he generally enjoyed taking his time, he was not in the mood for it this day.

Unbutton your dress.

She obeyed, though her eyes reflected the struggle she was putting up to refuse his power. Tears were coursing down her cheeks from the pain in her mind by the time the top of her gown had come undone.

He smiled as he reached across the small space between the seats and pushed the material down her arms. With a quick move, he ripped her undergarments so that yards of cloth lay around her waist as she sat with her heavy breasts and belly exposed to his sight.

He felt himself stir, but his sexual need was only secondary to his blood lust. The pulse in her throat was beating wildly, but the round globes that bobbed up and down in the rocking carriage caught his eye.

He pulled the garnet necklace from his pocket and clasped it around her neck, watching goose bumps form across her skin. It suited her perfectly, like little drops of blood; now she was his.

He loosened his grip on her mind enough for her to whimper, a sound that pushed him over the edge. Grabbing her arms he sunk his teeth into her breast and sucked.

Chapter 7

"I am very sorry my dears, but I will not be joining you this evening, I simply cannot get myself to leave the house in this condition." Lady Dewberry sniffled dramatically and held a white lace handkerchief to her pink nose. "Do take care of your sister, Mikhail. And for heaven's sake, do not go leaving her side now."

Mikhail raised the older woman's hand to his lips and smiled roguishly. "I will not let her out of my sight, though I must say that your presence will be sorely missed."

Her face turning the color of her nose, Lady Dewberry pulled her hand away and admonished, "Get on with you, you rascal."

Angelica stood by and watched the banter between her brother and her aunt with an odd sense of detachment. She had decided that morning that she had to have been mistaken. Her mind had likely played tricks on her; there was really no other explanation. But now that mind-reading men had been put to rest, the pressure of finding a husband had set in once more.

Her reasoning told her that she was making the right decision by not telling Mikhail. Her brother's heart would definitely suffer. Oh damn, damn, damn! She had to think. The viscount was out of the question now, so she had two other prospects to consider in more detail . . . and perhaps Lord Nicholas too, if he was rich enough, that is. She would have to ask around about him tonight, though discreetly of course.

Suddenly, going to the theater was no longer a happy prospect. Angelica found herself pining for Polchester Hall. There she could be free of all the unnecessary intrigue of London. Her mind could not keep up with the pace of the city!

"Angelica, did you say something?"

Angelica looked at Lady Dewberry and Mikhail who wore identically questioning gazes and realized she must have spoken aloud.

"I was just . . . saying that we might be late if we do not leave soon. As Louis the thirteenth said: 'Punctuality is the politeness of Kings.'"

Lady Dewberry nodded in agreement, but her brother seemed less convinced.

The carriage ride to the theater was a quiet one. Mikhail was as pensive as she was, and realizing that she had no clue what her brother was thinking disturbed her.

"Angelica, talk to me."

Angelica was so deep into her thoughts that it took her a moment to react to her brother's plea.

"I am sorry I have been distant, Mikhail, I do not mean to be, honestly." She was surprised when she realized how close to tears she was. What was wrong with her?

Mikhail reached across the small space and put his hand on hers. "Tell me, Angel, let me help. What has been going on? Are you still thinking about yesterday's occurrence?"

"I . . ." Angelica watched as Mikhail's fingers tugged on his shirt collar unconsciously. A quick look confirmed he was struggling for breath.

"Mikhail, are you—"

"I am fine, Angelica!" Noticing the anger in his tone, Mikhail took a deep breath and moderated his voice. "I am fine. You go on and tell me what is happening."

It felt like a betrayal not to explain, and yet, Angelica knew she could not risk Mikhail's health. No, she could not tell him, but she could not lie to him either.

"It is nothing really, and honestly I want to resolve this matter on my own. I have depended on you for far too long." Softening her tone she looked into the blue eyes that were so much like her own. "Understand me, please. I am twenty years old. Most women my age have several children, the least I can do is stop acting like one."

Mikhail pulled back, leaning against the leather material of the fashionable seats. If Angelica had not been watching him closely, she would have missed the indiscernible nod.

"We are almost there. Hand me your wrap, will you?"

Angelica handed over the dark green wrap that matched her evening dress but did not let go of it until Mikhail looked up at her in question.

"I forget to tell you sometimes that you are the best brother in the world."

For a moment, Mikhail said nothing and then sighed. He found it hard to accept that his sister did not want his help when she had relied on him her whole life. In truth, he liked taking care of her. That fact in itself made him wonder if maybe she was right. Perhaps he was too protective of her, just as she tended to be too protective of him.

Shrugging, he let a laugh cure his pensiveness.

"You are a minx, Princess Belanov. Keep your secrets, sister of mine, but if there is even the slightest possibility of some harm coming to you and you do not run to tell me, I will personally take a switch to your bottom!"

Angelica grinned, recognizing the idle threat for what it was. Feeling relieved, she turned to look out at the Royal Lyceum Theater.

"Do you think it was the least bit suspicious that Aunt Dewberry developed a condition right after she realized we were coming to this particular theater?"

Mikhail looked out at the throng of theatergoers lining up at the large doors and nodded.

"You know our aunt would not appreciate going to a theater less grand than Theater Royal. I doubt it matters to her that Henry Irving is starring in this new production."

Angelica agreed, and stepped out of the carriage just as a loud voice filtered over the crowd.

"Welcome ladies and gentlemen, to the production of *The Bells.*"

An hour later, all the feelings of love that she had harbored toward her little brother had disappeared. Mikhail had invited a friend to their box unbeknownst to her, and the man, a perfectly pompous lord with a perfect pedigree, was about to drive her crazy.

"So as I was saying, Lady Shelton . . . or should I call you Princess Belanov? Which do you prefer, my dear?" Tweaking his thin mustache between his thumb and forefinger, Lord Anthony Hettinger looked at her through his eyeglass.

Glancing at the curtains blocking the entrance of their private box for the fifteenth time in as many minutes, Angelica was ready to scream.

"I honestly do not have a preference," she said with as much calm as she could muster. She really did have to calm down because listening to Lord Anthony's thoughts was making her feel nauseous.

For the last hour, the man had been busily calculating how beneficial a marriage to her might be for him in terms of money, station, and social standing. He seemed to like the idea of adding a line of Russian nobility to his exalted lineage, though he was having a problem with her eye color.

In fact, a miniwar was taking place in his head about the negatives of possibly having blue-eyed children; the problem being that all of his ancestors had dark eyes, and he was not sure if he wanted to risk breaking that trend.

"Perhaps I should call you Angelica." Lord Anthony watched her face with avid interest after making that statement. If he thought she would give him leave to be more familiar with her, he was sorely mistaken. Determined to put him off, she made her voice sharper than it need have been.

"I hardly know you, Lord Anthony, and do not deem such familiarity proper."

When Anthony smiled, she knew she had erred. Curse

and rot! The man liked that she was prim and proper to the point of obnoxious. *Probably because he was the same way,* she thought rather gloomily.

Where could Mikhail be? It was scandalous to be left in the small cubicle with the man. When Mikhail did show himself, Angelica was planning to box his ears.

A prickling sensation on her neck had her glancing out toward the audience. People were milling about, using the intermission to socialize. Her eyes moved over glittering jewelry and freshly starched collars until they encountered the pair of eyes she doubted she would ever forget.

Chapter 8

Alexander sat motionless for a moment, taking in the face that had haunted him through the night. What did he want with her? he wondered. Something . . .

She looked stunning in her green evening wear. Her luscious black hair had been artfully swept up, leaving ringlets about her face to add softness to the look. It was her eyes, however, that set her apart from all the other beautiful women he had seen.

They were the color of the Mediterranean during a storm; a deep turquoise that sparkled with knowledge and with something more, something he knew well: pain.

He felt lust and then, unbelievably, anger when he noticed the man beside her. He wanted her he realized with clarity, he wanted her for himself.

"Alexander?"

Alexander did not take his eyes away from his black-haired witch as he asked, "James, did that visiting vampire report in?"

James shook his head no and pulled at his shirtsleeve. It was, overall, a frustrating day. They had found a flower girl who had seen a man fitting Sergey's description, but when Alexander caught the elusive figure he turned out to be an average ruffian.

They had handed the man to the police, as he was a thief and a villain, but all in all had gotten not a step closer to finding Sergey.

Refocusing his attention on Alexander, James responded. "No, she must have left."

"She did not."

Noticing for the first time that his friend's gaze was fixed on one of the theater boxes across from theirs, James scanned the seats. His brow furrowed in confusion.

"I do not see a vampire."

Alexander understood his friend's confusion. "She seems to be adept at blending in her aura. She is exuding human colors."

James was all attention at that piece of news. "Only an elder can do such a thing. That would make her our age, and yet we do not know of her existence? It is not likely, my friend."

"Speak to her yourself, James. She is the one with the green dress and the haunting blue eyes."

A suspicious look on his face, James scanned the boxes across from his own until his eyes came upon a stunning woman.

"It is not possible, Alexander. How could one forget having seen her?"

Alexander had not been able to figure out the answer to

that question either. She had to be an elder, which would mean they would have had to cross paths at the vampire gathering that took place once a century at the very least.

He had to put an end to this puzzle.

He directed his thoughts.

Good evening.

Angelica was so spellbound that it took her a moment to understand that she was hearing a thought in her head, a thought that was directed at her! Her eyes flared as she regarded her mysterious man.

Good evening? She sent the thought tentatively, having never conversed through thoughts before. What was happening? Had Lord Anthony succeeded in driving her crazy, after all?

I am the leader of the Eastern Clan. Perhaps you failed to find us upon your arrival, but I will need you to report in as soon as possible. We have a crisis on our hands at the moment that you must be notified about, and it will take the Northern Clan suppliers at least half a day to procure a ration of blood for you.

Angelica's eyes widened. *What?*

You need not worry, if you need a supply sooner than that, I will give you of my own, Miss . . . ?

Angelica was a hairsbreadth away from getting hysterical. She repeated Plato's preaching over and over like a prayer: "Nothing in the affairs of men is worthy of great anxiety . . . nothing in the affairs of men is worthy of great anxiety."

When that did not work, she shut her eyes and opened them again to find those of her mysterious man as if for reassurance. His gaze never wavered, but a moment later a sharp sting enveloped the front of her head.

She gasped in pain, and reached a gloved hand to her brow. The pain left immediately, and in its wake remained an odd sense of emptiness, as if something had been taken from her.

Alexander fought with the twinge of disappointment that he felt at his discovery. Just when he thought he had dispelled with that disturbing emotion, an odd sense of anger settled in its place.

"She is not one of us," he said somewhat needlessly. James had understood that well enough, having listened in on their conversation.

"The question is what *is* she if she is not vampire?"

Alexander shrugged, wishing the unwanted emotions that were coursing through his system could be dispelled with the movement.

"I have never encountered a human telepath before. At least not one who is that strong. Is it possible?"

James narrowed his gaze on the woman who was still staring in their direction, likely trying to communicate. The blocks that both he and Alexander had placed would keep her out, but the situation disturbed him. What was she?

"It is easier to believe she is a human with extremely developed telepathic abilities than to have to consider the possibility of a completely different race."

Before either of them could think on it more, a messenger boy ran through the curtains and into their box, almost tripping over himself in his hurry.

"Your Grace, a message!"

James reached out and took the folded missive. Alexander rose as he felt the tension building in his friend's body.

"Sergey, spotted outside the theater."

James did not have to say more.

Angelica fought with tears of frustration as the two men she had been regarding with such mingled confusion and hope got up and left their box. He was *like* her and she was losing him yet again.

"What do you think, my dear?"

For the first time in many minutes, Angelica remembered the presence of Lord Anthony. Though being rude was not something Angelica ever did willingly, she found that for the first time in her life she wished she could simply tell someone straight out that she did not wish to speak to them.

"Lord Anthony, this is painfully embarrassing, but I am afraid I must powder my nose."

Anthony looked at her with surprise before understanding gleamed in his eyes and his face took on its customary superior expression.

"But of course, Princess, your wish is my command."

Angelica said no more as the pompous lord escorted her out of the box and toward the ladies' room. She eyed the passersby with the hope of seeing the men or her brother. If only he were here to help her. Where in God's name are you, Mikhail? she thought furiously.

Once at the door of the ladies' room, Angelica turned to her escort.

"My dear Lord, do you think you might trouble yourself to fetch me a refreshment?"

Basking in the smile she had directed his way, Anthony bowed low.

"But of course, Princess. But of course."

Angelica pushed the door of the ladies' room with her white-gloved hand and waited for two heartbeats before stepping right out again. She had to find the men or find her brother and leave. Sitting through the entire second half of the play with Lord Anthony was simply not an option.

There were a few people milling about in the corridors connecting the upper boxes of the theater. Ladies were being escorted to the powder room, while a long line of formally clad gentlemen were speaking amongst themselves by the refreshment table.

"And here I was worried that this was going to turn into an exceedingly boring evening."

Angelica turned at the sound of the voice.

"Nicholas." Her smile was genuine, if a little distracted.

"I am flattered that you remember my name." At her sardonic look, Nicholas grinned. "All right, I expected you to. After all, how many men do you meet while hiding behind a large potted plant?"

Angelica laughed in response, but her eyes were busily searching the corridors.

"Now I find I am not flattered at all. What has you so distracted, my dear?"

"I am sorry, but I am looking for someone." She managed to calm herself enough to look Nicholas in the eyes. His thoughts had been coming to her all along, though she had been too distracted to decipher them till now.

Who is she looking for? Those eyes . . . so beautiful. Tell me your secrets, Princess. Come home with me.

The blush that stained her cheeks was automatic. Angelica did not have the time to analyze how she felt about his attraction to her. She found him attractive too, that was for certain. . . . Oh, she simply could not deal with all of this now. The men had likely left the theater, but maybe she could catch them outside. She had to go!

"Nicholas, I really am sorry, but I have to leave. My brother will be looking for me and—"

"Angelica?"

Angelica's eyes took in the disheveled appearance of her brother with relief. Had he been running?

"Mikhail, where have you been?" She held out an unsteady hand toward him and tried valiantly to smile. Mikhail took her hand immediately and squeezed.

"Looking for you," he said evenly as he regarded Nicholas. Catching his gaze, Angelica rushed to make the introductions.

"Mikhail, this is Nich—, Lord Adler. Lord Adler, my brother, Prince Mikhail Belanov."

The men shook hands, each assessing the other.

"It is a pleasure to meet you, Prince Mikhail."

"Pleasure is all mine." Mikhail inclined his head and tried not to wince as Angelica pinched him softly in his side. She was afraid Mikhail would want to question Nicholas to death and simply had no patience for it.

"Though I am afraid this meeting will have to be cut short. I have received word from my aunt, and Angelica and I need to leave immediately." The last of it was delivered to Angelica, and it was all she could do not to applaud his quick thinking.

"Well then, we must leave!" Angelica cast Nicholas an apologetic smile, "I do hope you will excuse us."

"But of course, Princess Belanov. London is not as large a city as one thinks. I am sure our paths will cross sooner than you expect."

Though the statement was rather odd, Angelica did not want to prolong the conversation by asking Nicholas what he meant.

"Well, good-bye then." She took Mikhail's arm.

"Good-bye." Nicholas inclined his head in her brother's direction, and a moment later they were heading down the stairs.

"Where have you been, Mikhail?" she asked the moment they were out of earshot.

"I've been looking for you!"

"Looking for me? You left me with that . . . that buffoon of a man and . . . Oh, never mind that now, can we go home?"

Thankfully, Mikhail did not ask for explanations as he nodded. They walked out of the theater and down the street to where their coach waited for them. Angelica saw no trace of her mysterious man or his friend, but she had not expected to. Too much time had elapsed since they had left their seats in the theater. They could be halfway to Scotland by now.

Mikhail was unusually quiet as he helped her into the carriage, his hair and cravat a mess.

Considering her own mind frame, she decided to give her brother the quiet he seemed to be wanting.

"Hopkins, please send a boy to box twelve with this message for Lord Anthony." Mikhail addressed the coachman as Angelica settled more comfortably into her seat.

Once that was taken care of, Mikhail signaled the driver to take them home. There was a moment of silence during which Angelica looked out of the carriage window and tried to clear her mind. She had to gain control of herself now. Losing her calm helped for nothing.

"I'm sorry I left you alone. I wasn't well."

The soft words uttered by her brother had Angelica turning to face him.

"What do you mean?"

Mikhail ran a hand through his ragged hair and closed his eyes. "I was getting a drink when there was a commotion at the bar. Two men were fighting about something or another. They both seemed to be foxed, trying to hit each other while two others were trying to keep them apart.

When I realized that I knew the chap holding one of the men, I decided to help out. It turned into a bit of a fight and then . . ." Looking at her with a strange expression, Mikhail breathed deeply. "I was just pushing one of the unaccommodating fellows into a hired hack when I felt the need to sit down for a little while."

Mikhail reached out for his sister's hand and looked at her worried face. "I am all right, Angelica, it was nothing. Nothing. I was being foolish, I should never have involved myself in such ridiculous affairs. I'm sorry for leaving you alone."

Tears finally spilled from Angelica's eyes. It was all too much. Lord Anthony and his impossible snobbery, her mysterious man who showed her so much, and then shut her off, and Nicholas, whose attention she should be cultivating because she needed a rich husband. And now to find that all the time she was getting angry and flustered, her brother was in pain and needing her help.

She held on tightly to Mikhail's hand, trying to give him some comfort and strength. "I am the one who is sorry. I should have guessed you would not leave me for any other reason. Promise me never to do such a foolish thing again, Mikhail; you're my only family. Without you there is no one."

Mikhail pulled her into his arms and smoothed her hair. "Hush now, do not cry. Everything will be all right, Angel. I won't be so careless again. I promise."

After a telling silence, Mikhail said somewhat dryly, "Come to think of it, if this condition did kill me, it might save me from all of your blathering."

Angelica laughed despite herself and hit her brother on the shoulder. "You are horrible."

Mikhail smiled, relieved that he had managed to stop the flood of tears.

"You do know that I am much smarter than you, Mikhail Belanov, don't you? Most everything I say has philosophic value."

"Your conceit is overwhelming. I hesitate to think what you would have done had you been born a man, Angelica. Actually I can envision it quite clearly." Mikhail's tone was somewhat sour, but his eyes sparkled with mirth.

Now that the crisis had somehow been avoided, Angelica focused on some of her earlier anger and asked with a frown, "What did you think you were achieving by bringing Lord Anthony along, anyway?"

Mikhail raised his brows in feigned innocence. "Whatever do you mean, dear sister? He is but a good friend of mine."

"Really?" Angelica asked suspiciously. "Then you will not mind if I ask you a few questions about him."

Mikhail nodded. "But of course."

"Does he have a house in London?"

"Naturally," Mikhail said slowly.

"He is from a good family, I suppose. No scandals waiting to surface?"

"None whatsoever," Mikhail agreed.

"He has a house in the country then?"

"Yes," he said more quickly.

"A big stable?"

"Yes."

"A large income?"

"Very large."

"And you met him yesterday?"

"The day before . . . you! Minx!" Mikhail laughed.

Angelica waved her hand as she concluded. "Well, he must be a very dear friend, indeed. Two whole days, imagine that!"

Mikhail shrugged as he pointed out: "It is no crime to want one's sister to marry well. He is far more respectable than half of the hopeful swine that drool over your hand at balls."

Angelica gave up the pretense of indifference. She too was looking for a husband, something she could not tell Mikhail as she had protested to the contrary far too often for far too long for him not to get suspicious at her change of heart. Either way her brother could choose his candidates with more care. "He is the most pompous man I have ever had the misfortune to meet. No, that is probably not true, but he definitely ranks among the top ten, Mikhail! Must you inflict such torture on me?"

Mikhail laughed, his eyes shining. "It is hardly torture, Angel, but I will try and discover if the man has his pomp-ousness under control before I choose another to introduce to you."

"You are impossible, Mikhail Belanov!"

Angelica turned once again to watch the streets of London rush by. Soon the trees and the sidewalks blurred until all she could see were a pair of haunting eyes. It alarmed her to realize how much she wished to see those eyes again. Being in her mysterious man's presence made her feel . . . she did not know exactly how, but it had to be good—did it not?— since she found herself thinking of him constantly.

Where are you? she wondered. Who are you?

Chapter 9

Angelica let her fingers rest on the piano keys for another moment before she reached up to make sure her coiffure had not come undone by her vigorous playing. Her hands trembled with released passion as she pushed several pins more firmly into place.

When sleep had come, the worry she felt the night before had disappeared together with consciousness. This morning she found herself considerably more relaxed and in control.

She had decided not to think about her mysterious man. If she did come across him again, she would question him, but if not, she would not drive herself crazy trying to find a man whose name she did not even know in a city as large as London. Mikhail's health was more important to her than anything else, and that meant that she could not expend energy on anything but finding a husband. And she had to find a husband quickly.

Feeling better for having made the decision to focus, Angelica stood and was moving toward the foyer when she saw the most beautiful peach-colored rose right outside the window.

She remembered very little about her mother, but Angelica did recall that peach-colored roses were her mother's favorites. On the spur of the moment, she changed the direction she had been going and headed for the kitchen, where she picked up a pair of scissors.

The rose would look beautiful on the dark wood of the dining table.

"Can I not be rid of you?"

Angelica froze just as she bent over to cut the rose. The soft breeze blew the hem of her dress about her ankles as her body tensed. She knew that voice, though until this very moment she had only heard it in her mind.

It simply could not be him.

"You are going to ignore me?" The amusement in his voice had her breathing slowly in and out. God, she was still bending over the rose, her back stiffening with every moment that passed. Why was she making a fool of herself?

"Hardly. You might notice I was doing something." Her voice came out just a little wobbly as Angelica snipped the flower expertly and straightened. A million things ran through her head as his face came into focus. He was so . . . elemental. There was no other way to describe the raw power of the man. His eyes left hers for a mere second as he looked toward the house behind her and back.

"You are Mikhail's sister, Angelica."

"Alexander."

It was an unusual response with a blatant disregard for

decorum. She did not respond, did not know how to. It was nerve-racking to be in his presence. He was like her, and she was scared senseless that he would disappear again without giving her a chance to ask the questions that had loomed in her mind for as long as she could remember.

"How do you know my brother?" she said after another moment passed. It was a legitimate question, but she was not really concerned about incidentals just then. He was standing in front of her and he seemed so steady. How did he look so steady when he was suffering from the same affliction as she?

He didn't respond, asking instead, "He is not a mind reader?"

"No," Angelica answered, feeling even more off-kilter. His being there, their conversation so far . . . it all felt like one extended dream. He was shifting as if preparing to leave. Who was Alexander? Did he only hear the voices when he was nervous or excited? Since when did he hear them? Would it get better? Worse? Before she could decide which of the million questions that popped in her head she would ask first, he spoke.

"You are the only one in your family with the ability?"

"The curse? Yes."

"It is hardly a curse."

She was about to make an equally unfazed remark, she really was, but then it occurred to Angelica that she had not heard a single thought. All this time that her heart had almost felt as though it were in her mouth, she had heard nothing, just as she had heard nothing in the theater after Alexander had turned away from her . . . nothing from *him* at least.

"How is it that I cannot hear your thoughts?"

Alexander cast her a confused look. "Because I do not choose to let you."

"You do not choose . . . what do you mean?"

"I block my mind."

Angelica ignored the fact that he spoke now as though he were speaking to a none-too-bright child. She was far too busy trying to calm her rising pulse.

"You can block others' thoughts from your mind?" Angelica felt an instant remorse for asking the question. She did not want to find out that it was an impossible feat.

Knowing that she would have to live with hundreds of voices in her head for the entirety of her life was worse than living with them and retaining the hope that one day she might find a way to block them all out.

"You cannot possibly mean that you do not know how to block thoughts." Alexander looked unconvinced, but when Angelica remained silent his eyes narrowed slightly. "No one could withstand the strain."

Taking a deep breath, Angelica tried to remain composed. Did it mean that he knew how? Could he teach her?

"Teach me. Please." It was the most important thing she had asked for in her life. Nothing else mattered. It did not occur to ask him why he was standing there, in front of her house. It did not matter how he knew her brother. She did not think of anything but this one thing. If she could learn how to do it . . . if she could shut off the voices, oh God, if only . . .

Angelica watched Alexander's expression and saw surprise come and go before he spoke.

"What will you give me in return?"

She did not hesitate. "Anything."

He nodded and appeared to consider for a moment before he spoke softly.

"I am going to enter your mind and retrieve a childhood memory. Try to stop me."

Angelica's eyes opened wide as she felt him enter her mind. It was as if a hand was pressing down on top of her head. It occurred to her that others could not possibly have the same feeling when she was reading their minds, otherwise they would know . . . they would look around or at least complain of a headache. At least Mikhail would have learned to recognize by now when she was reading his thoughts.

A picture of her father holding her hand and guiding her toward the stables appeared abruptly in her head. Alexander was seeing it too, she knew, he was seeing her past, her memories.

All of a sudden, Angelica became uncomfortable. She did not want a relative stranger accessing her memories, her feelings. She wanted him out, but she did not know how to get him to leave.

Think of a wall. Build it around your mind.

Alexander's voice was as clear as day, perhaps because he was so close. As she looked across the few feet that separated them, she realized that they were in full view of the street and likely presented an awkward picture to any passersby. They stood there, watching each other, not moving, not touching, not speaking.

But, she had to let go of all of that now. She had to concentrate on what Alexander was telling her.

She thought of walls, of bricks and of stones, but nothing

worked. Alexander was delving even deeper. She saw herself in Mikhail's room. He was six, she not much older and she was holding him as he cried.

No! She did not want him in her head anymore. Tell me how, I cannot block you!

Pick a place. A safe place. Imagine yourself there and then build your wall.

Angelica pictured herself in the woods close to Polchester Hall. The birds were flying, the flowers in full bloom, everything was so beautiful, so serene. She focused on the trees, and soon the space between them began to fill with brick tiles.

Every cube that followed the next made her feel more in control, more powerful. The bricks filled the gaps, moving up toward the tops of the trees with an ever-increasing speed. Soon they were all around her and she was in a well, unafraid and in control.

She opened her eyes and looked at Alexander. He looked back, a strange light in his eyes. He was out of her head, and the knowledge made her triumphant.

"Angelica?" Mikhail stood at the door, concern in his eyes until he saw Alexander.

"Alexander! I was wondering what was keeping you. I see you have met my sister."

"Yes, I have had the pleasure," Alexander said, but his attention was still firmly on Angelica. And then it hit her. She could not hear his thoughts, but neither could she hear Mikhail's. Her pulse was speeding, her nerves a-jitter, but she could not hear Mikhail's thoughts!

Nothing. She heard nothing, and the sweet quiet that came over her made her eyes fill with tears.

Peace, Angelica felt true peace for the first time in her life. Oliver Wendell Holmes would never understand just how meaningful his words had just become to her.

"And silence, like a poultice, comes to heal the blows of sound," she whispered the words too softly to be heard and yet they reverberated over her skin, making her shiver. The feeling was too great to suppress, too bewildering, too wonderful. Silent tears slipped down her cheeks and onto her dress with little splashes that filled the quiet around her.

Mikhail noticed her tears and was immediately by her side.

"Angelica, what is it?" He stood by her side, bewildered and unsure what to do as he took in the tear-streaked face of his sister. "Angel?"

Angelica could not bring herself to speak. How could she explain the enormity of the gift she had been given? It was like seeing for the first time, like breathing for the first time.

Thank you. Thank you. Thank you.

Alexander saw Angelica's tears and felt a tug somewhere in his stomach as he watched the siblings hug. He had lived many years and had come across such tenderness, such unrestrained love only a handful of times. Resentment mingled with discomfort as he realized he wanted to be a part of the scene. He wanted what they had.

Just as Alexander decided to leave quietly, Angelica pushed out from her brother's arms and wiped at her tears with fast movements.

"I am dreadfully sorry for having subjected you to my dramatics," she said quietly, and turned toward the door, "I bid you gentlemen a good evening."

Alexander watched his dark-haired witch disappear into the house and wondered what on earth had happened in the last minutes. He had finally met the woman who had haunted his dreams and had come to realize that she was a tortured soul. By all rights and purposes, Angelica Belanov should have been driven to madness, and that she was not mad showed him just how powerful her mind was.

In truth, the knowledge that he could not, even if he wanted to, penetrate Angelica's mind left him in awe. He had not come across a single vampire who could defy his will and now, this woman . . . she could keep him out even if he wanted in. It was an unsettling thought. An annoying one . . . but the gratefulness he had seen in her eyes made him soften.

A strained silence followed Angelica's departure and then the faraway notes of piano music filled the room.

"I don't quite know what happened there," Mikhail said quietly.

Alexander saw Mikhail's embarrassment and understood that the man was having trouble finding a way to explain his behavior.

"You do not need an excuse or explanation, Mikhail. I admire the devotion you have for your sibling."

"Well that is good then." Mikhail smiled, his face taking on a far more relaxed look. "Let's have some vodka, shall we?"

"I cannot stay long, but maybe one drink."

"Of course. I made you the list of men I know are interested in the jewelry business. I don't know why, but I would never have guessed that you were interested in jewels."

Alexander made no comment as the younger man led the way into the spacious house. When they were settled in a cozy study, Mikhail struck up a conversation but Alexander found he could not focus. His ears pricked up the distant strains of a haunting melody that held him firmly in its grip.

"It is how she deals with sorrow."

"What?" Alexander looked across the armchair at Mikhail. Though the man seemed to be a frivolous type at first glance, Alexander had recognized his intelligence easily, though obviously he had underestimated the man's perceptiveness.

"The music. It is captivating, no?"

There was no point in lying. He had been enraptured and he was coming to realize that it had probably shown on his face.

"Yes. It is beautiful." Swirling the clear liquid in his glass, Alexander continued, "Did I tell you about Murat Yavidoglu . . . ?"

The men were having a rather lively debate about the state of the Ottoman Empire when a servant entered the room to bring a folded sheet of paper to Alexander.

"A messenger brought you a note, sir. He did not wait for a reply."

Alexander took the missive as the servant left the room.

"If you will excuse me," Alexander said, and made to stand but was deterred by Mikhail's hand.

"Do not bother going to another room, I just realized that the music stopped. I am going to go check on Angelica. Take your time," Mikhail said as he stood.

Alexander nodded and waited until Mikhail left before scanning the note.

Chapter 10

Fear. Alexander could taste the filmy texture of it on his tongue long before he crossed the gravel to James's residence.

"Welcome, leader." The Duke of Atholl's trusted butler opened the heavy oak doors as he climbed the last of the marble steps. "Their graces are expecting you in the parlor."

Nodding, he moved swiftly through the grand foyer.

"Alexander." James moved away from a group of vampires. Worry had taken up residence in his eyes. Alexander looked around the room and counted thirty pairs of eyes, all wearing identical expressions.

"Another body?" he asked as James reached his side.

"A vampire."

His fingers pressed firmly into his palms, then released. There was more that James was not saying. The only thing worse than the death of one of their race . . .

"How did the slayer get to her?"

James did not look surprised that his friend had drawn the right conclusions about the murderer or the vampire's sex.

"We do not know precisely. She was a visitor from the Southern Clan. A messenger has been sent to notify Ismail of her passing. Her ceremony will take place this night."

That was the law, Alexander knew, but he wished they did not have to go through with a ceremony when they needed to be out there looking for the slayer.

He turned to face the vampires in the room. John, Christopher's father, was standing close by. Alexander beckoned the man and issued his orders.

"I need you to go to Scotland Yard. We need all the information we can get. Clues, prints, anything. This is a human; he is bound to leave marks."

"Yes, Prince." John was at the door when Alexander addressed the rest of the room.

"You have nothing to fear."

There was a considerable amount of shifting as the voices died down. Their fear was not gone, but they were listening, so Alexander continued.

"This is one man, but it would not matter if it were two, or ten, or one hundred. We have faced much worse before. Some of you were there, some of you were yet to be born, but know this. We did not end an age of vampire slayers to stand by and allow another to begin."

The air was decidedly lighter as Alexander stopped to look at the faces who now watched him with trust.

"Tonight, we all have a burial ceremony to attend. Tomorrow, we will hunt the slayer."

James stepped beside him and looked intently at his clans-people as his servants passed around glasses of red liquid.

James lifted his cup. "To our clan."

The blood in his glass swirled as Alexander followed suit. "To our race."

The room filled with voices as the age-old toast was completed. "To the Blessed."

"Everything is set for this evening. Though I wanted to check the grounds on which we will do the burning, but your men seemed disinclined to let me out of the house, James," Margaret, the Duchess of Atholl, complained as her husband and Alexander entered the library.

James pointed at the settee by a large window for Alexander to sit, then approached his irate wife.

"You know it is for your own protection, Margaret."

Margaret arched a skeptical brow and glanced at Alexander.

"Alexander dear, you have known me for a long time. What do you think? Can I manage to go to the woods and back without getting hurt?"

Watching the couple, Alexander decided it would be smarter not to get involved in their affairs.

"I am sure James has his reasons, Margaret."

"Oh, how drearily political of you, Alexander, you have become a clan leader, after all! You are just as stuffy as all the others."

Alexander took no offense, and James only snorted.

"If Isabelle or Ismail heard you calling them stuffy, they would be here in short order to prove you wrong, my dearest."

"Well, not stuffy then, but so serious."

"These are serious times, Margaret." James's tone had his wife walking to him.

"I know, love, and I am sure you and Alexander have much to discuss. I will leave you two in peace."

Alexander watched as James's eyes softened and his shoulders relaxed. His friend had transformed in only seconds from a worried leader with too many responsibilities to a young man with starry eyes, and Alexander envied him for it. He was tired of being alone, he realized, which in itself was a revelation. Alexander had always liked being alone. Well no, that was not quite true. Before Helena died, he had never been alone . . . but since she left his world, he had been content by himself. But now, now he seemed to crave more. . . .

"I will see you tonight, Alexander." Margaret's voice brought him out of his musings.

"Till tonight," he responded, though she had already left the room.

"I will begin compiling a list of possible slayers." James walked around the large desk at the back of the library and started going through drawers. "Unfortunately, we do not have much to work with as yet."

Alexander walked to the window and watched as one of the grooms walked a white stallion across the gravel.

"Do not worry about the length, James. Just make the list. I will find the bastard."

Coming up with parchment and quill, James nodded.

"We know that he is rich by the material from his coat the runners found hanging on a nearby branch. That means we could be looking for a rich merchant or one of the ton."

"How could he have known that she was a vampire?" Alexander wondered aloud. He turned from the window and watched the duke make quick black marks on a white sheet of paper. "If it were one of your clan, it is conceivable that the slayer had been watching. But she was a visitor newly come to London."

James blew on the ink, then looked up. "She was a visitor, yes, but she has been in England for a while. She was staying in a country residence just on the outskirts of London and visited us a handful of times. If he has been watching for a few weeks, he would have seen her before."

That made sense, Alexander supposed, but there was something about the murder that did not make sense. If the slayer had attacked anyone else, he would have likely had a much more difficult time of it, as the clan members had all been instructed to stick together. Even if the man had managed to get one of them alone, someone would have heard the cry for help. Someone would have seen something . . .

"Here you go. These are the first men that come to my mind. Since the beginning of Sergey's killing spree, there have been rumors of the killer being other than human. My clan members reported these men as spreading rumors of vampires."

Alexander took the paper, but he doubted the list would bring up any slayers. "Our slayer is not likely to go about telling stories."

"You are right, but it is a start."

Folding the paper, Alexander slipped it in his pocket and squared his shoulders. There was a lot to do, and little time to do it in.

"I will see you this evening."

James nodded as he stood from behind the desk. "When John gets back with the information, I will begin compiling a more comprehensive list. It will be done by tomorrow."

"Till tonight then."

"Alexander?"

Alexander turned as he reached the door of the library.
"Yes?"

"Be careful."

"I am always careful."

Chapter 11

Alexander walked into the National Gallery in Trafalgar Square, his mind on the meeting that would take place shortly.

Early that morning, he had been informed that a messenger would arrive with a list of possible slayers from James. In a spur of the moment decision, Alexander had told Kiril to send the informant to the Gallery, where he would be waiting for him.

Kiril had regarded him oddly upon the unusual request, but said nothing. It was as well, since Alexander had had no intention of speaking of his urgent desire to be surrounded by paintings.

It was odd, but for the first time in a hundred years, Alexander felt a shadow of his long-lost passion for art. Perhaps it had something to do with the music he had heard in the Belanov residence. The melody haunted him still; every note infused with a passion he had not felt in it seemed forever.

She haunted him still. What was it about Angelica Belanov that made him want her every time he saw her? She was as strong as she was beautiful, and Alexander caught himself thinking about her far too often.

A wave of nostalgia hit him as he walked the painting-lined walls and took in the familiar strokes and colors of a Rubens masterwork. Alexander remembered the weeks he had spent in Italy with Peter Rubens. The memories were so vivid, it was hard to believe that almost three hundred years had passed since those carefree days full of color and life.

Peter had possessed a vitality and inventiveness that came through his fingers and brush onto the canvas. A vitality that Alexander had envied and enjoyed.

Moving slowly from room to room, he let the art fill him the way it used to. Rembrandt van Rijn, Raphael Sanzio, Claude Monet. . . . Their craft surrounded him, teased his heart and made his fingers itch for paint and brush. And then the near euphoria faded as he neared the room where he knew they had displayed *Death*.

His footsteps echoed along the marble floors as he approached the painting. Would it still be in the same spot? Would it have faded like his very soul?

As he looked toward the corner of the room where *Death* should have been, he saw the woman. With hair like the night sky and a face that rivaled those of the most beautiful women of the past that lined the walls, she stood blocking his view.

He breathed in her intoxicating scent and wondered why he was not surprised to see her.

Angelica turned as he approached, as though she had felt

his presence. Her thoughts were locked in her mind but her eyes gave away her surprise.

"Prince Kourakin," her soft voice echoed in the large room. He watched her eyes as they softened. "I am so glad you are here."

Alexander felt pleasure course through him at her words, but said nothing. He had yet to decide what to do about his attraction for her.

"I mean, what a pleasant surprise." Angelica flushed with embarrassment. She was mortified by the words that had leaped out of her mouth unbidden, but she did not move. She wanted him to know how grateful she was to him.

"The pleasure is mine, Princess." Alexander bowed.

Angelica fidgeted at the ensuing silence. "What brings you to the gallery?" she asked at long last, finding nothing better to say.

Alexander was amused by her effort at conversation. She was nervous and for some reason that pleased him.

"I came to admire the paintings, what else?"

At the mention of paintings, Angelica turned back to the piece that had so riveted her only moments before. The colors were bold, exciting, and somehow very, very sad.

"Yes, it is beautiful, is it not?" she said, once again caught up in the torrent of emotions before her.

Alexander regarded her profile as he tried to imagine where she could possibly have seen beauty.

"I would hardly call it beautiful."

Angelica glanced at him in surprise, her back straightening at his sarcastic tone.

"And why not?" she asked.

He did not respond to her question. "Is the subject matter not a bit too virile for an innocent such as yourself?"

Angelica had no idea why he seemed to be taking pains to be contrary and condescending, but she was beginning to get angry. Too virile? She wanted to laugh. The faceless man in the painting was dying.

"Actually, no," she replied simply.

Alexander arched a brow. "You are not afraid of death?"

"No," she said again.

Alexander was surprised at the simplicity of her reply. She was serious.

"Is your faith so strong then?"

Angelica laughed, then covered her mouth with a gloved hand. The last thing she wanted was for Lady Dewberry to hear her and come barging into their conversation. Her aunt had dragged her to the gallery, but Angelica did not have to suffer through the woman's endless chatter about the fine points of baroque art . . . not again.

"It has naught to do with faith, Prince Kourakin; it is just that we die every day."

Alexander regarded her with interest. "I suppose you will explain?"

"The man who made this painting is dead. He died the very next day."

Alexander nearly smiled at the irony of her statement. Little did she know that "the man" was standing right beside her.

"How do you know that? The artist is unknown."

Angelica shook her head. "That hardly matters. We are who we are due to our experiences, so it stands to reason that we change constantly. And the person we used to be? That person has died." Pointing at the large canvas she said, "He died and whoever he was at that moment is no more."

Alexander knew she was right. The man who had laughed and loved, the painter who had enjoyed every moment of his existence was certainly dead.

She turned to regard him, her eyes willing him to take her seriously. "I was a different person yesterday, a person in constant pain. Now I am someone new. Similar, but different." Taking a deep breath she continued, "Yesterday I died and I am happy with who I have become. I have you to thank for it."

Alexander watched her in silence. He wanted to paint her, he realized. He wanted to kiss her until she looked at him with more than gratitude.

"Besides," she shrugged as she turned back to the painting, "I know for a fact that if heaven and hell exist, they are right here on earth, so what is there to fear?"

Heaven and hell were both right here and Alexander had tasted them both. He watched her watching his painting and knew that she had too.

"I doubt if many people think the way you do," he said finally.

Angelica shrugged, vaguely disappointed that he had not acknowledged her thanks. "They may not realize it, but they do. What do you think all women want?"

At his pointed silence, Angelica continued. "Love."

"Yes, of course," Alexander said sardonically. He had been thinking money, jewels, and attention.

Angelica ignored him. "Precisely, and what is love? Most people see it as something elusive that radiates from a member of the opposite sex, something they grab with both hands as tightly as they can."

"You see it differently, I presume?" Alexander was surprised to realize that he was interested in her unconventional thoughts.

"Love, to my way of thinking, is the emotion one feels when they meet someone who makes them be what they want to be. We feel love toward someone who shows us the light, who pushes us to become what we have always wanted to become but may have never realized. We love the person who makes us love ourselves."

Alexander considered. "So you cannot love someone if you do not love yourself?"

"Precisely," Angelica said, and smiled.

Alexander stepped closer to her and was gratified when she took a step back. "And how do you explain why even though we barely know each other, it is my fondest wish to kiss you till no thoughts remain in your head?"

"That would be lust," she replied breathlessly. She knew their conversation had gone far beyond the limits of propriety, but could not seem to walk away. "A very different emotion that is felt with much more frequency, though fleeting where love is not."

"Ah, Princess, I believe you are a romantic beneath all of your highly rational thoughts on love."

Angelica stood her ground, refusing to be intimidated by the predatory look on his face. "If it is romantic to hope that love may be everlasting, then I suppose I am."

"And what if you never find love? Will you die without experiencing lust?"

Angelica looked at his handsome face and his tumultuous

gray eyes and wondered how she dared to continue the conversation. He was obviously experienced, very experienced in lust, and she felt herself falling under the spell he was weaving.

"Then I will not have missed much," she said with false conviction.

"Are you suggesting that you can go through your entire life without being kissed and feel as though you have lived fully?" Alexander asked softly. There was only an inch of space between them now.

"A kiss without feeling is merely the touch of skin on skin; I have felt that before."

Deciding that the headstrong woman in front of him needed to be taught a lesson, Alexander pushed his fingers into her hair and pulled her into his kiss.

He swallowed her surprise as their lips molded against one another. Her hands grasped his shoulders to push, but held on as her head filled with his scent, his power . . . him.

Alexander groaned into her mouth, unable to believe what she was doing to him. His eyes closed as he angled his head and deepened the contact. Their tongues brushed and she whimpered, only serving to heighten his need. He wanted more of her, more.

The smell of her blood filled his head and had him pulling back.

Angelica touched her lips reverently as she looked up at him.

"Why, Angelica! There you are!" Lady Dewberry chose that precise moment to arrive. Before Angelica could form a coherent thought, Alexander nodded.

"It was a pleasure," he said with his face as impassive as it had been when he arrived, and then he walked away just as her aunt reached her side.

"Who was that, Angelica? You ought not to speak to men when no one is around, child! It is highly improper!"

Angelica watched Alexander disappear into the next room and turned to her chaperone. "That was a friend of Mikhail's, Lady Dewberry, Prince Kourakin."

"Oh." Lady Dewberry looked mollified upon hearing the prince's name. The rumor mills had been churning about him, and it was said that he was not only very eligible but that he also had a veritable fortune. "Well I suppose that is not so very bad, then, if he is a friend of Mikhail's, but it still would have behooved you to call me to your side when you were approached by a gentleman."

"You are right of course, Aunt Dewberry, I will endeavor not to make the same mistake again." Angelica smiled, although her mind was still with Alexander. Every time he was around she felt breathless and ready to fight, and when he was not she was looking for him.

And that kiss. He had definitely proved her wrong. Kissing was . . . so much more than she had imagined.

"Shall we return to the house?" Lady Dewberry interjected into her thoughts.

"Yes," Angelica replied. She wanted to be alone after what had just transpired. She needed to think. "I am very tired and would like to rest before dinner."

Chapter 12

"Henry?"

Sergey looked up and beckoned the man he had met only days earlier at a small dinner party in Kent.

"Sit, sit, Jonathan. We have been waiting for you, have we not, ladies?"

The two elegantly dressed women beside him giggled, their cheeks flushed from the wine he had been plying them with.

"I had no idea you had company. Had I known, I would have made myself more presentable!" Jonathan said as he took his seat at the dining table.

"Nonsense! Ladies, this is my good friend Jonathan. He seems to be under the impression that he is underdressed, but I say he looks good enough to eat. What do you think?"

The women said nothing, but another fit of giggles burst out of the one with the red hair.

"You like giggling, do you?" Sergey's blue eyes twinkled mischievously. He lifted her hand and brought it to his lips, turning the palm out in the last moment.

"Oh, Henry . . ."

The smell of her blood almost made him lose his head, but not quite. He would enjoy her, he decided. She would be dessert.

"And now," Sergey stood, rubbing his hands together in anticipation, "it is time for dinner!"

The ladies laughed and all three humans looked toward the doors, expecting servants with platters.

"I think your servants have misjudged the hour, Henry," Jonathan pointed out.

The blonde with a smattering of freckles spoke excitedly, "What will we eat, Henry, is it something special? Please do tell us!"

Sergey smiled as he stood and circled the table until he stood behind Jonathan's chair.

"I will not tell you, my dear. Why don't you let me show you instead?"

Sergey let his incisors grow as his fingers circled Jonathan's neck. The women sat entranced by the white points of his teeth gleaming in the light from the candleabra for another moment before they began to scream.

A sickening sound filled the room as Sergey snapped Jonathan's neck and grabbed the blonde.

"You wanted to know what was on the menu, my dear." Sergey leaned toward her as he held her from her waist. "Do you care to guess?" Fear sent the blonde fainting to the ground.

Disgusted with her weakness, Sergey let her drop for the

time being and moved toward the street door. He could hear the redhead pounding on it, trying to escape. Her hysteria tasted good.

So good.

It was too bad he could not take more than a few moments with her. Company would be coming soon.

"Oh God, oh God, oh God!" she saw him coming, her back to the door.

"Now, let us try that again, shall we, my dear?" Sergey smiled as he slipped his hand into his pocket. The beads were slippery in his dry palm. "This time you say, 'Oh, Henry' or even 'Oh, Sergey.'"

His hand dug into her throat just as she was about to scream.

"Welcome, my love, I have missed you." Sergey walked into the parlor where his guest awaited him. Disposing of the three bodies had been tedious, but he was in a good mood overall.

The woman walked into his open arms and held him tight. "You were right."

"I was?" Sergey's voice was particularly condescending, but the woman did not seem to notice. She was secure in the belief that he loved her. He had seen to that.

"You told me there would be slayers, and I have to admit that at first I thought you might be mistaken. But you were right. They cannot do this anymore; they have to be stopped!"

Sergey smiled inwardly, though he made sure that all she saw was concern on his visage. Human or vampire, women were just too easy to manipulate.

"Do not worry. We will stop them. Once the clans see what we know is true, they will stop hiding. They will fight back, instead of bowing to humans like slaves."

She pulled away the hand he had grasped, and paced. Sergey counted her steps and by the time she had reached thirty, he knew he had her. She was his now.

"Prince Kourakin is more than capable, why can we not go to him, Sergey?"

He deserved a crown for this, Sergey thought to himself with pleasure. Everything was working according to his plan.

"We cannot, love. They would judge me if I cannot make them see the severity of the situation. All I need is time. With a little bit of time I can deliver the slayer to the leaders and then they will listen."

She nodded solemnly.

"Your job is easy. Just make sure that the leaders do not find me, until I can rid us of our human predators."

"You mean to go after the slayer yourself?" There was uncertainty in her voice. Although Sergey had no such intention, it peeved him that she did not believe him capable of the task.

"Of course! I have killed plenty of humans who meant us harm already, have I not? I protect this clan far more effectively than our leaders ever could, my dear. They cannot do what I do, because they are bound by ridiculous laws."

It took a moment, but she nodded in acceptance.

"I have to leave."

"Yes, of course. Go home. And remember to mislead them. All you have to do is give me time and trust me. Everything will be all right."

Sergey watched her leave and listened to her receding steps. Laughter bounced off the rafters on the ceiling. Perfect, it was all perfect. She would ensure that he would not be found and give him the time to begin the bloodiest war mankind had ever witnessed.

Chapter 13

Angelica got dressed quickly in a riding habit of emerald green and set out, a footman following at a discreet distance. The horse she was riding was a beautiful gelding with an even temper and made the ride all the more enjoyable.

She smiled up at the sun and found herself on the verge of laughter. Sunshine three days in a row . . . the world was being kind.

Yes, she missed Polchester Hall, her house and her horse. Yes, she had to find a husband and quick. And, yes, she had met a man who attracted her to no end and confused her just as certainly . . . but she had decided to put all that aside, if only for a few minutes. Somehow everything inside felt calm and the richly decorated card that her maid brought to her room earlier had a lot to do with it.

Lord Nicholas Adler, a man she was almost certain she could

like and like well, had asked her to ride with him in the park.

It was a good sign. Nicholas was rich according to her aunt's wealth of knowledge. He was amiable and made her feel at ease unlike some other men of her acquaintance. He was also the type of man that she could keep at arm's length, the type of man who would likely desire some space himself and who would never have to discover the truth about her.

If all went well and Nicholas proposed, she would no longer have to worry about finances, hers or her brothers. And once they were married and settled, she could continue her life in the peaceful manner she had once led it. Reading and riding and playing her pianoforte—how she missed the calm of her old life.

Angelica breathed deeply as she was surrounded by the greens and browns of Hyde Park. In only a short time she would meet Nicholas and she would do her utmost to gauge what his intensions truly were.

"*Hooa,*" a distinctly disgruntled female voice pulled Angelica out of her musings. She turned around to look toward the closest entrance to the park, where a striking redhead was trying to regain control of her mount. The woman's features were truly extraordinary, eyes the color of a cloudless sky were the only soft features in the angular face with high cheekbones and a small sharp nose.

The lady was doing all the right things, but the horse did not look like it wanted to comply with her instructions.

Ignoring the footman who waited off to the side, Angelica turned her mount and inched closer to the pair. "Do you require some assistance?"

The redhead looked up and smiled, though the lines in the corner of her mouth spoke of the pressure she had to use to keep her horse in control. "Nothing to be done, really. A rabbit spooked him, so he is throwing a little fit. He will come around in just a moment."

As if on cue, her horse took two more steps backward and then quieted.

Angelica was impressed by the woman's steely nerves. No matter how trained a horse was, they were prey animals and therefore inevitably got spooked by one thing or another. She remembered a time when a jackrabbit crossed Shura's path during one of her afternoon rides. Angelica had nearly been thrown.

After brushing invisible specks from her riding habit, the lady with steel nerves set her horse moving and came over to where Angelica waited.

"Thank you for your offer though; my name is Joanna."

Angelica liked the open smile Joanna directed her way and responded with a smile of her own. "I am Angelica, and you are most welcome, though you obviously did not require any aid."

"I might have," Joanna said in all seriousness as she pushed some of her burgundy locks out of her eyes. "Damn hair always is in my way. Sometimes I just want to cut it all off."

Angelica laughed at the annoyed expression on Joanna's face. "If it is any consolation, it is absolutely beautiful."

Joanna's brows flew up as she regarded the woman in front of her. "A woman who is not eaten with jealousy in London? I believe you just became my best friend."

Angelica laughed harder and gestured toward the far end of Hyde Park.

"Care to join me for a ride, best friend? I have a little while before I am to meet an acquaintance."

Joanna saluted at her with her right hand and clicked her heels to get her horse moving. "Let us ride, shall we? If Peter here studies the grass just a little longer, he will give into temptation and start eating, and then I will have a big problem on my hands."

Angelica smiled and started her mare off across the grass, when she realized they were being followed only by her footman.

"You are unchaperoned?" she asked with some amazement.

Joanna laughed at Angelica's expression. "As much as I wish I could be, I am not. Thomas, my footman, that is, got waylaid a little while back. He'll catch up soon."

Angelica raised a brow at her new friend. "Waylaid? Is that another way of saying you outran him?"

Joanna grinned. "Well if you wish to get technical . . ." Shrugging, she changed the topic. "So, tell me where you have been hiding yourself. I am absolutely certain I have never seen you before and I have attended so many balls and functions recently I can barely stop smiling," Joanna said conversationally.

Before Angelica could reply, Joanna twisted in her seat and pointed at her cheek.

"Do you see that?" she asked dramatically.

Angelica tried to bite back a laugh as she regarded what looked like a dimple. "Yes?"

"Aha, exactly as I thought!" At Angelica's confused expression, Joanna looked at her intently. "It looks like a dimple, does it not?"

Angelica nodded.

"There you have it! I did not have a dimple in the beginning of this season, believe me. It is a sure sign of oversocializing!" Joanna exclaimed with relish.

Angelica could only laugh at her companion. Joanna had a wonderful penchant for the ridiculous.

"Why do you indulge in so many gatherings, then, if you despise them so?"

"A person who cannot live·in society, or does not need to because he is self-sufficient, is either a beast or a God," Joanna said matter-of-factly.

"Aristotle," Angelica said with pleasure. To have met a woman who liked quoting "dead people" as most females of her acquaintance would put it, was a delight, indeed.

"Exactly," Joanna replied, looking at her with renewed respect. "Now, I know I am not God and the alternative definitely bothers me. I would rather not be a beast either, so I socialize."

Angelica's mind drifted as the two of them continued riding between trees and across dappled ground. She hated socializing. Did that make her a beast?

"I am trying to pretend that that made sense, Joanna, but it is difficult."

Joanna laughed and brought her horse to a stop. "You and I, my dear, have to meet more often, far more often."

"She is hilarious, Mikhail, and I had such a good time." Angelica reached across the large breakfast table and grabbed at the silver dish containing the salt before her brother could pour another pound of the stuff on his eggs. "You know that is not good for you!"

Mikhail rolled his eyes and resigned himself to a spice-less life. "For all your little size, you can be a real tyrant, Angelica."

"Twixt Kings and Tyrants there's this difference known; Kings seek their Subjects good: Tyrants their owne."

Mikhail stopped in the act of cutting his eggs and shook his head.

"How on earth you are able to memorize all of those ridiculous quotes you sprout about, I have no idea! Where do they come from?"

Angelica sipped her coffee from the delicate porcelain cup decorated in flower prints.

"That particular one is from *Hesperides*, a work by Robert Herrick."

Mikhail chewed vigorously and pointed his fork at her. "I am going to lock the library door. No woman or man for that matter should read as much as you do."

"There you are in error, my sweet brother."

Grabbing the *Times* from beside Mikhail's plate Angelica grinned. "As I figure it, reading is key to knowledge. Knowledge is key to wisdom. And as our good friend Horace wrote sometime between 68 and 65 BC: 'Dare to be wise!'"

"Princess Belanov!" The disapproving voice of her aunt was enough to knock the cocky smile from Angelica's face. When she realized she was holding the *Times*, she thought furiously for a moment before she complained, "Mikhail, you have been playing with me. There is no picture on this page!"

Mikhail laughed as Angelica half handed and half threw the paper at him.

"Sorry, sister dear." He stood, taking the paper with him

and walked around the table. "I am off then. I will see you two ladies later, I am sure." Leaning down as if to place a kiss on his sister's cheek, Mikhail whispered, "Keep up appearances; there lies the test; the world will give thee credit for the rest."

Angelica turned as Mikhail left her side.

"Who said that?"

Mikhail kept walking, his smile growing wider as he heard his sister huff indignantly. She was altogether too smart, and Mikhail enjoyed leaving her to wonder.

He found himself laughing as he guessed at what Angelica would be doing that day: most likely digging through every book in the library to find the quote.

Angelica watched her brother depart and then turned warily toward her chaperone. Lady Dewberry had been dying to have the "marriage talk" with her for a few days now, and Angelica feared that the woman had finally worked up the nerve to deliver the lines she had been practicing.

"Angelica." The informality of the beginning would surely set the tone of the lecture. Angelica tried to get comfortable as her aunt took the seat her brother had vacated.

"In these last weeks, I have come to worry for you deeply, Angelica. For this very reason I want to speak frankly." Lady Dewberry took a deep breath as she leaned forward in her chair. Angelica regarded her with affection, noting how each of her silver strands was exactly in the right place.

How would life have been if she had not had her ability? Would she have been less willful? Would she have read less and followed more of the popular beliefs? Would she have married sooner . . . would she have been like Lady Dewberry; composed and even tempered?

"Your parents passed away a long time ago, and I know that was hard on you and Mikhail. I have tried to participate in your upbringing to the best of my ability, but I worry about you, Angelica, because you show no real interest in marriage. It is the most important thing in a woman's life.

Now, I have been going to functions with you so that I might direct you toward the eligible bachelors with good reputations. But my dear, you seem to be less than, how should I say, excited at the prospect of finding the right man, and it makes my job so much more difficult."

Angelica realized that her aunt was genuinely concerned for her future, and she felt a moment of regret at making her unhappy. But her aunt would not have to be unhappy for long, as she would be getting married soon one way or another.

"Your mother also took her time in getting married. . . ."

"She did?" Angelica sat up a little straighter. She had asked so many questions about her mother in the past, but her aunt had always been disinclined to speak of her departed sister. That she was doing so now, and revealing such a particular piece of information, had Angelica almost teetering on the edge of her seat.

"Yes," Lady Dewberry acknowledged, "but she had entirely understandable reasons, let me assure you. It was all a misunderstanding really. Our father, your grandfather, that is, had a spat with his brother, your great uncle Robert. Your grandfather refused to speak to him, and in a moment of extreme foolishness, Robert had your mother kidnapped and dragged off to his home in the highlands."

Angelica tried to picture her mother being dragged to the

highlands in some dark coach, but simply could not. How had she known none of this till this very moment?

Lost in memories, Lady Dewberry's expression took on a faraway look. "If that were not bad enough, the messenger that was meant to deliver the note that would get your grandfather to the highlands posthaste, disappeared never to be seen again. Though Robert sent other messages when your grandfather did not show, little did he know that his brother was off on a boat to the Americas because of a color-blind detective who swore he had seen your mother at the rail of the *Elisabeth* on its way to Boston."

"Oh my God! How long did it take Grandpa to find my mother?"

"Nearly two years."

"Two years!" Angelica could not believe it. Her mother had spent two years with her great uncle Robert waiting for her father to come and get her? What must she have felt? What had she done all that time?

"Yes, two very long years. So you see, it was hardly your mother's fault that she took her time in marrying. Actually when you think about it, the minute she came back to London she met your father and they were married within the month."

To Angelica's mind that was a rather quick courtship, but then her mother must have had her reasons. And, she reminded herself, her father had been the most charming man she'd ever met. Gorgeous, brave, strong, and smart, her father was a born diplomat and must have swept her mother off her feet. What woman would not have married him in a heartbeat?

"You need a husband, my dear, someone to look after you and give you children." Wrinkles formed on Lady Dewberry's brow as she picked up the thread of her lecture. "You do want children, do you not?"

"Of course," Angelica replied without hesitation. In truth, she wanted a child more than anything in the world, but that was something she never told anyone.

"Oh, good," Lady Dewberry said, and nodded approvingly. "Now I know that you have a penchant for quotes, so let me give you one, my dear. 'Thy husband is thy lord, thy life, thy keeper . . .'" The lady hesitated as she tried to recall the rest of the famous lines from Shakespeare's *Taming of the Shrew.*

Angelica waited a few moments more before quietly saying, "Thy head, thy sovereign; one that cares for thee, and for thy maintenance commits his body to painful labor both by sea and land."

"Yes, exactly." Lady Dewberry smiled. "That is precisely right. Now, I hope I can count on you being more attentive to my advice about certain gentlemen."

It was not a question, so Angelica did not respond, choosing to nod instead.

"Good. Now let us broach the subject of ladylike behavior. . . ."

Half an hour later, Angelica took in a ragged breath as she made her way to the library. The lecture had gone on for so long that she would not be surprised if the words *marriage, husband* and *children* popped out of her mouth spontaneously!

Little did her aunt know that she was making an effort along those very lines, and had even thought that she had made some progress until a little while ago.

Nicholas had been waiting for her where he said he would,

but he had acted quite odd. Only moments after she and
Joanna reached his side, he was telling her that he had a very
important appointment to keep and had left.

At least he had promised to make it up to her by taking
her on a carriage ride in the afternoon.

Closing the library door behind her, Angelica checked the
clock on the wall to make sure she was not running late on
her meeting with Nicholas.

"Another forty minutes." She smiled as she regarded the
book-covered shelves. She would find who had written that
quote that Mikhail had blurted out earlier.

"Princess Belanov?" The light rap on the door made her
look up from the book she had pulled from the nearest
shelf.

"Yes?"

A maid popped her head in the door and curtsied.

"Begging your pardon, Princess, but Lady Dewberry ex-
pects you in the drawing room. You have a gentleman caller."

"Thank you," Angelica said as the maid bobbed up and
down once more and left. A gentleman caller? She hoped
to God it was not that horrid Lord Anthony. She had been
informed that he came by almost every day. Thank God for
Herrings. The steadfast butler never budged once Angelica
told him she was not receiving.

Now as she neared the drawing room she reminded herself
that she had to be nice to whoever the gentleman was. Especially after the conversation earlier with Lady Dewberry!

Could it be Nicholas? He might be early. . . .

"There you are, dear!" Lady Dewberry exclaimed as Angelica entered the room. "Look who has come to pay you a call."

Angelica's mouth nearly dropped open upon the sight of

him. She tried a smile, but found herself thinking of their kiss and blushing instead. Why did the man have such an effect on her person?

For one tiny second, Angelica wished that Alexander Kourakin would pass Lady Dewberry's list of eligibility. She knew instinctively that with him she would never be bored. He was smart, well traveled, and if two days before was any indication, giving and understanding.

Most important, he already knew what she was, and he hadn't run in the opposite direction. He was like her.

The thought disappeared into thin air as soon as he stepped closer. The man was far too strong willed, far too powerful. He would never allow her any freedom and would expect complete obedience. Angelica doubted if she had it in her to obey without question.

No, no. Nicholas was a far better match. Plus, Angelica doubted that Alexander had any intention whatsoever of getting married and she needed to be married and fast. No, he was no marriage prospect, but he had given her the most invaluable of gifts: peace.

"Prince Kourakin." She curtsied almost imperceptibly and smiled up at the man who was more or less a hero in her eyes—a potentially dangerous hero. "I trust you are doing well this morning?"

He did not smile, nor did he send her the heated look she was becoming familiar with. Instead he turned toward Lady Dewberry.

"Can I offer you some tea?" her aunt asked.

"I would love some," Alexander responded.

To Angelica's utter surprise Lady Dewberry nodded and smiled. "Let me go see to that right now. Normally I should not leave my niece unchaperoned, but you are Prince Mikhail's friend, so I trust in your good judgment." Shooting Angelica a look that said "be polite," she left the room.

"Your good judgment?" Angelica watched her aunt leave the room in confusion. How had she agreed to leave her alone with Alexander?

Alexander did not seem to hear her or to notice her bafflement.

"You will stop what you are doing."

Angelica blinked up at the imperious man before her.

"Whatever do you mean?"

Alexander pushed on in his characteristically forthright manner.

"What I mean is you will stop seeing Nicholas Adler."

Confusion melted away as Angelica's temper began to rise. Who did he think he was, trying to tell her what to do?

"I have no idea where you arrive at the belief that you can tell me what to do. I will see whomever I please."

When Alexander recovered from her biting retort, his answer came as a growl. "You do not know what you are getting yourself into. This is a dangerous matter, and I will not have you traipsing around like a target waiting to be hit."

Angelica could only stutter.

"Have you gone mad? How can you possibly believe it might be dangerous for me to see Nicholas?"

It was only at that moment that Angelica realized she had no idea how he was privy to her actions. How had he known that Nicholas and she were so much as acquainted? Suspicion grew in her mind and her eyes narrowed.

"Are you following me?"

His laugh was short and degrading. "I have more important things to do. Now, this is my final word on the matter. I bid you good day."

Bowing curtly, he turned to walk out of the room and into his waiting carriage. He reached the door when a familiar tingling in his forehead had him turning his icy gray eyes to Angelica. She stood casually by the settee, tendrils of her black hair flowing around her face, looking as innocent as can be.

Alexander did not speak as he walked toward her. Angelica did not move, but stood unflinching in the face of his silent fury. He had no right, she kept reminding herself, to come into her home and give her orders. The man was insufferable and she would not be intimidated!

But it was hard not to feel fear when she saw the rage boiling in his eyes.

When Alexander's hands grabbed her arms and lifted her off the ground, Angelica could only let out a muffled shriek.

His voice was quiet and all the more dangerous as he spoke.

"Don't you dare try that again, do you hear me? The last person who tried to read my mind ended up in a lot of pain."

Angelica felt the power in the arms that dangled her over the ground like a doll. She saw the anger reflected in the steely gaze. She heard the growl that sounded like that of a lion's. She did not for a moment doubt that the man who had dared to breach Alexander's privacy had indeed felt a great deal of pain. . . .

Yet her fear disappeared. She was unafraid. She knew with a certainty she could not explain, that this man would not hurt her.

"Is my brother aware that you read his mind?"

Angelica had no idea where that had come from, but it seemed to cool Alexander's temper. He lowered her slowly to the ground, his eyes narrowing into mere slits.

"I am going to continue seeing Nicholas, with or without your blessing. And if you continue threatening and man-handling me, then you will have to be willing to give up your friendship with Mikhail because I will tell him of your ability."

"Have it your way, Princess." Alexander bowed yet again, but this time he stepped toward her.

Angelica found that for the first time throughout the con-versation, she was truly afraid. With his lips only a hairs-breadth away from hers, Alexander was more frightening than he had ever been.

And then he kissed her, and all Angelica could do was give in to the passion. This was no slow exploration as their last kiss had been, but a burning assault on her senses.

In two steps he had her against the wall. Her legs would have given out from under her had his body not been there to hold her in place.

"Alexander." It was a request, a plea, a desire. Her fingers slid into his hair as his head dipped lower, brushing kisses along her jaw, then her neck.

"Promise me," Alexander whispered.

His tongue slid along the sensitive skin behind her ear and she shivered.

"Wha-at?"

"Promise not to see him."

Her world spun as his fingers played along her spine. What was he doing to her? He wanted her promise . . .

"No." She pushed at his shoulders knowing the movement was halfhearted. She did not want his heat gone.

"You are playing with fire, Angel." His words were soft, almost a caress, and it was their clarity that caused Angelica to stiffen her spine. Though she could hardly form a cohesive thought, Alexander was obviously not affected at all.

He was watching her, his breath fanning the tip of her nose and cheek. She had to show him she would not be intimidated. She *was* intimidated, curse and rot the man!

"When we conquer without danger, our triumph is without glory. Pierre Corneille."

Angelica had no idea where that quote had come from. None whatsoever, although she was finding that under duress, all sorts of nonsense popped out of her mouth.

Alexander regarded her with an expression one might have mistaken for humorous and then stepped back. He looked like he was about to say something, but then, without another word he was gone.

Confusion and embarrassment overcame her all the same time. She should be feeling victorious, but instead Angelica found herself wanting his heat back.

She had wanted him to kiss her, she realized with some shock. What was the matter with her reasoning lately? Had Lady Dewberry's hour-long lecture made absolutely no impact on her? She was looking for a husband, which meant she should stay as far away as possible from men with whom there would be no future. Men like Alexander.

As she turned to make her way out of the drawing room, a thought suddenly occurred to her.

Alexander had said that he had caused a lot of pain to the

last person who had tried to read his mind. *The last person who had tried to read his mind?*

Angelica came to a standstill as the implications of the phrase hit her. There were others who could read minds. It was not just Alexander . . . there were others!

He knew others like her, but why would he not tell her about them? Did he assume that she knew?

Lifting her skirts she ran out of the room and for the door. She had to know. Were there others like her? Could it really be that she was not a freak, that she actually belonged somewhere or with some others like her?

Chapter 14

Alexander walked down the dark street, his mind racing. There were preparations to be made for the upcoming ceremony, the latest information on the jewelers had to be reviewed, scouts had to be questioned, but all he could think about was her.

Sighing, he ran a hand through his hair, his frustration coming to a boiling point. He had told himself countless times that exploring what was between him and Angelica Belanov would have to wait until after everything was over, but somehow he got himself tangled up with her again and again.

She was a distraction. A problem. And now she was spending time with potential vampire slayers!

When Joanna had reported that Nicholas Adler, a man on James's list of men who fit the vampire slayer profile, was very possibly courting Angelica, he had left everything and turned up at her home. He had not been thinking, he realized now, but all his attention had been focused on one objective: stop Angelica from seeing the man.

And what the hell had she done? She had looked up at Alexander, her arms akimbo, and she had said no. No one told him no!

Angelica Belanov made him want to break things and kiss her at the same time. How could she distract him in this way? He could hardly believe he had stood there in some godforsaken drawing room and fumed while she waited for him to explain himself.

Of course he had not. Not only because he could not, but also because he had refused to stand and explain himself to some little chit, no matter how insane she was driving him with desire.

Damn it, he had to stop thinking of her. It really was not all too important, as Nicholas Adler was one of the least likely prospects of the sixty or so men on his list. Nevertheless, he would see to it that Angelica would stop seeing the man. He would use Mikhail to influence her, and if that would not work, he would have the man leave London. Better yet, he would arrange for Angelica to leave London. That should ensure him some peace of mind.

The scent of blood turned his head left. He took four steps and knocked on the darkly painted door.

Name.

Alexander's mouth twisted into a sardonic smile for what was likely about to happen. He was not known for visiting such places, so they would not be expecting him.

Alexander Kourakin.

The door opened swiftly to reveal a gap-mouthed doorman.

"Welcome, leader."

Alexander inclined his head and walked past the man into the dimly lit hallway. He could hear the sounds of voices above a violin playing a soulful melody. The hallway opened up to a large room with high ceilings. Settees had been placed all across the space as well as a few small tables and chairs. A mahogany bar was set up by the back wall and a large staircase led to a second floor.

Vampires were scattered around the room, some sitting with others at the bar. Alexander spotted Kiril on a couch with a brunette. She was dressed, like most of the other females, in a black form-fitting sheer dress.

"Leader." A voice by his side drew his attention. Alexander looked at the woman, taking in her full breasts and luscious mouth.

"My name is Catherine. May I get you a glass of blood?" She smiled, her eyelashes sweeping her pale cheeks. A look around the room showed several males watching them with interest. She was desired by all of them and she knew it.

Alexander nodded, then turned back to where he had seen Kiril. He had not known what to expect while coming here this night, but now he realized that he should have known. The women surrounding him did nothing to stir his lust. Only Angelica did that to him.

Kiril.

Kiril leaned away from the woman he had been kissing and looked across the room. His eyes reflected his surprise.

My Prince?

We have things to discuss.

Alexander indicated the empty table in the right corner and Kiril nodded.

"Here you are." Catherine was back with a crystal glass full of red liquid.

"Thank you." Alexander took his drink and walked to the table where Kiril was waiting. He watched as the woman circled the room slowly. Several vampires stared his way. They would not disturb him, he knew. They would wait for an invitation.

Kiril leaned forward. "Prince?"

"I need you to do something for me." Alexander explained what he needed, all the while aware of the voices that were begging to be let into his mind. He kept them out but could feel them growing more insistent as the night progressed.

An hour later the heat in the room had risen to an almost unbearable degree. Black material littered the room and moans ensued from the naked bodies dancing to the age-old rhythm of life.

Alexander watched a male dribble blood over the back of a naked woman and then lick, his eyes the color of the liquid he swallowed.

He drained the last of his drink as his conversation with Kiril came to an end.

"Do you wish me to return with you to the house?" Kiril asked.

Alexander looked around. "There is nothing further to be done this night; you may stay."

Kiril inclined his head, his gaze getting caught past Alexander's shoulder. "Leader, we wait for you." Catherine was by his arm. Alexander had known she would approach. Several women stood behind her, their eyes glowing red in their excitement. He watched as Catherine slipped her arms out of her dress and let the skimpy material pool at her feet.

Kiril cleared his throat, unable to take his gaze from the perfection of Catherine's body. He waited for a reaction from the Prince, as did the women. It was true that a female vampire had the right to choose her mate at such a gathering, but a leader was an exception to the rule. A leader always chose.

Alexander sat unmoving for several moments and looked at the bared body before him. It angered him that her rounded breasts did nothing to stir him. It angered him that he had no desire for her or any of the women in the room.

He did not want her.

At the slightest tip of his head, Kiril stood from the table and rejoined his brunette.

Alexander did not speak as Catherine straddled his lap and kissed him. Hands stroked over his shirt, then on his bare chest.

The lips on his skin felt dry, useless. The hands caressing his stomach were cold. An image of Angelica came unbidden into his mind. She looked at him, defiance written across her face and desire in her eyes. He had wanted to kiss her in her parlor, kiss her until she could not speak. Then he would have stripped her . . .

He felt himself grow hard. He wanted Angelica, but he could have only them. Alexander slipped his hands under Catherine's hips and lifted her as he stood. A redhead swept her arm across the table, clearing it in one swift motion. He laid the body in his arms across the small surface.

His shirt was gone, removed by the three pairs of hands that now traveled the length of his body. They kissed him, hungry openmouthed kisses. He imagined it was Angelica's hands, her mouth.

Hair brushed across his shoulder blades, Angelica's black hair. A pair of breasts pushed against his back, her breasts.

He undid his pants and pulled the woman in front of him closer to the edge of the table. His eyes were closed as he spread her legs and entered her.

Angelica. Her name echoed through his mind as he pushed deeper. *Angelica*.

Chapter 15

"Great, just great," Angelica muttered grumpily as she opened her eyes to find her covers pulled over her head. She had meant to find Alexander and pound him with questions until he gave in and told her all she wanted to know, but had gotten sick to her stomach and slept instead.

Of all the rotten luck in the world, to have developed a sensitive stomach at such a time! And now she was suffocating under her own covers!

"Well good evening, sleeping beauty."

Mikhail's far too sunny smile came into focus as her brother pulled the material from her face and pushed several strands of her hair away from her forehead. "You are not sick, are you?"

Angelica refused to return his bright and chipper smile, reaching out to touch the stubble on Mikhail's chin instead. "You are not really walking around like that, are you Mikhail? How on earth will you impress the ladies?"

Mikhail ran his hand across his face and grinned. "This will hardly deter me. As it happens, the women of London find it makes me look more dangerous."

"They do, do they?" Angelica sat upright in her bed. It occurred to her that Mikhail might very well know where Alexander would be this evening. If only she could find a way to ask without being obvious . . .

When Mikhail only continued grinning, Angelica looked toward her window.

"What time is it?" she asked, trying to sound as casual as possible.

"It is almost past dinnertime, you lazy girl. You'd better get up and order a bath if you don't want to be late for the costume ball."

Drat! She had forgotten about the ball completely. The need to know about other mind readers warred with the need to go to the ball and find a rich husband.

She could tell Mikhail she wasn't feeling well and get out of going to the affair, which would likely be as boring as all the others she had been to but . . . The warm smile on her brother's face had her swallowing her excuses. Keeping Mikhail healthy and smiling just like this was more important than anything else. She needed to make an appearance at this ball and further her acquaintance with Lord Nicholas as well as some other eligible bachelors.

"What are you going as?"

"I was thinking a half-Russian, half-English aristocrat; you?"

"Mikhail, you are too funny for words." Sarcasm dripped off of Angelica's tongue. "Men have it so easy. They put on a pair of dark trousers and a jacket and voilà, they are acceptable at all occasions. Me, I must wear a costume, otherwise the women at the ball will cluck their tongues at me until I feel the need to hold them still."

"'I am not denying the women are foolish,'" Mikhail quoted with relish.

Angelica ignored her brother's grin and waved her hand so that he would step away from the bed. As she threw the covers aside and walked toward her closet she remarked, "You seem to have forgotten the rest of the George Eliot quote."

"Oh?" Wearing an innocent look, Mikhail watched his sister open her closet and discard one dress after another.

"The whole sentence reads: 'I am not denying the women are foolish: God Almighty made them to match the men.'"

Mikhail grinned. "*Hmm*, yes, I do seem to have overlooked that part of it. I am off then, Angelica, I will see you in a short while."

Picking a Grecian dress made of white and gold silk, she turned to her brother. "Run then, coward."

"I cannot believe that man!" Angelica grimaced as she looked toward the baron, who was now dancing with a blonde dressed as Marie Antoinette.

"Men are pigs. It is a fact, not a question." Joanna shrugged as she leaned over and patted Angelica's bare shoulder. "Although I have to give the man some credit, looking the way you do tonight it's a wonder he did not attempt to do more than just give your rear a little tweak."

Angelica shot her friend an annoyed glance, but did not comment. She was angry at herself more than anyone else. She had wasted considerable time with the baron, thinking that he was a possible candidate for groom, when the man wanted nothing more than an easy fling. She had to be smarter with her time; after all, she didn't have much of it!

Now, as the evening wound down, her feet hurt and she had made no progress. Nicholas had not turned up and it being a masked ball made it difficult to recognize most of the guests. How was she meant to find the marquis that was on her list of possibilities in the throng of colorful masks?

"Would you care to dance, my lady?"

Joanna covered a laugh as Angelica turned to the man who had approached her. He looked far too young to be a prospective husband.

"Thank you, but I'm afraid my feet are sore."

"Then perhaps I can bring you a refreshment, my goddess?"

Angelica heard the giggle that escaped through Joanna's fingers and tried valiantly not to roll her eyes in irritation. This was not funny in the least! She had to find a husband, and all she found were ridiculous boys and men who played at being boys!

"It is kind of you to offer, sir, but I believe I will retire to my home in a moment."

"Then perhaps I could—"

"No, you most certainly could not!" Angelica cut him off before he even suggested escorting her home.

"As you wish, my Venus," the boy bowed deeply and left, to her great relief.

"Oh my Venus!" Joanna deepened her voice in imitation of her unwanted gallant.

"Stop it, Joanna! You are terrible," Angelica hissed just as another gentleman approached. Older than the last and dressed impeccably in a green brocade jacket he bowed low over her hand.

"Princess Belanov."

Angelica glanced at her friend in question. Joanna mouthed a name at her behind a cupped hand. Trenson? That could not be; she did not recall a Trenson . . . oh, but of course. Angelica smiled suddenly.

"Lord Trenton." She inclined her head. Here was a real possibility. Lord Trenton was a widower and an exceedingly rich man.

Looking pleased to have been recognized, the lord held out his hand to her.

"May I have this dance?"

"Why, of course." Angelica caught Joanna's nod of encouragement as she walked out to the dance floor with Lord Trenton.

He put his hand lightly at her waist and began guiding her around the room in graceful circles.

"I have been admiring you for a long while," he spoke after a few moments of silence. Angelica was not quite sure how to react. Most of her acquaintances would flirt expertly at such a remark, but she was unpracticed in such matters.

"It could not have been so long, Lord Trenton, when I arrived in London only a short while ago."

"Call me Richard, please."

Angelica had a feeling that this familiarity was growing a bit too quickly, but she told herself to relax. She needed a husband, and this man might very well do.

"Do I seem forward, Princess Belanov? I do not mean to. It is just difficult not to be when you are clothed so . . . sensuously."

Alarm bells began to ring in her head. What was this man going on about?

"The way that silk clings to your hips, your breasts, it makes a man—"

"Stop!" Unable to believe what she was hearing, Angelica pulled lightly at her arms to bring the man to a halt. She had heard such thoughts in her mind before, but no one had been so blatantly forward with her. The man was obviously deranged, and he was not letting go!

"Lord Trenton, let me go if you please. I find I am no longer in the mood to dance."

Lord Trenton looked as though he was about to argue with her, then he came to an abrupt stop, his eyes glued above her left shoulder, his hands going slack around her waist and hand.

Grabbing at the opportunity, Angelica turned away from him and almost walked into the tall figure.

Alexander. She recognized him instantly. He was dressed in black, his only concession to the themed ball a black silk mask framing his eyes. Jaw clenched, his eyes boring into those of the man behind her, he looked like the devil. And then he looked at her, and lifted her limp hand so that the mask she had let drop once again framed her face.

Angelica felt movement behind her and knew Lord Trenton had left. Now it was only the two of them, standing amongst dancers that waltzed by them on either side.

She took a step forward. He put his hand around her waist, and they began to move.

He was a wonderful dancer, she realized quickly, effortlessly guiding her without seeming to push in the least. Her head barely reached his shoulder, so she had to pull back a little to see his face.

"Thank you for that."

Alexander said nothing, and soon Angelica began to slip out of her daze. She had been dying to speak to him earlier and now the questions in her head were there once more.

"I tried to catch up to you when you left."

"Oh?"

He was not looking at her, which made speaking to him that much more difficult, but Angelica was determined.

"Yes, after I . . . well after I made you mad, you said . . ."

"Don't ever do that again." He was definitely looking at her now. His earlier anger was still palpable, but she was too focused on her questions to care.

"You said that the last time someone tried to read your mind they got hurt," she continued.

"Angelica . . ." There was warning in his voice.

She had let her mask tip sideways, her eyes begging him to tell her what she needed to know.

"Are there others like me? Like us? Is that why you said that? Alexander, please tell me. I need to—"

His hand encased her jaw, his thumb resting against her lips to keep her from speaking. Suddenly Angelica could not think, she could only feel.

She had no idea how they had found themselves in the center of the room, but they were now surrounded by dozens of blurred faces and ridiculous costumes. The dance floor was impossibly crowded and no one seemed to be looking their way. They were alone in this crowd of people, his hands on her face and waist, both of hers resting on his arms.

"Alexander." His name came out a soft whisper. She was confused, lost in the moment. All questions had left her head, all problems flowing out of the open terrace doors on the sensuous notes of Mozart's waltz.

His thumb rubbed over her lips and she stepped closer, unheeding of the scandal she was about to cause. Suddenly she had the uncontrollable urge to taste him. The tip of her tongue trailed over the pad of his thumb. His eyes changed color, becoming a hot silver. He tipped his head forward and then stopped.

"Alexander?" She was slowly coming back to herself, a cold she had not felt before causing goose bumps.

"I need to leave."

"What?" The song had come to an end and couples were making their way toward the sidelines. How had she not noticed that the music ended?

"Go to your brother, Angelica."

She looked up at him, confusion bursting in her mind. He was right; she had to go to her brother. She had to think of Mikhail, she had to gain control of herself. Only a moment more and she might have ruined every chance she had in making a good match and salvaging their financial situation.

It was terrifying to realize that if it were not for Mikhail, she would not have cared. She did not care about what other men or society thought of her. She did not care about anything when it came to this one man.

"I need to go." She lifted the mask to cover her face once more and turned to walk off the dance floor. When she got to the edge and glanced back, Alexander was gone.

Chapter 16

Angelica had a lot of sneaking-out-of-the-house practice from the time they lived in the country and she had partaken in secret moonlight rides. For that reason, the two-story climb down from her bedroom window was no real challenge, though the dress she was wearing made things a little bit more uncomfortable than it was in the country where she would borrow her brother's breeches and shirt.

Although it was a mere fifteen-minute walk up Park Lane to get to Alexander's house, Angelica knew that getting there unseen might present a problem. She would just have to be very fast and stay close to the dark sides of the sidewalks.

Pulling the hood of her cape farther up to shield her face as her boot-clad feet touched the ground, Angelica ran to the gate and looked quickly up and down the street.

Not a leaf stirred on the deserted road.

Perfect.

Angelica grabbed two fistfuls of skirt in her palms and ran. Why she held her breath she had no idea, but it turned out not to have been such a good idea, since by the time she found herself at Alexander's gate, she was completely out of breath.

The gate was, quite naturally, locked.

Damn! Now what? If only the blasted man had bothered to read her note. The response she had received only a quarter of an hour ago was outrageous. It was penned by Alexander's assistant. Angelica remembered every word clearly as she had read the note over and over in disbelief.

Dear Madame,

Prince Kourakin is currently indisposed and will not be able to attend to your note until a later date. Rest assured that your message has not been read by me or anyone else in this household.

Respectfully,
Prince Kourakin's assistant

Well, if Alexander Kourakin thought he could get rid of her that easily, he had another think coming! He had made her forget herself at the ball, how she still did not know, but she would get him to speak about the other mind readers if it was the last thing she did! Angelica thought furiously as she looked around for inspiration. The dark mansion looked foreboding, the walls and gate around it impenetrable. But no, if she had learned one thing from all the books on warfare she had read a few years back, she knew that no structure, especially not a town house, was impenetrable.

As Angelica moved across the gate to the other side of the wall, a shaft of moonlight fell on her, illuminating her like a spotlight.

Casting an annoyed glance at the sky, she stepped back quickly. "It is the very error of the moon, she comes more nearer earth than she was wont and drives men mad."

The quip from *Othello* left her lips and traveled on the cool air around her.

What to do? What to do?

Spotting a rather large tree around the corner, Angelica almost clapped with glee.

"Perfect, perfect, perfect."

A particularly thick branch leaned on the top of the wall, and the moon had found no favor in this part of the grounds.

Taking one more look around her, Angelica tucked the skirts of her dress into her waist, exposing her legs to the cool air, and climbed. After one near fall and a few scrapes on her palms, she made it up to the wall and to the other side.

Now what? she thought to herself as she tried to keep from laughing. She really had to curb her impetuousness from now on. What misbegotten notion had landed her on Alexander's property in the middle of the night? Yes, she was angry, and yes, he had a lot of explaining to do, but could she have not waited a few hours?

All the years spent relatively alone, surrounded only by family and the staff, who were also family, in their own way had led to this outcome. She had apparently lost sight of how a lady had to behave as her aunt kept implying.

If truth be known, she did not care much for ladylike be-havior, but her aunt did. Sometimes she wished that she were more ladylike just for Lady Dewberry's benefit. The woman had put so much effort into her upbringing.

Oh, what was she thinking? Standing by the wall arguing with herself was likely the most ridiculous thing she could be doing at that moment, second only to being there to begin with.

Moving swiftly from the shadow of the wall to what looked to be the kitchen entrance, Angelica covered her mouth with her hand in order not to have a nervous laugh attack.

It occurred to her that trying to get past the front door at this ungodly hour was definitely not an option. How little had she actually thought all of this through?

As she looked at the kitchen door an idea came to her, and she thanked her lucky stars that Mikhail had bought her that naughty book for her thirteenth birthday. *Things That May Save Your Life* had been a book full of rough illustrations of things she should probably never have learned to do. Listening more clearly through doors by placing a glass on the wood and one ear on the glass . . . knots that will not come undone should one need to escape with linens through a window . . . and of course her favorite chapter: "Sixty-Four Uses for Hairpins."

Reaching up, Angelica removed a pin from her hair and proceeded to pick the lock on the back door. She had never actually employed this particular talent previously, and had always thought the usage of it somewhat shady, but if he was correct in his assertion that one would often be ashamed of one's finest actions if the world could see the motives behind them, then the opposite should hold true as well.

Yes, she was picking a lock and breaking into someone's home, but it really was for a good cause, and she would not be ashamed of her actions if given the chance to explain her motivation. At least she did not think she would . . . Was curiosity an honorable motive? She had to stop thinking so much!

The tiny creak that escaped as the lock opened seemed to travel the length of the house and back. Angelica held her breath, hoping against hope that no one had heard the sound. She did not want to be spotted until she could walk straight up to Alexander and have her say.

After a few more seconds Angelica pulled the door open and slipped inside the dark kitchen.

The room, like the rest of the house, was huge. It occurred to her that it must be very lonely to live in such a large house alone. Then again, she did not exactly know if Alexander lived by himself. *Was he married?* The thought had not occurred to her before now, and it sat like a dead weight upon her, bringing her to a stop.

He could not be married. Could he?

"Pull yourself together!" she admonished herself with a low voice.

Remembering that she had no idea if anyone else in Alexander's household had mind-reading abilities, she put a tight barrier to her thoughts so that no one could hear them. This was why she was here, she reminded herself. To find out if there were more people in the world like her and Alexander.

Excitement gripped her stomach as she thought of the possibilities. Gathering her courage, Angelica walked out of the kitchen and into a large hallway. The darkness was oppressive and had her shifting nervously from foot to foot.

Several doors loomed to the left and right, but only the farthest one had light shining from underneath.

This was it then, it was time to confront Alexander and find out the whole truth.

Angelica increased her speed as she approached the door with the light and brought her hand up to push.

An inner voice stopped her only a second before reaching for the knob. She stood, uncertain and confused, and then crouched down to look through the keyhole.

There was no way she could stop the gasp that escaped her shocked lips.

Chapter 17

Laying his hand on Christopher's frail shoulder, Alexander squeezed reassuringly. He could easily sense the boy's hunger and apprehension. Being tested in front of all four clan leaders had to be difficult for one so young.

Voices of vampires who had come from near and far this night filled every nook and cranny of the study. It was not often that the leaders of the clans convened. A coming-of-age ceremony such as this one did not normally require their attendance; one representative from each clan would have sufficed. Nevertheless, the leaders had come, not only to witness the ceremony but also to honor the passing of Christopher's mother, and others had come to see them.

Alexander had learned that Lady Katherine Langton was among the members of the Northern Clan who were sent to locate and apprehend Sergey several weeks ago. Lady Langton, like the other vampires in the group, had been found dead in the woods. Her ceremony had taken place with all Northern Clan members present as was their law, but now she was being mourned once more and her son celebrated.

"It will be over soon." Alexander spoke quietly, knowing the boy was listening to his every breath.

"I am glad," Christopher said as his stomach grumbled. His eyes searched the crowd, who had gathered in the now stuffy room, and found his father. He would make his father proud.

Turning, Christopher looked up at Alexander. "Will you stand with me through the whole thing?"

Alexander shook his head to indicate that he would not. "I will need to leave your side for a little while, but it will not matter, Christopher. You are a boy now, but in minutes you will be a man and a man fears nothing."

Christopher swallowed slowly and nodded his head. He would not disappoint Prince Kourakin, he would not be afraid.

"Alexander, shall we?" James asked from the middle of the room. At Alexander's nod of approval, the vampires around him stepped back until they formed a circle around three men, a woman and a boy who would soon be a boy no longer.

"In honor of Christopher's coming of age, the leaders of all four clans have united. Prince Alexander Kourakin, leader of the Eastern Clan. Grand Vizier Ismail Bilen, leader of the Southern Clan. Countess Isabelle DuBois, leader of the Western Clan. They have all come to honor Christopher and his departed mother." James spoke into the hush that had fallen over the assembly of vampires.

Taking Christopher by his arms, James positioned the boy so that he stood facing him and the other leaders. Many among the assembly looked upon him with compassion, they remembered well the pain of the first pangs of hunger.

"The laws of the clans of the vampire are clear. They were all established for the very survival of our race. Do you know them?" James addressed Christopher as he would a grown man.

"Yes," the boy responded, his voice shaking faintly.

"We are of a politics apart from humans. They have their countries, and we have our clans, but unlike their separate nations, our people live in harmony. The clans exist to strengthen the power of the law. In every other respect, we are one. Do you understand that?"

"Yes," Christopher said with more strength than before.

James nodded in approval, and both Alexander and Lord Langton stepped beside Christopher.

"You, Lord Henry Langton, father of Christopher Langton, have stepped forth as a guide. Do you intend to see through your duties of tutelage until such time as the leaders declare him grown?" Isabelle asked, her eyes intense and searching.

"I do."

"Do you understand you take responsibility for Christopher Langton and will therefore suffer the punishments he brings onto himself?"

"I do."

"And you, Prince Alexander Kourakin, leader of the Eastern Clan, have stepped forth as a second. Do you intend to see through your duties of tutelage should Henry Langton be unable?" Isabelle searched Alexander's expression as thoroughly as she had done with Lord Langton, her association with the prince not coming between herself and her duty.

"I do," Alexander responded without hesitating.

"Let all in this room witness. For all of Christopher Langton's transgressions, his guide will be responsible until such time as the young vampire is declared ready."

"We are witness," rung clear and true around the four walls as the assembly shifted slightly forward.

Isabelle nodded and Lord Langton stepped back out into the circle of observers while Alexander resumed his place next to the other leaders.

"Now, you will be shown the two sides of the law, young Christopher," Ismail spoke. He had arrived only an hour ago from the Ottoman Empire, bringing several of his clan members with him. Their brightly colored clothes and military apparel set them apart, though they were scattered amongst the crowd, shoulder to shoulder with all the other clan members.

"If you follow the laws, the laws will protect you. They will take care of you." Ismail looked to Isabelle, who moved forward.

She was a woman who had killed more men than she could keep track of. In her five hundred and some years, she had played the role of kitchen maid, shepherd girl, wife, queen, and empress. She had fought in battles and sung in drawing rooms. She was a respected member of the French aristocracy in the present century, but at that moment she was vampire: the Western Clan leader and the keeper of law.

She reached forward, her long brown hair brushing her arms as she pulled Christopher in an embrace. The boy was tense for a moment longer, before he gave into her warm embrace. She lifted him then, in her arms, like a young child, and covered him with her cloak.

James stepped beside them and reached out his arms. Isabelle passed the child-man to him without a word.

Christopher made no sound as he was passed to Alexander and then once again, this time to Ismail, who held him for a moment more before setting him on his feet.

The embraces had been symbolic, Christopher knew as much, but they made him feel good. Feeling the power in his leaders' arms, knowing they were capable of protecting him from all harm felt good.

"If you do not follow the laws, the law keepers will persecute you. Breaking our laws is endangering every member of this race. There will be no pity, no exception. The penalties are set." Ismail stopped speaking long enough to signal two vampires, who brought forth a bundle of cloth.

"There are two crimes for which you will lose your life: the killing of a vampire and the drinking of human blood. For these crimes you will be hunted down, and the life you have abused will be taken from you." After speaking the last word, Ismail looked at Alexander, who responded by stepping behind Christopher, who was looking at the bundle in Isabelle's hands with a transfixed expression.

Isabelle moved forward and shifted the clothes in her arms until the head of a baby girl was revealed. The young one was asleep, blissfully unaware of what was happening.

Christopher moaned as Isabelle brought the child within a hairsbreadth of his nose and then drew her away.

The smell of blood was strongest in the newborn of humans,

and Christopher, who had been starved for a fortnight, closed his eyes tightly against the pain in his stomach.

All was silent as the vampires watched while Christopher struggled against every instinct in his body.

His hands clenched as his incisors grew against his will. The sharp points resting against his lower lip egged him on, begged him to take what was right in front of him.

"Open your eyes," Ismail commanded gruffly.

Christopher followed the instruction unwillingly. His pupils were dilated, his sight sharpened to the point that he could see the veins coursing beneath the baby's skin. *What did it matter if he took one bite? Just a little one would not truly harm her.*

Perhaps sensing Christopher's thoughts, the child woke, her cries sending chills over his skin. He regarded the child whose tears streamed down chubby cheeks and hated himself for his thoughts. How could he have contemplated causing harm to the helpless infant?

Christopher did not realize that his body had been shaking until the trembling began to subside. He was ashamed of himself and felt more guilt than he had known in his short life.

Reaching his hands out, he looked up at Isabelle.

"Can I hold her?"

Isabelle smiled at him as she laid the baby into his arms.

The hand on his shoulder gave Christopher a start before he recalled Alexander's presence.

"You stood there to make sure I did not hurt her, didn't you?"

Alexander did not respond, signaling the same two vampires who had brought the child to take her away.

"You have done well, Christopher," James pronounced. "We come to the end of this ceremony. You have seen one side of the law, and now you must see the other."

James moved forward, but Christopher's eyes shot to Alexander. The boy knew what was to come, had been warned several times by his father, but now that the time was upon him he was more scared than he cared to admit.

"Christopher?"

Christopher looked back quickly at James, who stood before him. "Your Grace, I mean leader . . . I . . . could . . ." He stood, scared and uncertain, looking from his leader to Alexander and back.

"You wish Alexander to perform the last part of the ceremony?"

Swallowing, Christopher could only nod.

Alexander had not expected the request, though he did not let his surprise show. At James's nod, he cleared his mind and circled Christopher until the boy was directly in front of him. Due to the rarity of vampire children, he had not participated in many initiations and had never before found himself playing the role he was now. Although what was about to happen did not sit well with him, it had to be done. The boy had to understand that there was no mercy for those who broke the rules.

Alexander stood quietly for another moment, giving Christopher time to take another deep breath before he grabbed the boy by the throat.

Christopher had known what was coming, but he could not keep his heart rate from increasing as he was lifted higher off the ground.

He kicked reflexively as the pressure on his neck became uncomfortable, but the motion only served to make everything worse.

I cannot breathe! My neck will snap! The thoughts rushed through his mind and he struggled in earnest now, but Alexander's grip was unshakable.

Do not move, Christopher, I am not hurting you.

Christopher opened the eyes he had not realized he had closed and looked into the gray ones in front of him. It took a moment for the prince's message to sink in, but when it did, Christopher stopped struggling.

His throat was sore, but he suspected it was because he had kicked about more than anything else.

The look of approval he received was worth the pain in either case, Christopher decided. He closed his eyes. The prince had been right. He was a man now, and he might feel fear, but he was not going to show it.

As the calm settled over him, his hands unclenched and his body went lax. He was all right everything was all right. He was a vampire. He was a man. He could breathe. The pain was minimal. He would get through this initiation, he would.

When he opened his eyes, he found the prince's steady gaze on his own and recognized the pride. Alexander was proud of him. His dad would be proud of him. All would be right in his world.

Alexander lowered Christopher to the ground and stepped back. Complete silence ensued as the leaders stood silently, reading each other's minds.

"Christopher, the vampire," James said proudly.

"Christopher, vampire," the rest of the assembly echoed.

"To our clan. To our race. To the Blessed!" the toast marked the end of the ceremony. After every attendant had congratulated Christopher personally, and taken a moment to memorize his face, the guests began to file out of the house.

"Thank you for coming," Alexander said as he regarded Isabelle and Ismail.

"It was nothing." Isabelle smiled. "We are the ones who owe you thanks. How is the search progressing?"

Alexander looked toward James, who had stepped up beside him. They had agreed earlier not to mention the slayer and cause undo alarm. If things got out of hand, Isabelle and Ismail would be the first to be notified, but for the present moment, however, there was no reason to involve them when they had much to do in their own territories.

"Sergey is still in the city, and will not leave. Unlike what we thought before, he is not running. He is thirsting for a war."

"Good," Ismail said with satisfaction. "Against you, he stands no chance, my friend."

Isabelle put her hand on Alexander's arm and looked him in the eyes.

Alexander had only seen Isabelle occasionally after the night Helena died, but he had never been concerned for her. The women of their race seemed to weather depression better than the men, and Isabelle was the strongest female vampire he had ever met.

"Time."

Time. Alexander knew what Isabelle meant, and yet he had given up on the great unseen force long ago. No amount of time had warmed the cold that had entered his bones long ago. Nevertheless, he accepted the sentiment she passed to him silently. As leader of the Western Clan, Isabelle understood duty. As a woman who had never lost touch with her emotions, she understood grief. She might be too positive, but she understood . . .

"We are leaving then." Isabelle crooked an elegant finger at James. "You are absolutely certain, *mon cher*, that you will not leave that Margaret and come be mine?"

James kissed her swiftly and then shrugged. "I am sorry *ma petite*, but my amour is waiting for me at home with our baby in her stomach."

"Non!" Isabelle exclaimed with glee. The change from strong woman to happy girl was remarkably swift. "We will have to celebrate, James! A big party! Ooh la-la, the leader of the Northern Clan's child is coming! It will be a huge celebration. Grand! Oh, but I will have to speak with Margaret very soon and make preparations!"

"Yes, yes, Isabelle." Pulling at her hand, Ismail cast Alexander and James a harassed look. "If you want a ride on my ship, you'd better put that beautiful behind in motion. And no misbehaving on the boat, Isabelle, or I will lock you in my harem, you have my word."

Isabelle rolled her eyes, her hips swaying lustily as she followed Ismail out of the room. "You, *mon amie*, would be well advised to keep your harem girls far, far away from me. If I decided to have you as my lover, I would not stand for any human chits dancing around annoying me. . . ."

James could not help shaking his head as Isabelle's voice trailed off.

"Was she always this way, I cannot seem to recall."

"Definitely," Alexander replied. "Helena and she used to get themselves into the types of scandals that would become legendary. It was a hobby of theirs, I believe."

Surprise shone in James's brown eyes as the last of the vampires left the room. It was the first time he had heard Alexander speak of Helena in a century, but before he could comment, Lady Joanna rushed into the room.

"Forgive me leader, Prince, I am afraid we may have a slight problem."

Alexander's instincts sharpened at the possibility of danger. His ears picked up the sounds of the vampires that were leaving the grounds. One, two, three . . . four horses pulling a coach along the road by the gate, a street dog whimpering somewhere in the distance. . . . He turned to focus his attention toward the back of the house. Some of the pots were swinging on the wooden hooks they rested on, the floorboards creaked and . . . running?

"Where is Kiril?" The question was directed at Joanna, who bit her lip in concern.

"He said he heard noises and went to investigate. He is not back yet."

James turned his head in the same angle of Alexander's and listened to what the younger vampire could not hear.

"He's coming back."

Alexander's eyes narrowed as he tried to suppress the feeling of foreboding. Kiril was indeed coming back, his footfalls were unmistakable, but he was not alone.

"My Prince."

Three pairs of eyes took in Kiril's grim expression before moving on to his captive.

"I found her fleeing through the kitchen." Kiril kept his voice level as he explained, though the varying degrees of amazement and horror that found its way on his audience's faces made him want to fidget.

"I tried to read her mind and see . . ." Kiril did not finish the sentence, his inability to read Angelica's mind frustrating him beyond endurance. "She does not cooperate, and I'm afraid she saw much."

Chapter 18

Since the moment she had been dragged into the dreaded room, Angelica had not looked past Alexander's expressionless face. How could he stand there so calmly? He was a vampire, for God's sake. A vampire!

She had tried to come to grips with what she had heard and what she had seen while running toward the wall. None of it seemed even remotely possible, none of it.

But it was real; all of it was real. She had seen that boy's teeth grow, had seen his eyes darken as he stared at that poor baby. God, she had become immobile. During those dreadful seconds where she had been certain that they would kill the infant, she had not been able to think straight enough to even consider a rescue plan. She had left that baby to its own devices while she shook with terror.

Angelica shook still, hard enough to make her dizzy. Hard

enough to stop her from continuing her train of thought. She was not going to get hysterical again!

It had taken her a good five minutes to get her breathing under control after the first attack of panic, but she had no five minutes to spare this time around. If they thought she knew . . . what they were . . . they would kill her without qualm, she was sure of it.

She looks like she is about to run. Better hold on to her just in case.

"Do not touch me!" Angelica took a large step away from Kiril as his thoughts registered in her mind. Damn it, her nervousness was making her lose her grip on her block.

"Angelica, please, I do not understand how you came to be here, but cooperate and all will be well." Joanna stepped forward as she made the entreaty.

Not having noticed Joanna's presence in the room before now, Angelica gave a shaky sigh of pure gratitude.

"Oh, Joanna, I thought I was going crazy, I really did. I was beginning to think . . ." Something in Joanna's eyes stopped her desperate tirade midway. A moment of listening to her friend's thoughts clarified matters to an unwanted degree.

She can't possibly know. Even if she saw, her mind would not let her believe we are vampires. God, do not let her know. Do not let her know.

"But you were my friend! How could you be . . . ? I know you could not possibly . . ." Angelica stopped speaking. Her eyes went wide with hurt before they filled with ice. So nothing was as it seemed. Joanna, Alexander, and the other two, all of this was a setup somehow.

Alexander had deceived her, Joanna had deceived her, and

she . . . she had deceived Mikhail and Lady Dewberry. Was there no end to this charade?

All of a sudden, she just wanted to go home. To a time before she had laid eyes on Alexander. To a time before she had found out that she would soon be without funds. To a time when she would have only read about vampires in mythological encyclopedias.

Angelica looked across the room to where Alexander stood facing the burning fireplace. His thoughts were locked against her, as was his friend's. It was terrifying to realize how much he had come to mean to her.

A vampire . . .

God, she was going to die.

"Angelica?" Joanna's voice held a note of hysteria in it as she watched her friend sink to the floor. The rigidity in Angelica's shoulders was all that kept her from going to the young woman.

"This is no dream?" The words left Angelica's lips, but seemed a statement more than a question.

"No."

James's voice had Angelica lifting her head, her eyes unusually steady, her body calm.

"There is no need for any mind reading. I have seen enough." It was almost irritating how utterly passive acceptance made her. She was going to die, that was a fact, and now that she knew it, there was no point in fear.

James turned toward Alexander, his face as expressionless as his friends. In truth, nothing like this had ever happened before. There had been other humans who had stumbled upon the truth about their race, but none of them were mind readers. Their memories had been easy to alter. This woman's would not be . . .

"What do we do?"

Alexander looked at Angelica and felt like his skin was coming apart. The scent of her filled his lungs, her near hysteria a moment before had instilled in him the urge to protect, to reach out and hold her. *And to what end?* he thought to himself with disgust, since it was him she was scared of.

Nevertheless, his fingers itched to touch her, to assure her that he would not let anything happen to her. Yet he realized that he was not sure he could protect her. Tampering with the memory of a mind reader with her strength would be of no use, and no human could know of their existence. That was the law.

Alexander knew what he had to say in answer to James's question, and yet he stood frozen watching as a new Angelica emerged.

The scent of fear was swiftly becoming a mere memory as her expression turned icy in front of his eyes.

She stood slowly, proudly, from her position on the floor and regarded everyone around her with those cool blue eyes, as if looking at nothing more than dirt.

"We cannot let her go." James almost flinched as the words they had all been thinking echoed in the room.

Angelica only thrust her chin forward as her hands fisted beside her delicate muslin dress.

"But of course," Angelica said into the quiet that had followed. "After all, 'A dead woman bites not.'" She smiled at the irony of the pronouncement that had been made at the trial of Mary, Queen of Scots.

Lord Patrick Gray, she thought sardonically, you would be proud of the way you were quoted today!

Alexander's brows lowered at the picture of defiance she made. He was angry. At her, at himself, at the world . . . His anger was a living thing, and it took all of his energy to continue appearing calm.

"Is there no way around this, leader?" Joanna's distress failed to break through Angelica's icelike demeanor. "It is true that if she were a human she would be sentenced to . . . to . . . death," the word came out as a mere whisper, "if we could not void that part of her memory, but obviously the law is not applicable in this case. She is a mind reader, and a very strong one if what Kiril says is true. She would have as much to lose if she were to be discovered for what she was."

Alexander shook his head sadly, resigned now that there was only one way. "What she is, Lady Joanna, is human."

Angelica regarded the tall man who stood across the room and felt the sting of bitter tears. What had she expected from him? He did not know her, had only spoken to her a handful of times, why should he care if she lived or died? What crazy notion had made her think, even for a moment that he would save her?

Her heart ached, and she realized for the first time how close she had come to loving the stranger who had just condemned her with his softly spoken words.

She might die later this night, but Prince Alexander was already dead. To her, he was no longer.

Kiril hesitated for a moment, before joining the ongoing conversation. "Could we not ensure her silence somehow?"

James gestured for him to continue.

"If a vampire took responsibility of her, she could be excused."

"Responsibility for her?" James asked with interest. Although he barely knew her, he did not want to see the woman come to harm.

"Yes." Lady Joanna stepped forward, her eyes looking straight into Angelica's. "I would be responsible for her with your permission, leader."

Kiril frowned. "If she caused trouble, you would be the one to pay, Joanna, and I can hardly let you do that. I will—"

"You can hardly let me do that?" Joanna's angry retort was cut short by James.

"It is a grand gesture, Lady Joanna. I'm afraid, however, that you are not strong enough to contain the girl, and Kiril, neither are you."

"I do not understand," Joanna said quietly. She looked at Angelica as if she were trying to see something that would explain the power the others seemed to be afraid of.

Angelica, who had remained silent during the exchange, watched James as he moved about the room restlessly.

"Her mind is more powerful than yours, Joanna. Not only could you not perform your duties as a guide should she not desire to cooperate, but she could very well tamper with your mind. In fact, I am afraid that her mind is stronger than most all vampires in the clan, as Kiril has found out for himself."

Joanna closed her mouth, her eyes lowering as her hope that her newly acquired friend might keep her life was crushed yet again.

Angelica kept silent, not believing for a moment that she could do what the duke suggested. Nevertheless, she did not intend to point that out when they would most assuredly not believe her.

It really was a good thing not to have let her hopes rise with Kiril's suggestion. She did not want to feel fear again, and resignation was the only way to deal with the fear of death.

As detached as she felt at this moment of her life, she did appreciate what Joanna and Kiril had tried to do for her. Though she did not understand what a guide's responsibilities would be, or even if she could accept the proposal, she understood that the woman had been willing to take a great risk for her sake.

Mikhail. Her brother's name ran through her head. He would be so upset, if only she could spare him the pain. What if he had an attack? Oh God, no!

"Leave me with her." The deep voice that had been quiet for some time reverberated around the small room.

Angelica closed her eyes firmly, trying not to cry. Why were they doing this to her? Did none of them have a soul? Could they not kill her and be done with it?

She could not see Alexander from where she stood behind Joanna, but she knew how his face would look. Emotionless, as it always was, except for that split second where she had almost thought him about to smile just the day before.

There was a lot of shuffling about as the three vampires left without protest. She was alone with Alexander. Every instinct in her body wanted to lash out at him, to fight until he squeezed the last breath from her. But she could not. She had to beg him for her life, beg him for her brother's sake.

Alexander watched as Angelica stood quietly before him, her eyes trained firmly on the carpet beneath their feet.

Why did she not move? No woman he had ever encountered had faced death with such calm. But then, Angelica was different from any woman he had ever met.

Light from the fire behind him cast his shadow so that it touched her frame. He wanted to touch her, he realized. To protect her from everything, even from himself.

Nuisance! The woman was a damned problem!

"No human is to know of our existence."

Her face lifted, her eyes boring into his. Alexander saw exactly what he had expected to see in the depth of those blue pools: anger.

"Do you take pleasure in your torture?" Angelica's scathing words ran over his skin and cooled the ardor building in his veins.

"You hardly appear to be tortured."

Alexander failed to hide his surprise as she took a step toward him.

"Just kill me, God damn you! Finish it!" She stopped in her tracks, and it was only as her hand shot out for balance that Alexander realized how wrong he had been.

"Damn it!" With a muttered curse he closed the space between them and held her upright from her arms. His eyes searched hers as he willed her to understand.

"I will not kill you. Do you understand, Angelica? No one will harm you. You are safe."

Angelica made no response. Her eyes were glazed, her body shaking. She was in shock, he realized. What had spurred him to extend her misery? Why had he not told her that he would protect her?

Slipping his arms around her, he lifted her body as he called for James.

"Alexander?"

Rocking Angelica softly, Alexander grimaced in his friend's direction.

"Pour her a glass of that whiskey the highlanders brought with them."

James did so without question, and Alexander kept rocking gently.

"She is in shock," James said needlessly as he handed the glass of gold liquid to Alexander.

He tipped Angelica's head up in an effort to make her drink, but she would not cooperate. Her eyes had shut the moment her head touched his chest. *At least her breathing had evened out*, Alexander thought.

"What is your plan?" James nodded toward the body in his arms.

Setting the glass down on a cherry oak side table, Alexander sat in the armchair by the fire. It occurred to him that he had been in that exact position only hours before, but now he had the woman in his lap to contend with.

"I do not know exactly, but she will not be harmed, James."

Having guessed as much already, James took the seat across from Alexander. "I would not see her harmed either, but the law is clear."

"Yes. About certain things. The law says no human can know of us. It then gives us a way to fix things so that we need never to harm an innocent who happens upon us. We cannot fix her memory so that she forgets, and there lies the key. She is no ordinary human; she does not fit the definition."

"Alexander, she can still be dangerous. I did not want to aggravate things earlier, but did you consider that she may very well be in league with the slayer? We had not considered this before, but what if our slayer is female?"

Narrowing his eyes, Alexander regarded his friend.

"The slayer might indeed be female, but she is not a slayer. Do you think this is an act, James? She knew nothing of us. As far as I can tell, she is not even aware that other mind readers exist!"

Frustration had the Duke of Atholl on his feet. "Damn it, you are right. It seems I cannot think straight."

Alexander understood the sentiment. He was not thinking straight either, which could be the only explanation for what he was about to suggest.

"I will take responsibility for her."

"What?" James stopped pacing as he stared.

"She will stay here and will be my responsibility until Sergey is caught and the slayer is found. After that, there will be time to consider other alternatives."

Silence followed his proclamation, but did not last. The fire cackled, the wood beneath his feet groaned, and Angelica's heartbeat filled his ears. Alexander knew with utter certainty that peace had just walked out of his life.

Chapter 19

Angelica woke to the insistent knocking on her bedroom door. She groaned as she shifted in the large bed, pulling the covers more firmly around her body.

When no further sound ensued for the next several seconds, she sunk her head further into the feather pillows, convinced that the noise had been a mere dream.

Her hopes were dashed, however, as she heard her door opening.

"Allison, if that is you, please do not wake me."

Heavy footsteps had her frowning into her pillow. Her maid definitely treaded more softly than that!

"Mikhail, if the house is not on fire, I really do not want to wake up."

"There is no fire, no, but you need to get up either way."

Angelica's eyes opened into the darkness of the pillows she realized were not her own. That voice.

Memory crashed in on her with painful force and had her

jumping to the ground on the opposite side of the bed.

"You can put your hands down, Angelica. I am not going to hurt you."

Alexander looked sincere and tired, she noticed. That she had lived through the night was positive reinforcement too, unless . . .

Her hands flew up to her neck as she searched for marks.

"Don't be ridiculous. You are unharmed, and will remain so. I told you, you have no reason to fear me."

"I am not afraid of you!" Angelica straightened her back and pushed up the arm of the nightgown that had slid down her shoulder. "What? When . . ." She stopped herself before hysteria could set in.

Vampires. The word popped into her head and brought her close to laughing hysterically yet again. What a joke it all was. They could not be vampires, but they were. They were! And she was standing in a foreign bedroom, God only knew where . . . wearing someone's nightgown. Oh God!

Alexander sat at the edge of the bed, his sigh audible.

"This is a guest room in my house. Lady Joanna brought you the nightgown and helped you into it. You are under my protection and will not be harmed. Any questions?"

Angelica racked her brain for questions. She had so many, but where on earth would she start. *How is it possible that you are a vampire? How many people have you killed? How come you are not going to kill me?*

"What will happen to me?" She refused to sit, even though he gestured that she do so.

"No human is to know of our existence. Normally, that does not pose a problem, as we can make humans forget us should they accidentally discover us."

Angelica could not help interrupting him. "You erase their memories?"

Alexander nodded. "We cannot erase, precisely. We can just put suggestions into their minds that make them believe they did not see anything, or in some cases that they saw something else."

It was not hard for Angelica to believe that such a thing was possible. She knew better than most how the human mind worked. It would be simple enough to accomplish, if one could read thoughts and put thoughts into others' minds.

"We cannot make you forget, Angelica. The simple fact of it is your mind is too strong. So you are to remain here, until we can decide what to do with you."

"Here?" Angelica repeated the word somewhat stupidly. What on earth did he mean "here"?

"Yes, in my home. For reasons I will not get into just now, I cannot be here to watch you during the day, so you will spend the daylight hours with the Duchess of Atholl."

Angelica hardly heard his full sentence. She was a prisoner. *His* prisoner.

"I cannot possibly stay here. I cannot. My reputation would be shattered . . . marriage would become impossible and Mikhail. Mikhail!"

Her brother was probably frantically looking for her even at that moment! If he got too excited . . .

She came around the bed in an instant, her fear of him pushed back in the face of the danger her brother was in.

"Please, I cannot stay here. I need to go to my brother."

"Angelica, there is no need—"

"No, you do not understand!" She knelt before him and grabbed his hand. "Please, Alexander, please. I need to get to

Mikhail. He is sick. If he worries for me, he might have an attack and die!"

Pulling her up from the ground, Alexander stood and held her face between his palms.

"Look at me. Listen. I know of your brother's heart. He is fine. In fact, he is at the club right now with several of his friends, completely convinced that the two of you had breakfast together."

It took a moment for Angelica to calm herself.

"How did you know?"

His thumb stroked her cheek in an unconscious gesture meant to calm. "I heard the weakness when we first met."

Angelica became uncomfortably aware of his hands as her fear for her brother receded. Stepping back, she looked away from his intense gaze. It felt odd to thank him, when the whole situation was his fault to begin with, but she was grateful nevertheless.

Letting his hands drop to his sides, Alexander moved to the bookshelf at the opposite wall.

"Mikhail will never know that you are not spending your nights in your own home. You will see him often enough, no doubt, in the functions you will attend with Margaret. Now, I have to leave." He turned, a thick volume in his hands that he threw on the bed beside her.

"I seem to remember that you are an avid reader. It will occupy your time until this evening's ball, when you will meet Margaret."

Feeling much more in control, Angelica glanced at the leather-bound pages and back at him. "What is it?"

"Kiril will be here in my absence. You two met briefly yesterday, on your run out of the kitchen."

He had ignored her question, but that did not bother her. Memory of the night before had Angelica glancing toward the window. Perhaps after he left, she could climb down the window and make a run for it. But how far could she get? For God's sake, they were vampires. If she disobeyed them, they would probably kill her without a second thought.

Maybe if she grabbed her brother and her aunt and then got on a ship to some remote part of the world . . .

"Angelica." Her name sounded like a threat this time and made her turn quickly.

"Yes?"

"Do not try anything foolish. If you behave, you and yours will not be harmed."

Angelica tried not to look miserable at that pronouncement. She knew that Alexander had not read her mind. The man was just second-guessing her, and he was doing a very good job of it too.

Finding being predictable not to her liking, Angelica responded calmly. "But of course I will not. Thank you so much for the warning." She smiled sweetly and watched Alexander's eyes narrow to slits with some satisfaction.

"Behave." With that last word, Alexander walked out of the room and left her standing alone in the large chamber.

"Sheets." She muttered aloud as she moved into action. If Alexander thought she would sit here and wait for them to change their minds about letting her live, he had a surprise coming his way.

Intent on getting to the bottom sheets which she would tie together, Angelica threw the covers off the bed. The loud thud had her glancing at the book that had landed by her feet.

Curiosity, it gnawed at her and had her sinking to the ground though she knew she must not. The book was heavier than she had assumed, and far older.

She turned the pages delicately and came to the inscription.

> A Vampire walks unknown, a painful thirst upon him.
> He walks, but he leaves no mark, it must be so.
> One day he will come out of darkness, no more thirst.
> The Blessed will bring the light.

The simple sentences sent shivers down her spine. She turned the page.

I. The punishment for drinking human blood is death.

II. Humans are not to be harmed. No pain is to be inflicted unto them. Only in self-defense is it permissible to cause physical harm, and only when one's life is in jeopardy may one kill a human without punishment.

III. Humans may not know of the existence of the vampire race.

Angelica flipped forward, finding it difficult to get her mind around what she was reading.

VVII. In the event of the death of a vampire, a burial ceremony will be held. All members of the clan into which the vampire was born must be present as well as all vampires residing within said clan's territory.

VVlll. The burial *ceremony* is to *begin* with *the* reading of
the *dead* Vampire's . . .

Little specks of dust sprinkled the air as Angelica closed
the book and took a deep breath. That bastard! Whether
Alexander knew her better than most anyone in the world,
or he had just gotten lucky, the man had managed to find one
surefire way to keep her in that room.

She opened the book once more. The very laws that dic-
tated she be a prisoner or die were lying in her lap, and Angelica could do nothing but read.

Angelica had reached page twenty-eight when she heard
music.

Was Alexander back? She had so many questions for him.
So many things just did not make sense. The vampires who
followed these rules could not be the blood-drinking, mur-
dering shadows she had read about her entire life.

She had to talk to him. Captor or no, there was nothing
for it.

Grabbing one of the white sheets, she wrapped it around
her and made her way out of the room. The corridor was
long and awash with light. It was disturbing to find that she
had expected something dark and maybe damp.

"The bane of an overactive imagination." Mumbling to
herself, Angelica descended the staircase. The sight of the
parlor made her fingers shake, but she bit her lip and followed
the music down a hallway decked with burgundy wallpaper.
The notes became clearer as she stood before a door made of
darker wood than the rest in the house.

She could do this, she thought frantically. She could face
him. He was just Alexander . . . the man who taught her to

block thoughts. The man who kissed her in the gallery . . .

"This is not helping!"

With her hand on the doorknob, she listened for another moment. The door reverberated with the tentative notes from the piano and then she knew.

A soft shudder ran through her body, and she dropped her hand. It was not him. She knew without a shred of doubt that Alexander Kourakin would not do anything with such hesitation.

She imagined that if he was made to play the piano and knew not how, he would pound the keys until the sheer force of his will produced music.

Then who was at the piano? The curiosity that had kept her in the room upstairs now pushed her forward.

Angelica was surprised to see Joanna sitting at the piano, her brows furrowed in concentration as she tried to read the relatively easy piece by Mozart.

While her first instinct was to welcome her friend, she held her silence and watched. Joanna was a vampire, like all the rest of them, but she seemed so . . . normal. Having had the opportunity to know her better in the last few days, she knew that the woman had goals, dreams, likes, and dislikes that were no different from a human.

Tucking the observation away for the moment, she spoke above the twinkle of notes.

"Piano is not your forte, is it?"

The music came to an abrupt halt as Joanna turned, her face lit with a smile of relief. Unprepared, Angelica was surprised as the redhead rushed across the room and embraced her.

Pulling back, her eyes traveled over Angelica's face as if she were trying to see through the skin.

"I have to be honest; I was worried sick about you, An-gelica. I was almost sure that I would find you crying hysteri-cally or refusing to get out of bed."

Angelica smiled wryly. "I did give the latter some serious consideration, if you must know."

Joanna laughed before she sobered once more. "You are not angry with me, are you?"

Angelica shrugged as she led the way to the window seats. "I was at first, admittedly. But it is hard to remain angry with a woman who risked her own life to save mine."

Joanna's eyes took on a pleading quality as she took a seat. "I spent the whole night thinking about what happened, as I am sure everyone who was present did, and I realize that you might think I betrayed you by misrepresenting myself." Looking out of the window to the small backyard, Joanna searched for the right words. "You have to understand that we . . . Vampires are not free to divulge what we are to humans."

"So I learned," Angelica said with some bitterness.

Joanna frowned as she looked at her. "What happened yes-terday was a frightful ordeal for you, yes, but there are good reasons for our secrecy and our harsh laws. Do you believe that your race would idly stand by and allow us to live freely if they knew of our existence?"

Angelica's first reaction was to say yes, but she kept quiet. Would they, humans, be tolerant toward a completely differ-ent race when they still made slaves out of members of their own race for having different nationalities, or skin colors, or being of a different creed?

"We look like humans, we act like humans, and at the same time we have superior strength, eyesight, hearing, agility . . . they would brand us as predators that are after every-one's blood."

Angelica felt her friend's anger and her sadness. Could their laws truly have just cause?

"The *they* you are speaking of is my race. There are those of us who are deserving of your trust."

Joanna smiled a little sadly. "Vampires are just as bad judges of character as humans. Some would inevitably place their trust in the untrustworthy, and then what would happen? It takes only one person to spread the news of our existence, and then they will come for us with pitchforks and stakes as they have done in the past."

Angelica realized that what Joanna said was most likely true. It did indeed seem imperative for pure survival reasons for the members of the vampire race to be secretive. It did not, however, make it all right that they had wanted to *kill* her.

But, they had not killed, had they? Instead they had stood, looking for ways around their laws.

She had a headache!

"Wait a minute." Angelica stood, her eyes wide as she glanced out the window. "It is daylight, how can you be out and about in daylight?"

Taking Angelica's hand, Joanna pulled her back down to sit. "That would be because I have no problem with day-light."

Angelica said nothing as she waited for Joanna to explain.

Joanna cleared her throat. "Well, I suppose I should ex-plain, but I would not want to destroy all your preconceived notions. . . ."

"Joanna!" Angelica complained.

Joanna laughed. "Well, it is like this. Several hundred years

ago, when the leaders realized that the only way of coexist-
ing peacefully with humans was to keep them, I mean you, I
mean, you know what I mean . . ."

"Yes, yes, I am hardly offended!" Angelica urged.

"Well, was to keep them in ignorance of our presence. Realizing that wiping the idea of a vampire from the minds of
all humans was near to impossible, they decided to feed the
rumor mills instead."

·   "So the leaders spread rumors about vampires?" Angelica
asked confused.

"Yes," Joanna replied, "and soon it was common belief that
vampires could not walk in daylight or touch crosses. Everyone knew that they, or rather we, sleep in coffins and turn
into bats."

Angelica's eyes lit as comprehension dawned. "They made
it so humans believed vampires to be mythical creatures,
that way your neighbor who works during the day cannot
possibly be a vampire!"

Joanna nodded, and Angelica found she was impressed
with the simple solution the leaders had come up with.

"So, do you really hate garlic?"

Joanna laughed as she rolled her eyes. "I hate having garlic
breath, yes."

"Me too." Angelica grinned. "Though I do love the stuff.
It makes all the most unappetizing dishes bearable if not
tasty."

"To me, nothing seems unappetizing," Joanna said.

Angelica gave an unladylike snort and asked, "And how do
you manage to like everything?"

"It is quite simple," Joanna said, and shrugged. "I merely
wait until I am hungry before I eat."

Angelica cocked her head, trying to understand if her friend was serious. "How does that help the food taste better?"

"Hunger is the best sauce in the world," Joanna quoted.

"'Hunger is the best' . . . wait a minute, I know that line. It is right out of *Don Quixote*, Miguel de Cervantes's book!"

Joanna looked at her with frustration as she stood. "Can a woman not say a single thing that will not be attributed to a man?"

"Oh, come!" Laughing, Angelica realized that the afternoon was not turning out as miserably as she had feared. "Joanna, will you be attending this evening's ball?"

"Yes."

"Good." Angelica nodded. "I will need you by my side. I find I am somewhat afraid of meeting the duchess."

Joanna cut her study of a nearby painting to look back at her friend. "You have no need to worry, Angelica. Margaret is a fabulous woman. You ought not to even think of anything . . . just live your life the way you would ordinarily and view the rest as a temporary inconvenience. I am certain the leaders will soon find a way out of this mess."

Angelica wished she could have that much faith.

Chapter 20

"You did not tell me, James, that our Princess Belanov had a beauty to rival those paintings of Aphrodite you keep locked away in your study."

Heat seeped into Angelica's cheeks as she curtsied to the Duchess of Atholl. She had been a bundle of nerves all the way up the large staircase of the ducal residence. Meeting Mikhail beside their family coach and finding that he was under the impression that they had been together through the ride was an unsettling experience to say the least. Her brother spoke to her as if nothing at all was happening, and Angelica found it harder than she thought to reply equally unfazed.

Now, as she reached the end of the receiving line, her stomach was in upheaval and her cheeks had turned the color of a pale tomato!

"Oh do get up, Angelica. You do not mind if I call you

Angelica, do you? I am not a stickler for formality unlike my pompous husband, and we will, after all, be spending a good amount of time together."

Angelica cast a glance toward the duke, who had finished greeting her brother and was busily glaring at his wife.

"Do not mind my wife; she is pregnant," he said a few moments later as he took Angelica's hand. "Good evening to you, Princess Belanov. Thank you for coming."

The duke's eyes were kind as he regarded her, and Angelica realized she had trouble believing that he had been in Alexander's house only last night, ready to quite possibly condemn her to death.

"Thank you, Your Grace," Angelica replied politely.

"Oh call him James, dear. Don't be so formal!"

Although surprised once again at the way the duchess spoke with the duke, Angelica found herself close to laughter at the couple's exchange.

"Margaret, we are in polite company—"

Margaret cut her husband off without a qualm. "Nonsense, it is only Angelica. Look, even her brother has moved on to wait for her by—oh, bother—what was the dear lady's name?"

"Lady Dewberry." Angelica pressed her lips together to prevent herself from laughing.

"Yes, of course. In either case, my dear husband, only a fool would not realize that this darling girl has been deeply hurt by your tactless behavior yesterday night."

James frowned darkly at his wife as all humor fled from Angelica's face.

"What transpired was inevitable. You know our laws." He spoke softly to make sure no one overheard the conversation.

"Balderdash, James Atholl! Had I been there, as I'd wanted to be, I might add, I would have told you straight off that no one needed to even utter unpleasant words such as *death*."

James gave up trying to talk any sense into his wife, but he did take that moment to address Angelica.

"I am aware that you know very little about us or our ways, Angelica, but you will learn with time that there are good reasons for our strict laws, and we employ them even when we would rather not." When he saw that his wife was about to speak yet again, James laid a hand on her shoulder, effectively cutting off whatever it was she had been about to say.

The carefree air about him had vanished, Angelica realized, and had been replaced by the aura of the lord of the Northern Clan.

"Be that as it may, I am sorry for the distress you suffered at our hands. I assure you that now that Alexander is your guide, no vampire or human will harm you."

Angelica was not sure what exactly the duke meant, but she recognized goodwill when she heard it, and it did a lot to ease the resentment she still harbored.

"Yes, yes, mishmash," Margaret interjected lightly. Turning to face James she continued, "Darling, you will have to hold up the ranks here at the door. I am going to take Angelica for a spin around the ballroom."

"Margaret, we have guests to greet."

The duchess crooked her aristocratic brow at her husband. "And I am sure they will understand my absence, my love, when you tell them that I am pregnant." Linking her arm through Angelica's she moved them off before James could reply.

"Does he not get angry with you?" Angelica asked in wonder

as the woman beside her made a beeline for Lady Dewberry and Mikhail.

"My dear, he would be frightened to get angry at me in my 'condition,'" the duchess responded merrily.

"But what does the one have to do with the other?" Angelica wondered, baffled.

"Nothing," Margaret shrugged, "but my sweet James is convinced that pregnant women somehow become invalids. He will not let me lift so much as a porcelain plate, and lately he has taken to the belief that he must try not to anger me in any way lest it hurt the baby."

Angelica's laughter procured a shrug from the very eccentric Duchess of Atholl. "Of all his assumptions it is the only one that works in my favor, so it suits me to let him believe what he will."

"If you do not mind my saying so, Your Grace, you are not precisely what I expected."

Margaret smiled a dazzling smile as they reached the twosome they had been making their way toward. "Never say you had not envisioned a beautiful brunette with large breasts and an even larger stomach?"

Laughing, Angelica realized that however preposterous it might be, she was completely at ease. All the nervousness of the previous moments faded in mere moments beside this woman, who looked not a year over forty and was indeed beautiful.

"Your Grace, I see you have been kind enough to bring our Angelica to us." Lady Dewberry beamed like a satisfied mother hen. She was pleased that someone of as much consequence as the Duchess of Atholl had taken an obvious shine to her protégée and could not wait to spread the news.

"I am afraid I must disappoint you both for a while further. I have my heart set upon showing Angelica the rooms." Margaret smiled at the older lady and then at the young prince.

Mikhail looked with pride at his sister as Lady Dewberry quickly assured the duchess that it was no inconvenience whatsoever.

"If there is anyone under this roof that I would trust with my charge, it would have to be you, Your Grace," Lady Dewberry said with all sincerity.

"You wound me sorely, madam. . . . Am I not to be trusted with my own sister?" Mikhail asked with feigned, wounded pride.

Margaret laughed at the young man's jest as the elder lady scolded him. "Now you know that I implied no such thing, Prince Belanov! Why, I was only . . ."

Angelica reached out a hand for one of Lady Dewberry's and cast her brother a look that said "behave." "We all know you meant nothing close to what my tactless brother is implying."

"Tactless? I should tell you that I have—"

"Well-timed silence hath more eloquence than speech." Angelica cut her brother off with a quote from Martin Tupper.

Mikhail grinned, not at all put off. "Who was it that said that silence is the virtue of fools?"

"Most likely a man who liked to listen to his own voice," the duchess said, joining in the banter, then winked at Angelica.

Some time later, Angelica found herself sitting beside the duchess in a corner of the vast ballroom, observing the dancers as they glided across the floor.

It was the first moment of extended silence that the women

shared since taking their leave from Mikhail and Lady Dewberry, and Angelica realized with some amazement that she
had enjoyed herself immensely in the past hour.

The duchess, who had insisted Angelica call her Margaret,
was the most flamboyantly eccentric woman she had ever encountered. The woman said whatever she wished, whenever
she wished, and no one seemed to mind her outrageously
apolitical ways. In fact, she was quite certain after observing
the dozens of aristocrats she had been introduced to, that the
duchess was liked exceptionally well.

"You are deep in thought, my dear," Margaret commented
as she reached for her punch.

Angelica fingered the satin of her violet dress and wondered if she should breach the topic that had been nagging at
her all evening.

"If I may speak freely?"

The duchess clucked her tongue. "Do not be ridiculous,
my dear, speak your mind as I certainly do."

"I am just not certain of what I should do now that I have
a . . . protector."

Understanding her meaning, Margaret shifted in her large
chair until she was eye to eye with her. "What is it you were
planning to do before you obtained one?"

Angelica wondered how to begin to explain her situation.
As outspoken and willful as the duchess was, there was no
telling if she would approve of what she heard.

"I came to London upon my brother's insistence. He finished his schooling recently and was worried about my, well,
lifestyle."

The duchess arched a brow, a sure sign she wanted Angelica to expound.

"Our parents died when we were very young and our only living relative, Lady Dewberry, could not abide the country or children for that matter. . . . She would come to visit from time to time, but other than that, Mikhail and I lived with the servants.

When Mikhail went off to school and then university, I was left pretty much to my own devices, so I chose to do what I like to do best. I would read all morning, take rides across the country, and play my piano." Feeling a little awkward, Angelica tried to gauge by the duchess's expression if she found what she was hearing shocking. Angelica knew well that many would consider her upbringing scandalous at the very least.

The duchess said nothing but made a motion with her hand for Angelica to continue, so she forged on.

"So Mikhail insisted that we move to London, thinking, I believe, that once here I would evolve into some type of social butterfly and do what all women are supposed to do."

"And what, pray tell, are all women supposed to do?" the duchess asked with some amusement.

"Why, get married, of course. And believe me, Your Grace, getting married is the last thing I wish to do."

"I told you to call me Margaret!" the duchess admonished.

Angelica blushed but said nothing. It was difficult to shed years of ingrained rules of etiquette in a few hours.

"You still have not told me what it is you wish to do."

"Well, certain . . . events have made it so that marriage has become essential. So what I am looking to do is find a husband." Motioning toward the far end of the room where several young girls in white dresses waited patiently for a suitable male to ask them to dance, Angelica continued, "In that respect I am no different from those debutantes."

Margaret let out an unladylike snort. "Oh, do not make me laugh, my dear. The only thing you have in common with those poor girls is your sex. With your beauty, title, and fortune you can find a husband in a fortnight. In fact, I am not sure I understand why you have not."

Angelica touched her cheeks, which were surely flushed for the umpteenth time that evening and then shrugged. "At first it was because I could not find a man who I believed would make a good husband. Listening to their thoughts, I became convinced that they thought of nothing but . . . body parts while in the presence of a female."

This time the duchess did laugh, laying her hand atop her belly as she shook. "It is your own fault! You should not have read their minds to begin with. No wonder you are still unmarried! Men will be men, my dear. They look at your body first, but the good ones soon recognize your mind as well."

Acknowledging the possibility, Angelica continued. "It was not precisely my intention to approach the marriage market the way that I did. I did not know how *not* to hear thoughts until recently, when Alexander taught me."

Margaret laughed once more, a sound that seized when she saw the serious expression on Angelica's face.

"You are completely serious."

"Yes," Angelica said.

"Oh, my dear—" the duchess stopped herself midsentence, realizing that the woman before her would not appreciate pity. "I was told that your mind is powerful, but I now doubt that they knew just how powerful. Please continue,

Angelica. So what is it you desire to do now? Is it a husband you seek?"

Angelica did not hesitate in her answer. "Yes."

"Well, good!" Margaret clapped her hands like a young girl. "This should be no problem at all, and fun besides."

It was difficult to believe it was going to be as easy as Margaret was making it sound, but suddenly Angelica wondered if it was possible. What Alexander had said about Mikhail had held true. Her brother was in no way worried, or even aware of any changes. And Joanna had suggested she continue her life as usual . . . and now the duchess was saying the same thing. Maybe, just maybe, all of this was not going to be as difficult as it seemed.

"Do you really think I might be able to find a husband, even with . . . well, all of this?"

"Of course! You will be spending your days with me, my dear, and I just happen to have a schedule that involves a lot of socializing . . . with eligible bachelors."

Margaret's smile was infectious.

"Thank you, Margaret."

"You need not thank me, dear." Looking at her charge slyly, the duchess lowered her tone to a conspiring pitch, "Perhaps once we become better friends, you will tell me what it is that made you change your mind about marriage."

"Perhaps," Angelica agreed. She was not willing to share her monetary concerns with anyone, not unless she could not manage to find a solution to the problem on her own. *Marriage*. The word played in her mind and made her weary, dissolving her earlier happiness.

"There you are." The Duchess looked over her shoulder, prompting her to turn around.

"Margaret." Alexander bowed formally over her hand. "I trust you are well."

"Very well, as you can no doubt see." She patted her stomach lightly.

Alexander nodded in acknowledgment and then turned toward Angelica.

"Princess Belanov." He bowed.

"Prince Kourakin." She responded just as formally after a moment's quiet. Why did he affect her this way? Her body nearly shook at his nearness, her senses clouding with the distinct smell of him.

Alexander addressed Margaret though his eyes remained on Angelica's, "I do not have much time. When you see James, it would be a great help if you tell him I will be done with his initial list by the end of tonight."

Angelica did not understand his meaning, but she was too distracted to care. He looked divine in his formal wear, his black hair curling at his nape. What would it feel like to twirl one's finger in that hair?

Angelica realized she must have missed something when Alexander held out his hand. "Care to dance, Princess?"

She wondered for a brief moment if she had the right to refuse and then let the thought go. What did it matter when she would not have said no either way?

"Yes, thank you." She placed her hand in his, ready this time for the tingling feeling that traveled the length of her arm.

Within minutes, they were circling the dance floor to the strains of a beautiful waltz.

"How is your evening progressing?" Alexander broke the silence that had grown between them. She leaned back so that she could see his face as she responded.

"Is that a polite way of asking if I am causing the duchess trouble?"

Alexander did not respond. Although he only needed a few hours of sleep to rejuvenate his body, rest had eluded him and he was in no mood to indulge her with an argument.

"I see your fear of me has gone."

"I am not afraid of you, no." Angelica realized the truth of the statement as the words left her lips. Uncertain why that was so, she became uncomfortable and changed the topic. "The inscription in the book mentioned someone called the Blessed. Who is that?"

Twirling her around the ballroom, Alexander watched the men who watched him with envy. His annoyance was apparent in his voice as he responded: "The Blessed are a legendary race. They are to grace the world one day and save us vampires from our path to extinction."

"Extinction? I don't understand . . ."

"I have things to do. I am sure Margaret will be more than willing to answer all your questions."

Bringing them to a stop, he crooked his elbow and strung her fingers through it.

"Kiril will take you to the house. I had a few of your gowns brought to your new room, so you need not go home to change as you did this evening."

He walked them past two open windows. The spring breeze felt good on her face.

"But, how did you . . . ?" Angelica held her tongue. She could tell by the face of the man beside her that he was not paying attention. The arrogant lout! She would like to clobber him with a frying pan!

"Angelica?" He spoke her name almost softly as they were about to reach Margaret's side.

"Yes?"

"You look beautiful."

It was a good thing that Alexander left only seconds later, because Angelica's mouth hung open and her palms had begun to sweat.

"Dear, you are looking a little flushed."

Recovering from the warm pool she felt she had just dived into, Angelica focused her attention on the duchess.

"I am all right. I was just thinking, that is all."

The duchess watched her for a minute more, then beckoned forward a man Angelica noticed only now.

"Peter, this is Princess Belanov." Turning to Angelica with a sparkle in her eye, Margaret winked. "Lord Kingsly is the son of a good friend of mine."

Lord Kingsly took her hand and bowed low. "Would the Princess care to dance?"

Angelica looked from the duchess to the man smiling into her eyes. He was attractive by any standards, and seemed nice enough. She would dance with him, if only to get Alexander off of her mind.

"I would love to."

The time was reaching the early hours of the morning, when Kiril turned up to escort her home.

"It's amazing, is it not? Three o'clock in the morning and no one seems inclined to leave."

Kiril glanced around the crowded ballroom, but did not comment. "Are you ready to leave?"

"Yes, though I don't understand how this is going to work. Mikhail is still here and is bound to look for me."

"The duchess will tell your brother that you were tired and she took the liberty of sending you home with her coach."

Frowning, Angelica looked around for Mikhail, but found no trace of him.

"He might worry about me and go home himself."

"The duchess will dissuade him of the notion."

It was as simple as that, Angelica realized. Though daylight had brought with it some revelations that painted a far more peaceful picture of the vampire race than she had anticipated, it was difficult to digest the power they had.

A passage she had read this morning from the vampire Book of Law popped into her head. *Remember your strength. A slap could break their necks. A push, crush their bones. Be conscious always of the frailty of humans.*

"Angelica?"

Angelica looked up to find Nicholas beside her. She could not believe she had forgotten all about him! The last they had spoken, he was to call on her in the afternoon. Oh God, what to say? She had to fix it somehow.

"Nicholas, I—"

"Please, let me apologize." His eyes traveled to where Kiril stood beside her and back. Angelica had no idea why he was apologizing, but she realized that Nicholas would likely not explain if her *guard* did not give them some space.

"I'll come along in a moment, Kiril."

Kiril understood the implication of her words and moved away silently. Angelica refocused her attention on the lord beside her.

"I will not ask who that was, because it will smack too much of jealousy."

Angelica smiled and Nicholas shook his head. "That smacked of jealousy either way, didn't it?"

"Nicholas, you are incorrigible."

His eyes turned serious as he reached for her hand.

"You sent no reply to my notes. I admit that I was perhaps overzealous . . . but all I meant to do was show you I am serious."

Wishing she knew what he had written in those notes, Angelica pulled her hand lightly out of his grasp. She was glad Nicholas was serious, but such improper behavior would start rumors, and she would not risk that.

"I have not been well this past day and have not yet attended my correspondence. Do forgive me."

His brows rose. "And here I thought you had rejected my proposal."

"Your proposal . . . ?" Angelica could hardly get the words out. Was this it? Had he actually proposed to her on a note only a few days after meeting her? Why was she not elated? Nicholas was sweet, and charming, and so good-looking. Marriage to him would solve their monetary problems and Mikhail would not suffer another attack. . . .

"Angelica, I can practically see the cannons flying inside your head!"

He was laughing at her again, and Angelica found that this time she was not finding it at all humorous. It just was too soon. If she had had a little more time with him . . .

"Okay, stop it, really. I did not mean that type of proposal. I merely asked if you would allow me to accompany you to a dinner tomorrow night at the Summers' residence."

The relief she felt made her almost giddy.

"I, yes of course you can."

"Good, good. Then I will beg your leave till then." He took her hand once more and raised it to his lips.

"Till then," Angelica replied, then turned toward the large doors that led out of the ballroom.

"Angelica?" Nicholas called out as Kiril reached her side once more.

"Yes?"

"That other proposal will come soon enough."

Chapter 21

The first rays of dawn broke through the black skies as Alexander sat silently in his parlor. His boots propped on an ottoman, he watched the second handle of the clock above the fireplace. He was tired, but sleep would not come.

The preliminary list of possibilities had turned up no slayers as he had predicted, but it rankled nevertheless. It seemed nothing in his life was meant to be simple.

Angelica. It was funny how she had become synonymous in his mind with *difficult*.

She made him want, and it was a condition he felt obligated to fight. He could not afford to be distracted, not now, not when his people were in danger and he had responsibilities to fulfill.

The expression on her face as she had knelt before him that morning came before his eyes. She loved her brother, of that he was certain. He could have asked her for anything at that moment and she would have consented. Some might have considered her devotion foolish, but Alexander understood.

He would have died for Helena, if only he had been given the chance. Somehow he believed Angelica would do the same for her brother.

"Damn woman!" She was under his roof and under his skin. She was slowly driving him mad. Just a room away from his own, he could imagine her sleeping peacefully, her hair spilled across the pillows . . .

"Alexander?"

For a moment Alexander was convinced his mind was playing tricks on him, but then ten toes peeping from under a white sheet came into his line of vision.

"I heard some noises and thought. Well, I don't know what I thought. It's not like there could be anything scarier out there than . . ." Her voice trailed off as their eyes met.

"Vampires?" Alexander asked softly.

He watched her readjust what looked like her bedsheets over her shoulders. Her discomfort was palpable, but he did not put her mind at ease. It was time she heard about Sergey. There *was* danger out there, and she had to be on her guard.

"Sit down, Angelica. Since you are awake, there are things I need to tell you about."

She nodded, much like a docile child, and Alexander wondered how she managed to do that. How did she look so fragile one minute and so strong the next?

"Yes?" She was watching him, a little warily he noticed with satisfaction. When she looked at him with that defiant tilt of her chin, he found it especially hard to resist her.

"You should know that I came to London for a specific purpose. There is a vampire out there who has broken our laws, and his name is Sergey. I am here to find him and bring him to justice."

"Which laws did Sergey break?"

"Many. The first two to begin with."

Angelica's eyes looked into the darkness beyond the windows behind him. "He drank human blood." She was not asking him, so he said nothing. It occurred to him that it might have been a mistake to give her the Book of Laws. Her memory was far too good, and with her ever curious mind she was likely to ask too many questions.

"You are going to kill him, aren't you?"

"Yes." There was no point in lying. When he found Sergey, he would be brought in front of an assembly, and it would be up to Alexander as the leader of the clan Sergey was born into, to carry out his punishment.

"So you spend your days trying to find him?"

"Him and a slayer."

Angelica shivered. "A slayer?"

"A human who is aware of our existence and has decided we need to be killed."

"I am sorry."

Alexander saw her sadness and did not understand.

"Why? It is not your fault. There are human murderers just as there are vampire ones."

She shrugged as if she did not quite know either.

"I am sorry you have such difficult responsibilities. It cannot be easy to kill anyone, even with a wealth of cause."

Her words were innocent, naive even, but they made him feel warm. He stood and held out his hand.

"Come, you need your sleep and I have things to do."

Angelica took the offered hand without hesitation. They were silent as they climbed the stairs to the upper hall.

"Kiril will take you to meet Margaret in the morning."

She nodded, the action dislodging a strand of hair into her face. Before he could think it through, Alexander reached out and tucked it behind her ear.

He saw the surprise in her face and then passion. He barely contained a groan as his body burned for her.

"Good night, Princess." He turned and reached his door as a thought stopped him cold.

Do not go.

Alexander took in the view of her parted lips, the passion in the depth of her blue eyes, and the confusion. . . . She could not know what she did to him, for he had mastered the art of hiding his feelings. He had thought he had mastered the art of not having feelings, but Angelica had proved him wrong.

He took two steps toward her. She moved back, startled, and ended with the wall to her back. Placing his hands on either side of her face, his gaze drifted to her soft mouth, then back to her eyes.

Angelica held her breath. He could hear her heartbeat getting faster. He could see the uncertainty in her eyes, the struggle, but he was through with questions, hers and his.

He put his own doubts away as he leaned into her, placing his lips on hers. The contact was electrifying. His lips were soft and hard all at once as they brushed across hers. Her eyes closed gradually, her shoulders losing some of their tension.

Alexander recognized her inexperience instantaneously,

but the knowledge did nothing to cool his ardor. He cupped her face with his hands, slowly ravaging her lips.

Open your mouth for me.

Angelica did as she was told, then jumped when he slid his tongue into her mouth.

Alexander. He heard the desperation in her thought and felt it in the fingers that clung to him.

His kiss grew more passionate at her sigh, deeper. Alexander forgot all about her inexperience and pressed his body more firmly against hers. It was as if he were kissing for the first time again, the feelings were the strongest he had had in almost two hundred years.

Come to me, he thought forcefully, *tonight, be with me.*

Angelica came to her senses slowly as his request registered in her mind. What was she doing? God, she was kissing a vampire. No, he was the leader of a clan of vampires. She had to be losing her mind; that was the only explanation.

"Stop," she said softly as she pulled away. Alexander stepped back immediately, transforming in front of her eyes into the composed man he always was. His body straightened, his expression growing bland once again. Angelica looked at him and was not entirely convinced that she had not imagined the whole episode, until she saw his eyes. They remained hot, the way her body felt . . .

"I can't," she said, feeling stupid and confused. She was gratified that he had listened to her request, and yet a part of her wished he would kiss her again. "I . . . ," she began, but nothing followed. Her brain scampered to put things into order. If she was with Alexander, she would be giving up any possibility of marriage, and then Mikhail would suffer . . .

"Go to sleep." Alexander's voice was cold. The fire was

gone from his eyes, and he was back to being the arrogant prince.

Angelica looked at him and realized that his being a vampire did not bother her half as much as his arrogance. Curse and rot the man! How did he manage to be so infuriating?

"Good night then!" she said, her confusion neatly turning into anger.

Alexander caught her arm as she turned to open her door. His face was no longer bland as he looked upon her.

"You told me to stop and I am holding myself back. Explain to me the cause of this anger. Or perhaps your annoyance is with yourself for having kissed a vampire?"

"I am scared!" Angelica admitted on a half shout.

Surprise registered on his face. "You are scared of me?"

"No," Angelica said on a quieter note, "of what you make me feel."

When he said nothing to that revelation she kept talking, uncertain how precisely to explain or why she was even trying to.

"I never wanted someone before, and wanting you scares me."

Alexander was quiet for a long moment.

"Go to sleep, Angelica."

Angelica looked at his face, which seemed softer to her somehow and more dear. As innocent as she was, she knew the meaning of his statement. Alexander Kourakin was backing away.

Feeling very young and foolish, she nodded and entered her room.

* * *

"Here are the plans for tomorrow's search." Joanna threw a parchment on the table between them. "They are getting closer. You would do well to move to another house."

Sergey smiled slowly. It was such a pleasure to manipulate.

"Thank you, my dear. Without you, I would not be free to find that murderous slayer. Tell me, have they made any progress in that area?"

Joanna looked genuinely distressed as she paced the marble floor of his foyer.

"No. No, they have not, although I am certain the prince will any day now. He is . . . formidable."

"That he is," Sergey agreed as he thought of Alexander Kourakin.

"It is really unbelievable that a living legend can be so, well, approachable."

"What do you mean?" Sergey leaned against the wall as he made his voice casual. He had been watching the prince for a while now and was keen on any information Joanna could give him.

"Well, just the way he was with Christopher, for one . . ."

"The boy who just had his initiation?" Sergey realized he had erred when Joanna shot him a suspicious look and improvised quickly. "You told me about him a week ago."

Seeming to believe him, Joanna continued. "Yes, that boy. The prince was so gentle with him. Usually he is so curt. He speaks little, and never smiles, but with Christopher he was almost gentle."

A smile began at the corner of Sergey's mouth before he cut it off. This was perfect. Just perfect!

"I see. Well, Joanna, you should probably get going. It will be morning soon and you do not want to be missed." He opened the door to the brisk dawn air, eager now to have her gone.

"You are right, of course." Pulling up the hood of her cloak, Joanna passed by him and disappeared into the early morning fog.

"Christopher." Sergey said the name out loud. Little Christopher had apparently won the prince's affections and that was simply perfect.

Alexander Kourakin was his key to success. The strongest of all vampires, the warrior who had killed dozens of slayers in a mere night, he would be the one to win the upcoming war for the vampire race. Sergey knew through stories passed down, that the night Alexander had ended the age of vampire slayers, his sister had been murdered. It was rage that fueled the warrior's arm, so Sergey would provide the prince with fuel for rage.

Tomorrow he would pay a call to the vampire slayer. Sergey had led the killer straight to that visiting vampire and the results were perfect: the weak vampire's death brought them closer to war. Now Sergey would make sure the slayer killed the boy and thereby guaranteed the cooperation of his strongest ally.

Chapter 22

Kiril helped her down as Angelica stepped out of the ducal carriage.

"The duchess and Lady Joanna are waiting for you inside." He pointed at a small establishment that was known for its delicious scones and aromatic tea.

"Thank you, Kiril."

"You are welcome, Princess. I will be by later to take you back." Having said so he motioned her to the café and stood his ground. Angelica knew he would not leave until he was certain that she had gone inside, and the knowledge almost made her smile.

Inside the building, several women sat around tables draped with white lace tablecloths and laden with china plates and teapots.

Angelica looked around the crowded room until a flash of

red caught her eye. Joanna was really very easy to spot with that glorious hair of hers.

"You are very much like a flame," Angelica said as she lowered herself into the seat beside her friend.

"There you are!" Joanna turned to her happily. She had been waiting with ill-concealed impatience while she eyed the pastries strewn around the tables around her. "God Angelica, I am sure to gain one hundred pounds this very afternoon if I give in to the urges that have gripped me."

"The little tarts do look divine, don't they?" Angelica responded with a little laugh. "Perhaps we should ask the waiter if he might bring us one of everything they have got!"

"Do not even suggest it," Joanna said with mock horror. "I will do it; you know I will."

Both women were silent as a waiter, having noticed them, pushed a cart bearing dozens of different cakes, tarts, and other delicacies, toward them.

"Is there anything I can offer you ladies from our pastry selection?" the man asked politely.

Angelica almost laughed as Joanna laid her gloved finger across her mouth while she considered. After several seconds of complete silence, the redhead pointed at several items on the tray, not once glancing at the waiter's face.

"We will have this, this, this, and this. Oh, and this too," Joanna said with utmost haughtiness.

"Oh, Joanna, you had to see his expression!" Angelica laughed after the waiter had taken his leave, announcing he would bring their tea at once.

"I honestly do not care one bit. The establishment will be making a little fortune from us, what else do they want?"

"True." Noticing the third set of china at the table, Angelica realized the duchess was not present for the first time since she arrived.

"Where is the duchess?"

"Really, Angelica, I told you to call me Margaret!" The duchess approached the table at that very moment. A waiter rushed forward to hold her chair as she sat herself down.

"So, what did I miss?"

"I just asked for everything in their kitchen, other than that nothing, Your Grace," Joanna said.

"Well, that is good, but I doubt if it will be enough. I feel as though I have a starving colony in my stomach." Margaret complained just as four white-gloved men placed trays of delicacies on their table. "Oh good, oh this is so good. If they keep these coming, I am going to be a very happy woman today."

Angelica bit her lip, then forged ahead. "If you are in such a good mood, then perhaps I could ask for a favor?"

The duchess lowered the piece of scone she had been in the process of putting in her mouth. "Angelica, you know you need not ask for any favors. Just ask me for anything you want and if I can, I will help you."

"Okay, well, do you remember our conversation yesterday at the ball about husbands? Well, one potential suitor has asked to escort me to a dinner this evening at the Summers' residence, and I was wondering if it would be at all possible for us to attend. I know I cannot go without you and—"

"Say no more. Of course we can go. I had nothing else planned, so it is a far better option than doing nothing. I'll send a note over to the Summers and get invitations. All you would have to do, my dear, is arrange to meet your bachelor at the dinner."

"Oh, thank you." Angelica was quite relieved to hear that all would go according to plan. After what had happened that morning, she knew she had to stay as far away from Alexander as possible and focus on finding a husband. Though Alexander was unlikely to approach her in that way again, not after having rejected her the way he did, Angelica would not risk it. If this morning taught her anything, it was that she was incapable of clear thought when Alexander Kourakin was kissing her.

She reached for a pastry.

"So who is this man?" Joanna wanted to know.

Angelica swallowed and washed the lingering taste of crumpet down with hot tea.

"His name is Nicholas . . ."

"*Hmm*, Nicholas," Joanna repeated, her eyes closing. "I knew a Nicholas once. We met in a little village on the outskirts of a large French city."

Margaret laughed with delight. "It seems we all have Nicholas in common, dears. Dark brown hair and night black eyes. It has been over three hundred years, but I still remember those eyes."

"Three hundred?" Angelica could only stare in complete surprise. Why had it not occurred to her before now that vampires did not live the temporary lives humans did? "Are you immortal then?"

"Oh no," Joanna was quick to say. She added a lump of sugar to her tea and stirred slowly as Margaret began on her fourth scone.

"We can live up to six hundred years or so, though most vampires do not reach such seniority."

"Why not?"

Joanna sipped her sweet tea and then shrugged. The withdrawal of passion is not something she liked thinking about, just as she supposed humans did not like thinking about death.

"Living for so many years is not as simple as it seems," Margaret interjected, her eyes sad as she thought of her many friends that had chosen to move onto another world. "There comes a time when darkness starts to overtake the soul and nothing is satisfying any longer. How long do you think a writer can write before doing so no longer gives him pleasure?"

Angelica did not know the answer. She could not even begin to imagine living for such a long time in truth.

"I used to write. For a hundred years or so of my life, it gave me joy as nothing else could." Putting her cup back on its saucer, Margaret shrugged off the ache of melancholy. "I have not touched a pen in many years. The words that used to bring me joy no longer touch my soul."

Shaking her head as if to clear it, the duchess laughed. "Listen to me making everything sound so tragic. I have a lot of joy left in me yet."

Angelica did not want to continue with the subject that obviously made both women at the table uncomfortable, but she did not understand and she had the feeling that what she was missing was important.

"I do not understand. Does a vampire die when they lose their passion?"

Joanna shook her head in the negative. "No. The loss of passion leads to the loss of will to live. By the time most vampires reach their fourth century, they choose to move on."

Suicide. Angelica understood what Joanna was saying,

though she could not understand why anyone would do such a thing. As long as one was alive, there was hope for happiness wasn't there?

But then, perhaps if she spent a hundred years in misery she would have thought differently.

Something Alexander had told her just two days ago drifted into her consciousness.

"Is this somehow connected to why your race is dying out?"

Both vampires regarded her with surprise and had her explaining.

"Alexander mentioned it awhile back but then he would not explain."

Margaret pushed her plate away in a gesture that signaled she was full. "It does, yes. You see, the women of our race only become fertile after their fifth century."

"But most choose to move on before that happens?" Angelica asked.

"Precisely," Joanna put finality to the word. "Now let's eat!"

Angelica tried to make sense of everything she found out, but realized soon enough that she was simply too tired to think anymore.

She gave herself into the hunger that had been gnawing at her for the next few minutes until she noticed Margaret and Joanna were staring at her in surprise.

"What?" Angelica asked over a mouth full of chocolate soufflé.

After another moment of silence, the duchess laughed. "Good God, Angelica, you have one large appetite for such a slim girl!"

Shrugging, Angelica bit into a scone.

"Not really, I only get very hungry when I'm very tired."

Joanna looked surprised for a moment, then seemed to shake the thought away.

"I am going to the bathroom, dears. Do not finish the crumpets, Angelica. I have yet to start eating in earnest!" The duchess left the table amongst laughter.

Angelica turned to Joanna a moment later.

"What was it that surprised you a moment ago?"

"Oh, nothing really, it's just that it is the same with *us*. We only get hungry when we overexert ourselves physically."

"Oh." Angelica mulled that over in her mind, then smiled. "So I suppose some of those people at parties who I've seen sneaking away with mountains of food must have been vampires."

Joanna smiled though her tone was soft. "I do not think so, Angelica. Our hunger is for a different kind of nourishment."

"Oh."

Angelica felt foolish and a little imbalanced. It was so easy to forget that Joanna was not human. Her friend was a vampire and vampires lived hundreds of years on nourishment of a different kind.

Joanna put her hand over Angelica's. "We do not drink human blood."

"I know," she said, and nodded, but her voice came out as a squeak.

"It is really not as horrible as it sounds. Most of the time it is served out of glasses . . . like red wine."

"Joanna, stop please. I know you mean well, but the analogies are not making it easier to, well, digest." Angelica gave her friend a wan smile.

"I suppose you intended no pun?" Joanna said dryly.

"What pun, I . . ." It took a moment for Angelica to figure out what she had said, then she laughed.

"God, Joanna, you are impossible."

"Thank you, I have been working at it for centuries!" was the glib reply, and Angelica laughed harder.

Chapter 23

"You look beautiful."

Looking down at the pale green material of her dinner gown, Angelica wondered why her heart did not skip a bit as it had when Alexander had uttered the same words.

"Thank you."

Nicholas put fingers lightly under her chin and lifted her head.

"You are insincere, Angelica. Where has your mind wandered off to?"

Angelica was surprised that Nicholas could read her so well, but then she likely shouldn't be. After all, he was more attentive than most, and so gentle. Yes, he was gentle and sweet and looked especially dashing in his evening wear.

She had to be crazy not to be affected by this man that several of the ladies in the Summers' receiving room were even now watching with interest.

"I admit to being a little distracted, but I am flattered that you noticed."

"And by your tone I gather you are surprised? Why, Angelica, when you know how interested I am in you?"

Angelica was saved from having to answer as a footman approached them with an apologetic look.

"My lord, a message."

"Excuse me, I will be right back," Nicholas said as he took the missive and left the room.

Annoyed with herself for feeling slightly relieved, Angelica turned to find her brother amongst the group gathered by the windows. She still felt guilty every time they met for allowing them to manipulate him.

"He is divine." Joanna nudged her as she looked toward the door from which Nicholas had just left. "I did not notice when we saw him in the park the other day, but now I see pretty clearly, sweetheart. If you decide you do not want him, pass him to me!"

"Do you see the Dutchess anywhere?"

Joanna lifted a brow. "Does that mean you are keeping him?"

"Joanna!" Angelica complained. Her friend was impossible when it came to the male species, vampire or human.

"Oh, all right, I'll leave you alone. In fact, I think I'll do it literally since your Mr. Lovely is coming this way."

Angelica closed her eyes and hoped her cheeks were not flushed as Joanna left her side.

"What was that about?" Nicholas asked jovially, but she could tell there was something wrong.

"Joanna was simply being herself."

"Oh? If that is enough to make your cheeks that becoming

shade of pink, then I think I shall have to speak with her and gain some pointers."

Laughing, Angelica pointed at his chest. "If you follow through on that thought, I will not forgive either of you. Now tell me, was it bad news?"

Nicholas turned serious. "In a manner of speaking. My mother is sick; she has been for a while now, but it seems she took a turn for the worse."

"I am so sorry, Nicholas!" Unconsciously, she reached for his hand. "Do you need to go to her?"

He was watching her face intently as he nodded in the affirmative. "I am sorry to leave, but glad to see your concern."

"Of course I am concerned. I wish you only the best." Angelica knew it was true. Although Nicholas did not stir her the way Alexander did, she was coming to care for him. Perhaps with time they could grow to love each other even?

"Then I will leave you in the capable hands of your brother and Lady Joanna. Will you convey my apologies to them?"

"There is no need to apologize," Angelica assured him. "Take care of your mother."

Nicholas bent over her hand. "Be careful, Angelica, or I will snatch you off to Gretna Green and wed you before you have time to reconsider." He waited for no answer, and for that Angelica was glad because she would not have known how to answer.

She wanted to wed him, did she not? Considering she had to get married and fast, she had to be ecstatic at the way her relationship with Nicholas was progressing. She was happy about it. Really, she was, but ecstatic was pushing it.

Alexander! It was all his fault. Why did she have to meet him? Couldn't he just stay away? But even as she had the thought, she looked around the room in hopes that he might have come, after all.

She spotted Mikhail, but chose not to go to him. The duchess had yet to arrive, and Joanna was busily flirting with a man Angelica had not been introduced to, so it was one of the rare moments where she could be alone.

"Dear Princess Belanov, your brother has been regaling us all of your accomplishments on the pianoforte. Could we possibly convince you to play for us?"

So much for a moment alone. Angelica looked over at her brother, who was standing several feet away speaking with Lady Summers. Lord Summers was watching her hopefully, his double chin all the more pronounced because of the pleading tilt of his head.

"But of course, Lord Summers, it would be my pleasure," she replied.

Clapping his hands, Lord Summers turned to face the seven people who stood in clusters. "I am happy to announce that Princess Belanov has agreed to regale us with a musical performance while we wait for the last of our guests to arrive. Lady Summers, if you would lead the way?"

As Angelica followed the party into the music room, she understood why Lord Summers had been so eager to have her play. The room was majestic. The entire length of one wall was composed of windows that reached from the floor to the very top of the high walls. A sleek grand piano had been placed at the very center of the glass wall that looked out to a beautifully lighted garden. The seating arrangement created for an audience was unique as well. Unlike the single chairs that were more commonly lined up for musical interludes, the room contained only comfortable couches that had been placed to form a semicircle, providing each listener with a view of both the piano and the gardens beyond.

The delighted exclamations from his guests made Lord Summers's face light up with pleasure.

He guided Angelica to the piano as the rest of the party took their seats.

"We have sheet music from several composers available for you to choose from, Princess. Did you have a particular favorite?"

"Mozart," Angelica said without hesitation.

"Ah, a popular choice, although I must say that it is a little unconventional for a woman to desire to play his works," Lord Summers's commented as he shuffled through a pile of sheet music that had been left by the piano.

Angelica held her tongue. She knew from experience that many men believed Mozart's compositions to be too powerful for a woman to play, but that did not concern her. As long as she did his work justice, she was satisfied.

"I will not be requiring the sheets," Angelica said politely.

Lord Summers's hands stilled as his eyes rounded. "You will play from memory?"

"Yes," Angelica responded simply.

Having nothing else to say, Lord Summers nodded and moved off to join his wife on the settee closest to the piano.

Adjusting her seat so that the slick soles of her shoes rested comfortably on the pedals, Angelica twisted so that she could address the audience who had gone silent.

Mikhail sat toward her left with a young girl who looked like she was about to faint dead away. Lord Summers's daughter was selected as Mikhail's dinner partner this evening, and Angelica did not doubt her parents would like nothing better than a match between the two of them.

"I will play Fantasy in D Minor, a composition by Wolfgang Amadeus Mozart."

There was some shifting, which Angelica ignored as she placed her fingers on the piano keys. Taking a deep breath, she flexed her wrists once, then she began.

The air filled with music and time ceased to matter as Angelica let herself drift into a different world. This was a beautiful world, a harmonious world . . . a world without worries.

The flawless playing enchanted even the most skeptical of the guests against their wills. Notes drifted, the grandfather clock in the hallway ticked to the tempo of the tune, and as the piece ended, it was followed by uproarious applause.

"Amazing, my dear, absolutely wonderful," Lady Summers said as she touched her handkerchief to her eyes. "Will you not play another?"

Angelica looked at Lord Summers as several of the other guests repeated the request.

"We would love for you to grace us with more," Lord Summers implored.

Angelica nodded and turned toward the piano, then hesitated. The lamps that lit the garden provided such a wonderful light. Perhaps it was an utterly ridiculous notion, but she decided she would ask nevertheless.

It had to be the duchess's influence, she thought ruefully as she turned back toward Lord Summers.

"I was thinking, Lord Summers, that perhaps you would

not mind if we extinguished the lights? I am not reading the music, and the garden will look that much more beautiful would you not agree?"

"That is a wonderful idea!" Lord Summers exclaimed to Angelica's relief. "I will tell the staff to take care of it this instant!

Angelica watched with some amusement as gentlemen assured the ladies that they need not be afraid of the dark while next to them. Mikhail, on the other hand, did not seem to do any consoling, as Miss Summers looked excited at the prospect of a concert in the dark.

Alexander heard the music and knew without a doubt that *she* was playing.

"It is beautiful, is it not?" Margaret whispered, her hand on her husband's arm as all three of them followed a maid to the music room.

He did not hear James's response, he was captivated. The music filled his chest and brought all of his senses alive.

It was breathtaking, just like she was.

For a moment Alexander contemplated turning around and leaving. James had convinced him that he needed a break from the search and that he should join them for a small dinner party. Had he known, however, that she would be there he might have reconsidered the offer. Every time he saw her, it became harder to resist the temptation.

The temptation of touching her. The temptation of kissing those lips. The temptation of making her his.

The morning before, he had managed to walk away from her, but barely.

Yet he did not leave. Could not leave, and within moments they came to the entrance of the room from which the music poured.

Alexander was surprised when he realized she played in darkness. He could make out several figures sitting on couches around the large piano, which was partly illuminated by moonlight.

Margaret shifted beside him, as they all stopped and watched.

Angelica was in the dark, her body an extension of the instrument that seemed to have captured her soul just as she had captured his. No one so much as breathed as the notes poured from her.

As her fingers touched the keys one last time and held, total silence reigned.

Be mine.

He sent the thought before he could rethink what he was doing. He wanted her as he had never wanted a woman. Many vampires had human lovers; it was not uncommon. If she became his lover, it would make his obligations as her guide that much easier to fulfill.

Yes, she was innocent and had seemed uncertain, but she wanted him too, of that he was sure. Once they were lovers he would visit her when he wanted to and soon this irrational desire for her would leave his system so that he could start concentrating during the day once more, something he had not been able to do since meeting her.

Be mine. The thought that entered her head had Angelica pulling her hands off the piano keys. Had she allowed her block to slip as she played? The voice had sounded like Alexander's, although she had to be mistaken. Not only was Alexander not there, but he would never have thought those words.

Her eyes swept the audience as their applause broke out. She had simply gotten carried away with the music, she reasoned. It happened to her often enough. Once she had gotten so caught up while playing *Alla Turca* that she could have sworn she heard trumpets and drums.

"Incredible!" Lord Summers raved as several servants lit the lights in the room. "That was absolutely fantastic."

"Thank you." Angelica found herself blushing under the profuse praise. The applause had yet to dwindle and she found herself becoming self-conscious.

"Oh, and here are the rest of our guests!" Lord Summers exclaimed as he caught sight of the duchess. "Your Graces, how good of you to come, and Prince Kourakin, what a wonderful surprise! You are all very welcomed."

Angelica's eyes widened as she caught sight of Alexander. He was here! But he could not have possibly sent her that thought, could he?

Mikhail blocked her vision of the gorgeous man who stood at the other end of the room commanding the attention of every female present.

"That was wonderful."

Her heart, which had skipped a beat at the sight of Alexander, now did an awkward dance as she worried her lower lip. The smile on Mikhail's face was almost heartbreaking, the distance between them even more difficult to bear. If only she could confide in him.

"Thank you." Her brother reached forward and pushed a pin more firmly into her coiffure.

"You always did play with an unladylike passion," he re-marked, "but I could not be more proud."

Emotion overwhelmed her, and she wished that she could wrap her arms around her little brother as she had done so many times in her life.

"Mikhail, I love you. I don't believe I say that enough."

Mikhail took his sister's hands and looked down at the fingers that procured such magic.

"I love you too. I do not quite understand it, but I have missed you these past days."

Angelica understood it, far too well, but she could say nothing.

Mikhail laughed and patted her hand. "Anyway, where is Nicholas?"

Glad for the change in subject, Angelica shrugged. "He had to leave. His mother got sick. He asked me to apologize in his stead."

"That's strange, I thought his mother—"

"Good evening!" Joanna smiled as she appeared beside Mikhail.

Distracted, Angelica turned to her friend.

"Joanna, I don't believe you have been formally introduced to my brother."

Mikhail sketched a bow and smiled. "Mikhail Belanov at your service."

Joanna laughed, her eyes shining with appreciation. "Call me Joanna, and it is my pleasure really. I have heard a lot about you, Prince. May I just say that if you will make as fabulous a husband as you do a brother, I have several good friends whom I would love to introduce to you."

Mikhail did not bat an eye at the very unconventional introduction, though Angelica cleared her throat and shot her friend a pleading look.

"Joanna, really . . . ," she began on half a laugh, but was cut short by her brother.

"You are married then, Lady Joanna?"

Angelica could not believe what she was hearing, and Joanna was laughing! Oh, they were completely outrageous!

"Both of you stop it this instant! Someone will hear you and that will be the end of my reputation," she whispered.

Joanna cocked her head and looked at her questioningly. "But you are practically married already to that handsome devil, so what need do you have of a shining reputation?"

Mikhail laughed as Angelica shook her head in complete frustration. Thankfully, Lord Summers chose that moment to announce that dinner was served.

Mikhail excused himself, making his way to Miss Summers, who stood waiting to be escorted to the dining room.

Lady Summers appeared by her side, just as Joanna started complaining about her dinner partner.

"Oh my dear, I am so sorry, Lord Adler had to leave due to an emergency. Oh, but you probably already know that and oh you poor dear, I hope you are not overly put out." The woman looked very upset at the turn of events, and Angelica found herself trying to put her at ease.

"Do not worry yourself, Lady Summers, please. I understand completely."

"She can have my dinner partner," Joanna put in. "After all, it is quite acceptable for a widow to be seated on her own."

Angelica gave Joanna a sour look.

What are you doing? she thought with some annoyance.

Joanna's laugh echoed in her mind before her friend explained.

I am seeing if I can get rid of the stuck-up man Lady Summers has stuck me with. I had to sit with him at an earlier dinner party; completely intolerable ego.

Thankfully, Lady Summers protested on Angelica's behalf. "Oh, but Lord Jeffrey has already taken such a shine to you, Lady Joanna. Look how he waits at the door for you to finish your conversation!"

"It really is no trouble at all, Lady Summers," Angelica said before Joanna could further her plot to get rid of her unwanted dinner partner.

Lady Summers looked relieved. "Well, that is so nice of you to say dear, although you must be so upset! I will have your brother come and escort you immediately after he has seated my daughter."

Angelica was about to tell the woman that suited her perfectly when she was forestalled.

"If I may have the honor?"

Alexander's deep voice drifted across Angelica's skin, causing goose bumps. She was coming to resent his ability to sneak up on her in this manner.

"Prince Kourakin!" Lady Summers was radiant as she turned to him.

"Having arrived unexpectedly, I too do not have a partner," Alexander explained.

"Oh, but you have thrilled us all by coming, Prince Kourakin, truly. All of my friends have been dying to get you to attend their parties and not one managed. They will be so envious. And poor Princess Belanov was going to be unescorted! You are our hero, Prince Kourakin, a true knight in shining armor!"

Black armor, Angelica thought darkly.

"Princess?" Alexander said, and held out his arm to her with a mocking gleam in his eye. Had he heard her thoughts? No, it could not be, her block was in place!

Angelica laid her hand on his arm, trying not to notice the rigid muscle that bunched beneath her palm.

They made their way to the dining room in silence where he led her to her seat at the center of the long table.

"There you are!" the duchess exclaimed as Alexander took his seat beside Angelica. Margaret, who was sitting across the table, shook a finger at her. "You never told me of your accomplishment on the pianoforte!"

James, who sat one seat to his wife's left, held up his hand to indicate he did not want more of the bread that the server was offering. "The music was indeed most gratifying. We will have to ask you to play more often from now on."

"Thank you for your kind words, I would love to play for you more often," Angelica said as a plate of soup was placed before her.

"A toast," Lord Summers said, raising his glass from the head of the table, "to our pianist!"

The guests followed his lead and soon everyone was drinking to Angelica, while she turned quite pink.

"You have been well?"

Angelica was surprised by the low-pitched question.

"Why should I have not been?" she responded, annoyed that he was acting out of character. Where was the cold man she had gotten used to?

"Perhaps you have been thinking of me."

Angelica nearly dropped her spoon. He could not possibly know that she thought of him constantly. Moreover, where did he get off being conceited enough to imagine that she would? She was about to deliver a nice put-down when he continued.

"I have been thinking of you."

Angelica coughed as her spoon dropped into her bowl with a small splash. Fearing that she would not be able to control the volume of her words, she resorted to thoughts. He let her in.

What on earth do you mean?

I mean that I cannot seem to concentrate from thinking of you.

He could not be serious, it just could not be. He had refused her the morning before, hadn't he? Was this a game then?

She closed her mind and decided to make conversation with the others around her. The duke and duchess were speaking with Lady Summers, while Joanna seemed to be doing her utmost to ignore Lord Jeffrey.

"As pleasant as music is to the ear, one wishes that the women of our great country were encouraged to have a more diverse frame of knowledge. The world is a very large place, don't you know? When I was in India . . ."

Angelica stopped listening to Lord Jeffrey's account of his travels until she heard Mikhail say, "My sister's area of expertise is hardly limited to the pianoforte."

Angelica wished Mikhail had not engaged the pompous man in conversation, when it was not worth doing so. He was the type that cared for no one's opinion but his own, and was hardly worth the energy.

Nevertheless, the guests seemed to have sensed the ten-

sion that was building and had quieted so they might hear
what was being said.

"My dear Prince Belanov, I hardly meant to insult your
sister. But one cannot expect the lady to know of more prac-
tical things. Say, for example, that the capital of the Ottoman Empire is Constantinople."

"I assure you, Lord Jeffrey, that my sister—"

"Please, Mikhail," Angelica said at long last. She could tell
that her brother was angered enough to say something that
could quite possibly cause trouble, "I think this is simply a
misunderstanding."

"And what kind of misunderstanding would that be, Princess Belanov?" Lord Jeffrey said with a laugh.

All eyes focused on Angelica as she tried to keep her
temper in check. The man was quite possibly the most conceited man in creation.

"I believe, Lord Jeffrey, that you are under the mistaken
impression that music is of little consequence," she replied
smoothly. She did not want to turn the conversation onto a
personal note, for if she did she might find herself wishing
she had not spoken to begin with.

"Tell me then, Princess, how music is so consequential!"

The condescending expression Lord Jeffrey sported was
just annoying enough to create in Angelica the desire to wipe
the smirk off his face.

"Queen Elizabeth had Thomas Dallam build an organ,
which she then sent to Sultan Mehmed the third in 1599.
She did so as a political gesture, having heard from her informants who reside in Constantinople, which in Ottoman
Turkish is officially called Konstantinniye by the by, that the
sultan enjoyed music."

Lord Jeffrey scoffed, although Angelica noticed that Joanna was grinning at her.

"In 1828, Giuseppe Donizetti, the brother of the famous opera composer Gaetano Donizetti, became the director of the Imperial Military Music School upon Sultan Mahmud the Second's request. Yet another instance where politics was played through inconsequential music."

This time Lord Jeffrey's laughter was shorter.

"Finally," Angelica continued as neutrally as she had been speaking thus far, "you may remember the current sultan's trip to Europe not four years ago. Abdulaziz, who donated handsomely to Richard Wagner's Bayreuth funds I might add, attended a performance of Auber's *Masaniello* right here in Covent Garden. A performance that allowed for several informal *political* conversations of import, as the *Times* wrote the next day."

Lord Summers laughed as he raised his glass in Angelica's direction for the second time that evening. "Come now, Lord Jeffrey, I believe the Princess has proven her point quite adequately. Your knowledge of music as well as of Ottoman political figures is most impressive, my dear."

"Thank you," Angelica said. If a few bits of information had managed to put Lord Jeffrey in his place, she was more than gratified, although she sorely disliked getting into a close argument with the man.

As she picked up her spoon to resume drinking the soup that had no doubt gone cold, she noticed that Alexander was staring at her oddly.

"What?" she asked with frustration. Would she not have a moment of peace this night?

"Nothing really," he responded. "It is just an interesting experience to watch you show your claws."

Angelica frowned. "I was doing no such thing. You must have seen how Mikhail was about to argue with the man, I just wanted to keep that from happening."

"So you argued with him yourself?" Alexander asked, amusement in his tone.

"That was not an argument!" Angelica insisted.

"Whatever you say, Princess," Alexander said as she glared at him.

"I am curious to know if the very knowledgeable Princess Belanov can answer me this: Who ruled France in sixteen hundred and forty-five?" Lord Jeffrey said loudly, cutting off all conversations yet again.

"If you are looking for a competition, Lord Jeffrey, I am willing to oblige." Alexander's cold words had her glancing at him in surprise. His face was bland, as if the matter was not important at all, but Angelica knew that Alexander never spoke needlessly.

"Oh come now, Princess, must you hide behind the prince then?" Lord Jeffrey laughed haughtily.

Angelica caught the worried look James cast in Alexander's direction. Was Alexander losing his temper? It was impossible to tell by the look of him.

Angelica kept her silence as she put her hand on Alexander's knee and sent him a thought.

I appreciate the support, but please do not engage with this man. He is a ridiculous fool.

I will not allow him to upset you.

Angelica tried not to read too much into his statement,

but she could not help the warmth that enveloped her.

He cannot upset me, he hardly matters enough to be able to have that kind of effect on my person.

Alexander nodded curtly, though it was obvious to Angelica that he did so with reluctance.

"'Ah, she wavers, she hesitates; in a word, she is a woman!'" Lord Jeffrey quoted. Several of the guests joined his laughter, more out of relief that the tension between the two men had subsided, than humor.

Out of the corner of her eye, Angelica saw the duke lay a restraining hand on Margaret's arm. It was the last straw!

"If you are fond of Jean Racine, perhaps you will like this quote," Angelica said softly. "'The happiness of the wicked flows away as a torrent.'"

"'There is a method in man's wickedness, it grows up by degrees.' Francis Beaumont," Lord Jeffrey responded, unperturbed.

"Interesting is it not, that a man's wickedness grows up?" Angelica smiled at those around her. "When 'Men are but children of a larger growth.' John Dryden." Several of the women laughed and even some men smiled.

"'Man is a piece of the universe made alive.' Ralph Waldo Emerson," Lord Jeffrey exclaimed with relish. Several guests laughed openly this time, smiling for having found this rare entertainment.

"Do you think it wise to group all men in one mold, Lord Jeffrey, when there are Napoleons and King Arthurs in the world? I would think that Quintus Horatius was right when he wrote that every man should measure himself by his own standard."

At this, several men snickered while the women laughed

gaily. Lord Jeffrey turned slightly pink at the implication of her statement.

"You would think, Princess Belanov? Has thinking become your hobby then, after the piano?" he said maliciously, giving up all pretense of humor. The company grew quiet, realizing the atmosphere had grown sour.

Alexander stiffened beside her, but Angelica forged on.

"Now, now, Lord Jeffrey. I believe it was also Ralph Waldo Emerson who wrote that men lose their tempers in defending their taste. Obviously your taste in women runs along ones that do not think too much, but there is really no need to get agitated because I am not such a one."

Lord Jeffrey looked decidedly red by then, glaring across the table as if he were trying to burn a hole through Angelica's eyes.

"The two great duties of a virtuous woman are to keep home and be silent."

The silence was deafening as Lord Jeffrey's slanderous words reverberated in the room. Sensing Alexander was about to rise, Angelica thought quickly.

"I thought, my dear lord, that you were mocking me only minutes ago for keeping silent in the face of your challenge."

Picking up her napkin, she patted her lips dry and took a sip of her wine. Alexander's anger was a physical thing and she found herself thanking God that he was remaining silent. The look she had seen in his eyes a moment before was rivaled only by that of her brother. The tense silence around her continued, but a devil in her head would not let her leave it alone.

"Your weakness shows in your inability to make up your mind," Angelica continued conversationally, "and I will admit to a weakness of my own. I have oft read George Herbert's words, but not till now did I understand them: 'If a donkey bray at you, don't bray at him!'"

Red up to his ears, Lord Jeffrey stood with indignation, "Why you—"

"If you know what is best for you, Lord Jeffrey, you will leave this very minute." Alexander's voice was cold enough to crack ice. Lord and Lady Summers looked as though they were ready to expire on the spot while both her brother and the duke had stood, adding to the threat.

Lord Jeffrey looked around him grimly seeing not a single sympathetic face in the crowd, and then stormed off.

"I am so terribly sorry," Lord Summers apologized as the duke and her brother resumed their seats, "it was our fault for inviting him. We should have known he would cause trouble, as he seems to do at every affair he frequents. Being a relation of my wife's we felt obligated, you see . . . We are so sorry, my dear."

Angelica's anger had ebbed away and now she felt a certain amount of guilt herself at having caused her hosts grief. "Please, do not apologize. I should not have indulged my tongue that way, no matter what form of insult he delivered."

"Oh, do not be ridiculous, child," Margaret spoke up, "you only said what everyone at this table would have liked to say, and you did so very eloquently, I might add."

At that, everyone at the table laughed agreeing whole-heartedly with the duchess's sentiments. Everyone but Alexander, Angelica amended in her head. He had remained quiet after delivering his threat.

"Are we ready for the next course then?" Lady Summers

smiled, now that her guests were once again conversing among themselves. Though the few minutes of tension had not been pleasant, she knew that her dinner party would be the talk of the ton for a while to come and people would line up to attend her next one.

A tingling sensation let Angelica know that Alexander wanted to speak with her.

Yes?

Tell your brother you wish to go home.

"What?" Angelica whispered fiercely as she stared at the man beside her. Alexander did not even look her way. He just sat there drinking his wine!

Tell him or I will drag you out of here myself.

But why . . . ?

Now Angelica.

I . . . fine!

Angelica?

Yes, what?

Kiril is outside, he will follow you. Once your brother believes you have slept he will take you home.

You mean to your house.

Go.

There was no use in arguing. The blasted man would drag her out, she just knew he would!

Gaining her brother's attention, Angelica tried to signal him that she wanted to leave, but Mikhail just kept looking at her with questioning eyes.

Giving up, she concentrated on sending him her request as a thought.

Can we go home now please?

Mikhail blinked at her in surprise, then nodded as he turned to his dinner partner. A moment later, he stood from his seat.

"Lady Summers, Lord Summers, I must beg you for your leave," Mikhail said apologetically.

"You are leaving, Prince Belanov?" Lady Summers asked with considerable disappointment in her voice.

"I am afraid I must."

"That is quite all right, quite all right. We are just glad you were able to attend and blessed us with your sister's presence to boot!" Lord Summers interjected.

Mikhail looked around the room, bade his farewells, and held his hand out for Angelica. Within moments they were out the door.

Chapter 24

Angelica crept down the stairs, her bare feet making no sound as she made her way to the library. It was humiliating to realize that fear was what kept her from sleeping.

She had dreamed of a doglike monster that was out for her blood. No matter how hard she had tried to avoid the vicious beast, she had failed until he had caught up with her. It was as his teeth were about to sink into her throat that she had woken up. And then had failed to go back to sleep.

Reaching the window seat that had become her favorite spot of late, she shifted the curtains so that she could see the house across the garden.

After a few minutes, she sighed. No matter how hard she stared, she could not see anyone patrolling the gardens although she knew they had to be there. Kiril had told her of the vampires that guarded the house that afternoon, probably to dissuade her from trying to escape.

Not like she would try, but Kiril was ever cautious!

"Angelica?"

Alexander's voice came to her softly in the dark room. She did not know why it was important for him not to realize she was frightened, but it was.

"Yes?" she replied, purposefully straightening her back. She had no idea why he had forced her to leave the dinner party, but once she had reached the house her anger had abated. She had not particularly wanted to stay. The only thing that rankled now was his attitude.

She shifted as he walked toward her. Her nightdress brushed the tops of her feet, reminding her of her state of partial undress. Angelica's first impulse was to cover herself with her hands, but that would only attract his attention to places she did not want him looking. In either case, it seemed ridiculous to be peevish about her state of dress especially when the white gown covered her from neck to toe.

"What are you doing out of bed?" he asked as he reached her side and looked at the seat beside her.

Noticing his gaze, Angelica pointed. "Go ahead. I just could not sleep, that is all. Why are you awake?"

Alexander looked out of the window, spotting the vampire beside an old oak tree.

"I do not sleep much," he replied at long length. His gaze traveled over her nightgown and back out the window.

Angelica nodded, easily accepting what would have shocked her only days ago.

"Are you planning to tell me why you made me leave?"

Although his tone was level, she could hear the anger in his voice. "You challenged that man and made yourself a target for his violence."

"He challenged me!" Angelica protested.

"You should have desisted from taking him up on it."

Growing angry all over again, Angelica stood up. "He deserved to be put down, Alexander, and you know it!"

"You made him angry enough to entertain the thought of seriously injuring you, Angelica." Alexander still watched the darkness, and his calm made Angelica even angrier.

"He should have tried!"

Angelica froze at the expression Alexander leveled her way. "I would have had to kill him if he did."

He was serious. He would have done just as he said he would, and that was why he had gotten angry, Angelica realized. Alexander must have been reading Lord Jeffrey's thoughts and seen that the man meant her real harm. He was angry because she had nearly provoked a man into trying to hurt her.

She lowered slowly onto the settee.

"He was going to hurt me?"

"He was planning to try."

"You mean, even after he stormed off—"

"I dealt with him." Alexander cut her off. Angelica did not doubt him for a minute.

"You went after him?" It was a whisper.

Standing, Alexander offered her his hand indicating that she should follow suit. Angelica hesitated only a moment before placing her fingers in his. He would not have harmed Lord Jeffrey, she knew. Alexander was the protector of vampire laws; he would not have broken them. He must have dissuaded Lord Jeffrey in a different way.

"It is time you slept."

The statement brought a blush to her cheeks. Memories

of their kiss came unbidden, but she pushed them forcefully away.

He stopped at the bottom of the stairs and waited for her to climb them. When Angelica reached her bedroom door, he had vanished as quietly as he had come.

As she crossed to her bed and got under the covers, she wondered what he did during the hours that most humans slept.

He was not going to sleep, of that she was certain. Would he go back downstairs to the library and read?

Pulling the covers more firmly around her, she told herself to stop thinking and attempt to sleep. Closing her eyes, Angelica visualized sheep in a pasture. Some grazed while others trotted along the hill she pictured clearly in her mind. The sun was shining and Angelica felt herself relaxing into the mattress.

Perhaps she would be able to sleep, after all, she thought as she watched the sheep with their soft coats lying in the bright sunlight. Angelica felt herself slipping away, just as a wolf appeared, his fangs bared.

Her breathing uneven, she sat up in bed, her eyes traveling to the corners of her room as if she expected the wolf to materialize at any moment.

"This is not going to work!"

Throwing aside the blankets, she made her way to her closet, sorting through clothes until she found a day dress. She would go to the library and pick out a book, but if she was going to encounter Alexander again she was going to be fully dressed.

"What are you doing?" Alexander's deep voice came to her from her door.

Surprised, Angelica dropped the dress she had been holding with a small squeak. "Are you crazy, creeping up on me like that on this night of all nights?" she said fiercely.

Alexander did not look the least bit remorseful for his actions, but walked up to her instead, bending down to pick the dress off the floor.

"Were you planning to go somewhere?" he asked suspiciously.

Angelica snatched the dress back.

"To the library if you must know. I did not tell you before but I have been having nightmares. Every time I close my eyes to count sheep a wolf chases them away."

She knew she was sounding ridiculous, even childish, but she could not help it. She looked at Alexander, ready to face his unrelenting gaze when her jaw almost dropped in surprise.

"Did you just smile?" Angelica asked in awe. Her eyes had gone round as she saw the curve in Alexander's lips, and if she had not been mistaken, he had a dimple on his right cheek!

"No," Alexander said stiffly, his expression bland as it ever was, but Angelica would not be put off. She had been looking for something else to think about and this was the perfect outlet for her overworked mind.

"I do believe you have a dimple!" she said with a small laugh. Reaching out, she touched his right cheek before he turned his face away from her.

"Stop it, Angelica!" he commanded fiercely.

Feeling almost lighthearted, she teased him.

"I will not, until you admit that you smiled."

Alexander's brows came together as he stared at her. "I will do no such thing. Now get back to bed."

"Oh, come!" she cajoled. "Just one smile."

Holding the hands that had once again made their way toward his face, Alexander tried to intimidate her with a glare; which failed miserably.

"You do not smile like that, Alexander." Pulling her hands out of his loose grasp, Angelica touched the corners of his mouth and lifted upward. "It is more like that." Her voice went soft as awareness of him filled her. He was so strong, so vital, and so male.

Stepping back, Alexander cleared his throat.

"You need to rest. If it will relieve your mind, I will sit in that chair by the window until you sleep."

Angelica nodded mutely, trying not to show how much his dismissal hurt. He was right, of course, but it still stung that he could be so impartial while she wanted him so much.

That, Angelica Shelton Belanov, is a blessing, she reminded herself. Getting back into bed, she closed her eyes and listened to him shift about the room and sit as he had promised.

Breathe slowly, think sheep . . . After ten minutes of trying her best to sleep, Angelica realized she could not ignore the feelings in the pit of her stomach.

"Alexander?" she said softly. He was silent so long that she thought he might not respond. She heard him sigh before he finally responded.

"Yes?"

Angelica ran her hands along her arms, thinking that even his voice managed to make her shake.

"I cannot sleep."

She heard him shifting before she felt the sag in the mattress that told her he had come to sit beside her. She turned and looked up at his face, which was cast in shadow.

"Are you still afraid?"

"No," she replied honestly.

"Then what is the problem?"

"I . . ." Angelica closed her eyes and wondered how she had gotten herself into this fix. Although, she supposed it was ridiculous to keep her thoughts from this man. He had taught her to block thoughts, had saved her from becoming prey to vampire law, and had done God only knew what to make sure she came to no harm at the hands of Lord Jeffrey.

"I know that you do not want me anymore, but I cannot seem to stop thinking about . . . well, about kissing."

"Kissing?" Alexander repeated slowly. Even in the dark, Angelica could imagine his raised brow.

"Yes." She had admitted to half of it, so Angelica figured that there was no harm in coming out with the rest. "Kissing you."

Alexander sat silently for a long while, and Angelica began to wonder if he would say anything at all, when she felt his fingers on the part of her leg that had become uncovered.

His hand was hard and rough, sending tingles along her skin as it moved up her leg, dragging her nightgown in its wake.

Before she knew how it had happened, the covers had lifted and Alexander lay beside her.

She said nothing, not wanting to break the spell that had been woven.

His head propped over one elbow, he continued to raise her gown until her skirts were bunched around her waist and her white cotton panties were bared to his view.

Although every move he made filled her with ecstasy, Angelica felt the need to cover herself.

Alexander caught her hand.

"Do not," he spoke softly as he kissed her fingers. "You are beautiful."

His fingers resumed their leisurely travels, and soon they came unbearably close to her oversensitive breasts.

"Alexander," she whispered urgently.

Leaning forward, he pulled her body firmly against his and kissed her until she could not think. Angelica was lost in feeling, her mind let go as her body experienced each new sensation with relish. He was so hard all over, like a rock . . . her protector.

Suddenly his clothes bothered her. She wanted to feel his skin as he felt hers.

Angelica was working on the sixth button on his shirt when Alexander stilled. He stopped kissing her and pulled back to listen.

"What . . . ?"

"Quiet," Alexander commanded as he listened. Angelica heard nothing but the sound of branches rustling in the wind.

"There is a vampire approaching the house," Alexander said as he slipped out of the bed.

Remembering the vampire Alexander was looking for, Angelica looked toward the window with a worried expression.

"A friendly one?"

"Yes."

Sitting upright in the bed, Angelica clutched the sheets to her breasts as he reached the door.

"You are not leaving, are you?" Her voice betrayed her lingering fear.

"I will be back in a minute, do not worry."

Angelica nodded as she lay down again. Her eyes wide

open, she stared at the ceiling above her bed and counted slowly.

She had reached sixty-four when Alexander returned.

"Is everything all right?" she asked hesitantly. The fear that she had become familiar with in the last hours was draining out of her, leaving behind exhaustion.

"Everything is all right."

Coming back to the bed, Alexander lowered his body down beside her and pulled her into the crook of his arm. "Sleep now, I will keep you safe."

Angelica accepted his protection with the same ease she had accepted his touch. She snuggled closer to him and closed her eyes as an odd thought occurred to her: Alexander Kourakin was the only man who made her feel safe.

"Alexander?" She opened her eyes to the darkness of his shirt.

"Hmm?"

"What will you do when your job here is done?"

"Go back to Moscow."

Taking a deep breath, Angelica worked past the sudden tension in her chest. When the pain had eased to a dull ache, she closed her eyes once more.

Sleep finally claimed her.

Chapter 25

"I am really glad that you do not mind. When Kiril brought me Nicholas's note this morning, I could not think of anything to do other than to ask him to come here." Angelica realized that she must be talking at a rather fast pace, for she had run out of breath. Aiming for a little more dignity, she straightened her shoulders, picked up her cup of tea, and sipped.

"Angelica, it is quite all right for you to receive callers here and I will not have you feeling awkward about it. My home is your home, my dear, and your Nicholas is most welcome," the duchess said over a mouth full of scone. "Now what do you think is so urgent that he simply had to see you today?"

Putting her cup down, Angelica contemplated the message she had received. "Perhaps it is to do with his mother. I believe she is quite ill, so he might have wanted to inform me personally that he is leaving for a while?"

"Sounds reasonable," Margaret said.

That was probably the reason Nicholas wanted to see her, and Angelica only wished that she felt more regret at the thought of his departure. She should, by all rights, be upset that he would not be around to hasten their courtship; after all she needed to be married in all haste. And yet, Angelica could not muster up the sadness that was required of her.

Oh, she did feel sadness, but it was not for the right reasons. Since she woke up that morning, all she could think about was Alexander. He would be leaving to Moscow and that made her heart ache inexplicably.

You ninny! Is it not about time that you admit it? You are in love with him!

"Angelica, did you hear me?" The duchess was watching her intently.

"I, no, I was thinking . . ."

Margaret's laughter filled the room and helped Angelica's tense shoulders relax. When had she gotten so stiff?

"Yes, I can see you have not been listening to a word I said. But that is quite all right. While you have been off in your thoughts, I worked my way through those delicious pastries." Patting her belly lovingly she laughed and said, "This little devil makes me so hungry!"

Angelica watched the duchess lay her hand protectively over her stomach and wondered if she would ever have a child of her own. "Do vampire babies look like human babies?"

The duchess smiled and said, "Absolutely. Our babies not only look like human babies, but they are exactly like them."

"What do you mean by that?" Angelica asked, confused.

The duchess stretched her bare feet out on the sofa. She

had always had a special affinity for this particular room of James's house and was glad now that Angelica had wanted to see it. Tall ceilings, tall windows, and long couches, she almost felt as though she was outside when in the library.

"I mean that our young do not need blood nor do they have any of our species' abilities. Both begin to express themselves when the child reaches puberty."

Angelica was surprised. "But why—"

"Just a minute," the duchess cut her off with a raised hand. Angelica watched as the older woman closed her eyes. The seconds ticked by but no explanation was forthcoming.

"Your Grace, are you all right?"

Margaret opened her eyes and nodded. "I told you to call me Margaret and I am fine, it was just James."

"What?"

"I mean I was just speaking to James, he is on his way."

Angelica kept regarding the woman with incomprehension until it dawned on Margaret that an explanation was necessary.

"Forgive me, dear, I forget that you are not one of us. You see, when two vampires are attuned to one another, distance becomes insignificant. We can communicate regardless."

"So you can speak to any vampires at any time?"

"No, I am afraid not," Margaret said with regret. "Being . . . attuned takes a very strong bond. Most can only achieve such a bond with family and of course with their life mate should they be lucky enough to find one."

"Life mate?" It was as if Margaret was speaking a foreign language, Angelica realized. Every explanation led to even more questions.

"I suppose it is a vampire equivalent for true love."

Angelica remembered how Mikhail had heard her calling to him at the theater.

"Is it possible that I might be able to communicate that way?"

Margaret considered, then said, "I have never heard of a human who could, but with your mind, who is to say?"

"Your Grace?" the butler spoke from the doorway, his presence cutting their conversation short.

"Yes?" the duchess inquired.

"Lord Adler has arrived. He is waiting for Princess Belanov in the receiving room."

"Oh yes, of course. Thank you, Thomas."

An odd fluttering began in her stomach as she stood to go to Nicholas.

"I should be back momentarily."

Gesturing with her hand for her to leave, Margaret smiled. "Go, go, and then come back and tell me all about it."

Nodding, Angelica made her way to where Nicholas waited.

"Angelica!" Nicholas moved forward to bring her hand to his lips. He seemed a little flustered, Angelica realized, but that was understandable when his mother's health was in jeopardy.

"How is your mother?" She followed him to a large blue canopy and sat beside him.

"Better, thank you, though not in perfect health I am afraid."

She watched his handsome face as worry passed over it, then was pushed aside. He leaned back and regarded her with warmth.

"You look wonderful as always. I would have thought you were too clever for a naive color such as pink to suit you, but incredibly enough it does."

She arched a brow. "This color is called pale rose; it is hardly pink."

Nicholas laughed and she joined him in his merriment. He really was such fun that perhaps she would miss him, after all.

"You must be wondering about the urgency of this meeting."

He had turned very serious, Angelica noted.

"Yes, indeed."

Taking her hand once more in his Nicholas nodded solemnly. "Then I suppose I should not make you wonder any longer. Angelica, I woke up this morning and I knew that there would be no one else for me."

Angelica could only stare, as he knelt beside the canopy and looked up at her with a self-mocking smile.

"Even speaking to your brother this morning was not as difficult . . . Who would have known that I would one day willingly do this?"

Finding her voice, she looked down at him. "Do what, precisely?"

Nicholas laughed, though it was not the honest, jovial laugh she had gotten used to hearing from him. There was uncertainty in the sound, and hope.

"I am asking you to be my wife, Angelica."

Chapter 26

Angelica sat quietly, her feet propped on an ottoman, a rather large volume of *Mythical Creatures* on her lap. The pages facing upward contained pictures of bats and a cartoon of a man with fangs and bloodshot eyes, but Angelica was not reading the article on Romanian vampires. Instead, she was staring out the windows of the library.

She did not notice the rain or the particular darkness of the day. All she saw was the face of the man that had kissed her the night before, the man who would more than likely never kiss her again.

She did not understand why that thought made her morose; after all, she could not seriously want a vampire to kiss her, could she? What was so special about Alexander Kourakin in either case?

He was handsome, yes, but so were many other men she had met recently. He was powerful, but that too was a trait he shared with others. He had absolutely no sense of humor, which was definitely not a *good* trait.

As she compiled the list in her mind, Angelica began to brighten. She was not losing a single thing by not being of interest to the annoying man, because he had no redeeming qualities!

"Ha!" Her voice bounced from bookshelf to bookshelf, finding its way back to her once more.

Well, perhaps his concern for his people was a redeeming quality, she thought somewhat hesitantly. And, there was the way he had saved her life, albeit in an untraditional manner.

Perhaps his concern for her safety and the way he had stood up for her against the arrogant Lord Jeffrey could be considered examples of his good qualities. . . .

Curse and rot the man! Why did he have to be kind and thoughtful and caring and powerful and handsome and intriguing and so utterly impossible!

"He is a vampire!" she said, as if hearing the words aloud would make her feel different about him. They did not.

"It is not as if it matters anymore, either way," she grumbled as she gave up any pretense of reading the book and put it on the floor.

"Angelica?"

Kiril posed the polite question as he stood at the library door with a silver tray in one hand.

"Alexander is back?" Angelica said before she could stop herself. After Nicholas left, she had asked to return to the house and she had been waiting for Alexander since.

"The prince is not here, no," Kiril responded in his usual stoic tone. "I just had the cook make tea for me, and I wondered if you might like some."

Surprised and delighted, Angelica regarded the tray in his hand and smiled. "Why yes, thank you, Kiril. That is awfully kind of you."

"It was no trouble." Kiril shrugged, but Angelica detected the soft pink in his cheeks. He moved forward and put the cup of tea on the stand beside her seat before she could get up.

"Thank you, Kiril."

He was by the door again and it looked as if he would leave without another word when he stopped.

"It is my pleasure, especially when I have caused you some trouble of late."

Trouble of late? Angelica understood what he meant and was stunned. If that was an apology for almost getting her killed by preventing her escape that fateful night, then it was a poor one. But Kiril was probably not apologizing for he would not feel he had done anything wrong. He was merely telling her that he felt bad at what had happened as a consequence of his doing his duty.

"Thank you," she said once more, and then just as he was taking his leave, Angelica stopped him. "Wait. Actually, I was wondering if you might answer a question for me."

"I can try," Kiril said, and nodded as he stepped back into the room and took the seat closest to hers.

"I was just wondering about the poem in the beginning of your Book of Law." Angelica thought back to the poem and recited: "A vampire walks unknown, a painful thirst upon him. He walks, but he leaves no mark; it must be so. . . ."

Kiril joined in with a faraway look in his eyes, "One day he will come out of darkness, no more thirst. The Blessed will bring the light."

"What does it mean?" Angelica leaned forward, her curiosity getting the better of her as Kiril shifted in his chair.

"You know by now that we vampires cannot live without blood." Although it was not a question, Kiril waited for her to nod before continuing.

"The poem tells of that thirst that we feel until the end of our lives. How much blood we need changes according to what we are doing. A vampire could go a day or two without blood if he did not overexert himself or get injured in some way. Nevertheless, without blood, we die just as you would die without food."

"Yes, I see. And you 'leave no mark,' does that refer to the fact that we, I mean humans, do not know of your existence?"

Kiril shrugged. "I assume so, yes."

"And the Blessed? What is that?"

"The Blessed?" Kiril laughed. "That comes from a very old prophecy and is likely just a fairy tale."

"Tell me, anyway," Angelica insisted. She had been wondering about the Blessed since the first day that Alexander gave her the vampire Book of Law to read.

Sighing, Kiril gave in. "You will have heard that it is very difficult for vampires to procreate. We are not compatible with humans for that purpose, and most of our people die before they reach an age where they can have children. Well, it is said that there will be a human bloodline that will be compatible with ours.

The children from such a union are the Blessed. They are the ones that walk the earth as half vampire, half human. They would not have the thirst as we do, they would not need blood."

Angelica thought for a moment, but she could not figure out how the Blessed would bring "the light" to the vampire race. "How would the Blessed be different from humans then, Kiril? Why are they so important?"

A wry smile appeared on Kiril's face. "You misunderstand, Princess. The Blessed are vampires, but they do not have our weaknesses. They do not need blood like we do, but if they were to get hurt, a little drink would heal them. Because they do not need blood, they age faster than we do, so they mature faster than we do. The Blessed would not live as long as a normal vampire, but they would mature like a human. A female could get pregnant after her twentieth year, a male could inseminate after his. If the Blessed would arrive, a new vampire race would be born; one that would not have to hide from the rest of the world. And in most vampires' minds, they would end the hopelessness we feel."

Hopelessness. It was difficult for Angelica to view the men and women she had met recently as hopeless. It was almost impossible to think of Alexander that way. But then, a part of her understood the toll of having to hide what one is from the world.

The ability to read minds had made Angelica look for refuge within four walls. She had sought out her piano and had read hundreds of books out loud as though the men and women long dead might speak to her. She had craved companionship from sheets of paper, and only now did she realize that she had been hiding because she had not known what else to do.

She was only twenty and one and she had nearly given up on the world. What must it be like to feel this way for hundreds of years?

Alexander. His name came to her once more with force. No amount of time or strain could bring him down, and she understood the reverence she had seen directed at him more fully now. Angelica had heard that he was the strongest vampire alive, but no matter what Alexander's physical strength was, his mind was where his true power lay.

And he had taught her how to be powerful in return. He had given her control of herself and perhaps without even intending to, pulled her out of hiding.

"I must get going now, Princess." Kiril's voice pulled Angelica out of her thoughts and she smiled at him.

"Yes of course, thank you, Kiril."

"You are most welcome," he said, and bowed, then left the room as quietly as he had come.

Angelica leaned back in her seat and picked up her cup of tea. It was a revelation to realize she was no longer angry about all that had transpired. In fact, if she were completely honest, she would have had to say that she was more honest and comfortable with the new vampire friends she had made than any others she had had before.

The rain continued to drizzle, the last drop of tea was consumed, and the ticking of the second handle on the grandfather clock finally lulled Angelica to sleep.

"Who are you?"

Angelica opened her eyes, but could not see a thing until her eyes adjusted to the dim lighting in the room. When the boy finally came into focus, recognition hit.

"You are the boy from the ceremony!"

He frowned at her as he moved closer to the chair and squinted.

"You are not a vampire!" he exclaimed with pride.

Trying to clear her sleepy mind, she looked around the library. "How do you know?"

Christopher plopped himself into a chair across from hers. "Because you are sleeping. We vampires sleep very little, well when we get a little older. I still sleep more hours than most vampires because I don't have all my powers yet."

Storing that piece of information, she nodded. "So you are still developing your powers?"

"Yes." Christopher smiled. "I had my initiation just a week ago! Oh, wait, I heard about you. You are that mind reader, aren't you?"

"I suppose," Angelica said in a manner of agreement, "though you can call me Angelica, if you like."

Eyes alight with curiosity, Christopher leaned forward in his chair. "They say that you are such a strong telepath that no vampire can enter your mind. Not even the prince!"

"Is that what they say?" Angelica wondered who was talking about her and in such terms.

"Well, actually that is what my father said, right before he told me I should not tell anyone else." His expression turned suspicious. "How come you are in the prince's house?"

"He is taking care of her." Kiril came in at that moment and not a moment too soon. Angelica would have no idea how to respond to that particularly sticky question.

"Have you introduced yourself to Princess Belanov then, Christopher?" Kiril asked the boy as he came up beside his chair.

Christopher blushed and he shook his head in denial. After a small nod from Kiril, he stood and came to stand in front of Angelica.

"I am sorry for my rudeness, Princess. My name is Christopher Langdon."

He was heartbreakingly sweet, and so young Angelica realized.

"If I may call you Christopher, you may call me Angelica."

"Okay, Angelica." Christopher smiled, his earlier embarrassment quickly fading. Gesturing at the room he continued with childlike enthusiasm. "Isn't the prince's house grand? And he is protecting you, that is so great. He helped me too, you know? During the ceremony and all."

It was easy to see that Christopher worshiped Alexander, and she felt for the boy, she really did.

"He is a very caring man, I mean vampire."

"He is the strongest vampire in the world!" Christopher corrected. "My father says that if I behave I might . . ."

A piercing scream cut Christopher's words and had Kiril starting out of the room.

"Kiril?" Angelica came out of her seat.

"It came from down the street. The guards are not here, I have to go and see what is happening. Stay put."

With that, he was gone. Angelica and Christopher looked at each other.

"Who do you think that was?" The boy's fear was palpable, so Angelica sat back down and shrugged as if she had not a care in the world.

"Likely a silly woman who saw a mouse or some such." She knew she had said the right thing when Christopher chuckled and resumed his own seat.

"You are pretty nice for a human."

Angelica rubbed her arms as a cold breeze traveled over her skin. Where was that draft suddenly coming from?

"Well, thank you, kind sir, you are not such a bad sort yourself for a . . . what on earth?" Angelica watched in disbelief as a dark shadow leaped out from behind the long curtains. "Christopher, move!"

Reaching for the boy's arm, she grabbed him and pulled just as the figure in the dark cloak buried a blade into the soft material of the armchair.

There was no time for thought. In the moment that it took for the attacker to recover from the surprise, Angelica lunged herself at the weapon.

"Run for help!" Angelica screamed as she held onto the hilt of the dagger with all her might. Christopher ran from the room at the same time that a booted foot kicked Angelica forcefully in the stomach. Bile clogged her throat, but she forced it down and, imbalanced, went for the knife once again.

A gloved hand grabbed at her hair, twisting until she was level with the attacker's knees. Angelica winced before the knee made contact with her ribs. The pain was excruciating.

Falling back, Angelica doubled up in pain and tried to look up. She managed to see the knife come loose, and for a moment her fear suppressed pain as the shadowed figure of her aggressor stood still, likely in contemplation.

A moment later, the black boots were making for the door and Angelica knew the slayer had decided not to waste time with her.

"No!" She grabbed at the feet with all her might, her ribs protesting with sharp jabs of pain.

"Bitch!" The venomous hiss pierced her ears right before a hard object slammed into her skull.

Black, everything lost its color as consciousness deserted her.

* * *

"Is she all right?"

Alexander closed the library door behind him and turned to James, who had been waiting in the hallway. "The doctor is with her now. She was knocked unconscious and is likely in shock, but he is not overly worried. Her ribs are likely bruised but not broken. He says she should wake up soon."

James nodded, then looked down the corridor.

"I sent Christopher home with his father and an escort of four. He wanted to stay with her. He says she saved his life."

Having talked to Christopher, Alexander knew just what had happened. Did the woman have no sense, flinging herself onto the slayer's back the way she had? She could have been killed! Damn it, she could have died!

"We have to think this through. Why would the slayer attack Christopher? And how on earth did he manage to find the boy in your house, the one time in days that your guards were not at their posts!"

Anger threatened to consume him, but Alexander held back. "The bastard sent Christopher a message from me, telling him to come here. He knew the guards would not be there. The woman who screamed must have been paid to do so. Everything was staged perfectly. He knew everything."

"Except that Angelica would be here. When I got home earlier, Margaret told me that Angelica had wanted to leave early for some reason. She said the princess wasn't feeling too well."

Alexander cursed under his breath. She was under his protection and she had gotten hurt. If Kiril had not returned when he had, she might have died.

"Alexander . . ." James's look was steady as he continued, "This was not your fault. She is all right."

The doctor came out of the room, diverting their attention.

"She will be fine, Prince Kourakin, all she needs is rest."

"Is she still sleeping then?"

The elderly man nodded. "But you have nothing to fear. The lady came to for a few moments, long enough to ask about a young boy. I did not know what she was speaking of, but I told her that he was just fine upon which she asked if you were here. When I assured her that you were, she went right back to sleep."

"Thank you, Doctor," Alexander said gratefully.

"I believe my work here is done," the doctor said, and smiled. "If you would be so kind as to call me a hack."

"We would not hear of it! Please allow me to escort you home, Doctor," James interjected. "I will speak with you later, Alexander."

Alexander saw them off, then returned to the library. Kiril had laid her across one of the larger couches, and there she still was, sleeping as peacefully as a babe.

But she had come close, so perilously close, to dying, and it was his fault. She was his to protect, and he had failed her.

His head aching, he crossed to her side and knelt beside her. Angelica, beautiful Angelica, brave Angelica. She was special, so different . . . she touched him as no one ever had.

"Wake up, sweetheart." His tone was soft, the words an enigma even to himself. He did not recognize the man who wanted nothing but to hold this woman close and kiss her till they became one body.

"Angelica, wake up."

She did not stir.

"Angelica, please." The plea tore from his chest. She had to wake up. He could not stand being without her, not for a moment more.

Holding her head between his hands, he lowered his lips to hers and kissed her softly. "Wake up."

He kissed her again, his fingers slipping into the luscious-ness of her black hair.

"Wake up."

He felt her body begin to move as he kissed her cheeks, her eyes, her nose and found her lips once more. When her lips moved beneath his, he pulled back long enough to see those deep blue eyes that looked at him so sweetly. Then he kissed her again, and soon she was writhing beneath him, demanding the satisfaction only he could give her.

"Wait, Alexander." She turned her face, her hand on his chest as she tried to catch her breath.

"What is it, sweetheart, did I hurt you? Tell me where it hurts."

Angelica looked at him, her smile sad. "No, I am fine. I . . . Christopher?"

"He is fine."

"And, and the . . ."

"Slayer." Alexander helped her finish her sentence, know-ing she probably did not realize yet whom she had faced.

"Oh God . . ." The happenings of the evening came rush-ing back and she closed her eyes.

"Angelica, do not. It is over. You are unhurt."

She flung her arms around his neck and held on as tears

racked her body. Alexander lifted her gently, and cradled her in his lap.

"It is over, sweetheart. You did well."

She turned her face up to his as the tears subsided. Alexander used his thumb to wipe them away.

"Better?"

"Yes." Her voice was hoarse; her eyes staring at his lips with an intensity that made it impossible for him to resist temptation.

"I am going to kiss you, Angelica." It was only fair to warn her, because Alexander knew that this time he would not be able to stop when she asked him to so uncertainly.

When she said nothing, he tipped her chin up and urged her to look at him.

"I may not be able to stop this time."

Angelica swallowed visibly. "Alexander . . ."

"Yes?" He could not believe that this woman had him wrapped around her finger. He felt like he could do anything for her, if only she demanded it of him.

"I . . . I'm engaged."

Chapter 27

"I am engaged." Angelica closed her eyes as the words left her lips for the second time. Alexander still said nothing, only looked at her as if he were trying to discover . . . something.

"Alexander?" She could not stand his silence any longer, but what did she expect him to do? Stand up and demand that she undo it, that she marry him instead.

Would she marry him if he asked? Was it even possible? It had to be, since Margaret had told her of several of her previous husbands. It had to be possible. And Alexander was an elder, past his fifth century, so they could grow old together. Vampires only lived six hundred years, did they not?

Nervous laughter bubbled in her throat as she attempted to cool her racing mind. Nothing mattered, nothing. If he asked, she would marry him. In the blink of an eye she would be his wife. But he did not look as though he was going to ask any questions.

Alexander stood slowly and turned away from her. Angelica wanted to call out to him again, to ask him to understand. She wanted him to know that she had not agreed to marry Nicholas because she loved Nicholas. No. She had agreed because she had to marry. There was only one man she loved . . . but pride got in the way.

They were silent, his back to her, until an approaching carriage pushed Alexander into action. He said nothing as he left Angelica in the room.

She was not afraid. Alexander would never have left her alone if the approaching man or woman was dangerous. She was not afraid, but she was tired.

"Princess?" Kiril appeared at the door just as she put her head back on the pillow. "I am sorry to disturb you, but we have to leave."

"Leave? But where to, Kiril, what is happening?"

Kiril looked apologetic as he held the door open for her. "I was not given permission to say. I'm sorry. Please, come with me now."

As her anger rose, Angelica realized that rage was a better companion than heartbreak.

"Oh, Angelica, I am so sorry about what happened! You must have been so frightened." Joanna moved toward Angelica with her arms spread wide, her concern written across her face. Angelica stood from the settee and hugged her friend.

"The fear was not half as bad as this nefarious waiting, Joanna, I would be ever so much better if someone would explain what I am doing here." Angelica gestured vaguely at the duke's guest room, where she had been shown to upon her arrival at the residence.

"No one has spoken to you?" Joanna looked surprised as she followed Angelica's lead and sat.

"No, will you tell me what is happening?" Angelica asked with frustration. She had not seen the duke, the duchess, or Alexander after having been escorted from the town house by Kiril, who had also conveniently disappeared.

"It is a case of bad timing I am afraid," Joanna began, "that is what I presume is being discussed downstairs by the elders."

Angelica watched Joanna struggle with words and felt herself get tense. What could possibly be worse than a crazed vampire slayer on the loose?

"A vampire passed on yesterday afternoon," Joanna said finally.

"I am sorry, Joanna. Did you know him, or her?" Angelica said sympathetically, her hand covering that of her friends.

"Oh no, it is not like that, Angelica. She was a hundred years older than I, and spent most of her time on the Continent. I did not know her well at all."

"Then what is wrong?"

"Well, the vampire who died was born into this clan. She was in Kent when she died and her body is even now being brought to London for the ceremony that will take place. The proceedings will take all night and into the morning. It is law that all vampires born to the clan and in the clan's territory must attend." Joanna looked at Angelica, as if waiting for her to come to some conclusion. When Angelica merely looked on with incomprehension, Joanna tried once more.

"We must all attend the ceremony, Angelica. If the slayer decides to come back for you now that you have caused him so much trouble, none of us will be able to be there to protect you."

Angelica blinked a few times as the meaning of the words dawned on her. She would be left without protection?

"Then I will have to go somewhere where he cannot find me," she said slowly.

"I'm afraid that is not possible either. The prince managed to keep you from the consequences of our laws only by assuring the other leaders that you would be under his constant watch," Joanna said with regret.

"But I am not under his constant watch!"

"That is true, but when he cannot be with you, you are always with one of us. He entrusts us with you, Angelica. If you were to escape, or cause trouble, the prince would be held accountable."

Angelica could not believe she had not known this until this moment. If she had run, Alexander would have paid the price? Why had he agreed to such terms? Why?

"So, I cannot leave?

"For you to be able to leave, the prince would have to accompany you and—"

"He cannot," Angelica finished woodenly.

Joanna stood up, her agitation clear. "It just is a run of pure bad luck, but you need not worry, Angelica."

Angelica smiled wryly as she watched Joanna.

"Is that why you are wearing the carpet thin?"

Joanna stopped immediately. "No, I'm doing *that* because

I am a foolish woman. In all honesty, Angelica, it will be all right. The prince would not allow anything to happen to you. We will not allow anything to happen to you."

Angelica wondered what choice Joanna would have in the matter if the elders should decree that she would be locked up and left to her own devices.

"Angelica?" The duchess came into the room, and the smile on her face made Angelica feel a little better. "There you are, and Joanna, good; your timing is superb."

Angelica, having decided that she would ask no more questions as they led to only further confusion, held her tongue and let Joanna do the talking.

"What has been decided?" Joanna asked, but Margaret ignored her and thrust the dark cloak she had been carrying with her into Angelica's hands.

"Now my dear, I am going to have to ask you to keep very quiet and to have no fear. Nothing will happen to you or anybody else."

Joanna's voice was incredulous. "She will attend?"

Angelica regarded the cloak in her hand with wide eyes. She was going to attend a vampire ceremony! After the first ceremony she had witnessed, the idea was not a pleasant one.

"But only vampires are allowed to attend the ceremony . . . it is forbidden . . . ," Joanna continued with confusion. "How will they convince the others to allow it?"

Margaret gestured for Joanna to keep her voice down as she locked the door behind her.

"It is not forbidden exactly. Alexander and James have been going through The Book of Law for the last hour. There is nothing that states that only vampires may attend the ceremony, though that is the natural assumption as humans have never been allowed to know of our existence."

Joanna caught onto the idea. "Since Angelica has a guide and is therefore allowed to know of us, she can attend the ceremony."

"Precisely," Margaret agreed. "But the others cannot know of it. James fears it will lead to complications and there simply is no time to explain to everyone who is coming, the details of the situation we find ourselves in."

Angelica, who had been quietly listening to the exchange, found she was incapable of retaining her silence. "So what you are suggesting is that I pretend to be a . . . one of you?"

The duchess turned to her with compassionate eyes. "You have nothing to fear, Angelica. I will instruct you in everything you need to do. Most of the time you will simply be required to listen; that is all."

Angelica looked from Margaret's smiling countenance to Joanna's concerned one. She would have given a lot to read their minds.

Angelica clutched her cloak around her as another gust of wind blew through the trees and threatened to lift the material, thereby revealing her naked form beneath. She had balked when Margaret told her she would need to remove her clothes; after all, she could not remember being naked in front of anyone . . . ever.

I am not naked! she told herself as her fingers clutched more tightly around the black material.

It was no consolation that the hundred vampires who stood around her, equally unclothed beneath their cloaks, did not seem to care about the wind or even the cold earth beneath their bare feet. Their attention was fixed on the body, which lay in the center of the semicircle their clan leader had ordered them to make.

"Step forward, reader, and tell us of her life," the duke said, his voice carrying over their heads and far into the quiet woods.

Angelica watched as a short man with long blond hair and a hooked nose stepped in front of the body and faced the gathering. She shifted her weight to get a better look at him and then bit her lip in pain. Her eyes raced from right to left to see if anyone had noticed her stupidity.

The nettles and twigs on the ground did not bother the vampires, but they sunk into her soft skin and lodged themselves painfully in every which way.

Returning her attention to the little man who now lifted a little black book in his right hand, Angelica heard the onlookers draw in a collective breath. What was in that book that could ensure such undivided attention?

Angelica did not have long to wonder. The man began to read.

"I was born in 1384, Poland, where I was named after Queen Jadwiga. In 1422, I took the name of Eleanor Cobham, became first mistress to, and then second wife of the Duke of Gloucester, regent under council in England, uncle to Henry VI."

It took Angelica a moment to realize that what she was hearing was an accounting of the life of the dead vampire. Thirteen eighty-four, the date seemed so unreal to her, so distant. How had this woman lived for so long and as whom?

"In 1441, I was accused of witchcraft and put into prison, whereupon I moved to France and took the name Isabelle

Periene. I married a farmer named Jean Lordeaux and stayed with him for thirty-three years."

It occurred to Angelica that Alexander was over five hundred years old. What had he done in all that time, where was he born and what was his real name? Was Alexander the name he had taken only recently?

Questions ran through her head at lightning speed, prompting her to raise her fingers to her temples. She had to stop thinking, she reminded herself. This was supposed to be the easy part of the ceremony. The part where all she had to do was keep silent and listen.

"In 1735, I moved back to France and took the name Jeanne-Antoinette Poisson and in 1741, I was married to Charles-Guillaume Le Normant d'Étiolles. Four years later, I was mistress of Louis XV of France and remained by his side until 1764, when I left for Germany."

Angelica's eyes widened as she recalled a history book in which Jeanne-Antoinette Poisson was mentioned. The woman had been better known as Madame de Pompadour and was frequently accused of having caused the Seven Years' War!

Counting to ten slowly in her mind, Angelica tried to calm her racing heart before someone noticed. Could they see her inner turmoil, she wondered suddenly, did it change the color of her aura as many Eastern medicine books suggested?

Her eyes searched for Alexander and found him at the center of the circle, his face impassive as he listened to the recital of Jadwiga's life. Could he tell what she was feeling through her aura?

Angelica realized that she did not want to know. Even if it was the case, she had absolutely no desire to know.

Movement drew her gaze back to Jadwiga's body. The man who had read the little black book had moved back into the semicircle, and now two male vampires were approaching the center with bowls of liquid in their hands.

Angelica watched as they let the liquid drizzle onto the body, one moving from the feet to the belly and the other from the head.

After the bowls were empty, the men moved to her head and Angelica breathed deeply. She had been told about this part of the ceremony so that she would not cringe.

The sharp edges of the knives in the men's hands glistened as they bent over Jadwiga's head.

Do not close your eyes, do not close your eyes, Angelica thought desperately as the desire to turn away almost overcame her. She focused on the face of one of the vampires leaning over Jadwiga. He looked to be in his early thirties, but he could be two hundred years old for all Angelica knew. Two hundred years. What would she do with that time?

As the man stood from his crouched position, Angelica's eyes moved to his hands of their own accord. He still held the dagger in his left hand, though now it was stained, and in his right were Jadwiga's teeth.

Angelica felt queasy. She followed the man's progression until he put the teeth into a velvet pouch.

Why would they do such a thing? There had not been enough time for questions earlier, but now Angelica felt the need to know. She had to understand, then maybe she would feel less sick.

Her eyes traveled the length of the semicircle once more and found Alexander. He was looking directly at her, and she had to force herself to remain in place while every instinct in her body told her to run to him. All she wanted to do was crawl into his arms and have him protect her, from Sergey, from any other vampire that might mean her harm, from human men . . . from the world. How she had become so dependent on him, she did not know, but she felt safe with him, at peace.

A dark-haired woman stepped out of the circle and in front of the body as two others came forward with torches. Goose bumps crawled across Angelica's skin as the woman opened her mouth and began to sing. Her voice was hauntingly beautiful, and the song, though wordless, spoke more clearly of pain and longing and eternity than any other she had heard.

One by one, the vampires turned away from the body and moved off into the woods. Angelica followed suit, but not before she saw the torches being dipped toward Jadwiga's body.

She walked slowly, her mind on the body that burned behind her, her eyes fixed on the rising moon. It seemed bigger than it had ever been and tinged the woods in shades of red . . . blood red.

Within minutes, Joanna and Margaret appeared beside Angelica.

"Your feet?" Margaret asked with a low voice, her eyes on the vampires that were scattering in all directions, most making their way back to their homes.

Angelica realized that her mind had been too full with the smell of burning skin to notice anything else.

"I have been too preoccupied to notice." Her whisper procured a smile from both women.

"You are doing very well, Angelica, I am proud of you,"

Joanna said a quarter of an hour later. They were nearing a path where a carriage waited to take them back to the duke's residence.

"We are proud of you," Margaret joined in. "Remember that half of it is over."

Angelica nodded her head, and the three of them remained quiet as they got into the carriage.

Margaret looked at Joanna and then broke the silent spell that had come over them. "There is something that we did not mention, Angelica. We did not want you to be dreading this moment, so we thought it prudent to mention it as late as possible." Shifting a little, she put her hand on her rounded belly and continued. "The ceremony of death is a celebration of life and passion. It is a time where we remember why life is worth living."

Angelica could not fathom how removing parts of a corpse and then burning it helped in furthering such a cause, but she said nothing.

As if reading her mind, Margaret smiled at her and said, "Her teeth were removed because they will be kept in the chamber of history along with our books. They are so that we remember that she once lived. Her body however, had to be burned so that it rejoined the earth and so that no human would come across it, ever."

Joanna gave Margaret a look of urgency, which Angelica did not view as a good sign. Whatever they had kept from her, it could not be good. She was tempted to read their minds to find out what was happening, but she could not do that. She could not just intrude in such a way; they would never forgive her.

"Most of the clan has dispersed to other houses; only a

select few have remained behind to complete the second part of the ceremony in the leader's house. The two closest kin of Jadwiga will lead the affair; it will be a celebration of passions. There will be music and art and . . ."

The duchess was cut off as a vampire opened the door of the carriage that had rolled to the stop. Angelica wanted to ask what Margaret had been about to say, but it seemed it was too late. All three of them were ushered out of the carriage and into the manor.

"Joanna?" Angelica whispered fiercely as they followed several vampires, which she had never before laid eyes on, to the receiving room at the end of the hallway. Her eyes searched for James, Kiril, and Alexander, who she knew would be present.

"Do not worry," Joanna said softly as they entered the room.

Several sarcastic responses came to Angelica's mind, but she kept them all to herself when she saw what had been done to the room.

Ten chairs had been placed in a circle at the center, a large candle behind each seat. The rest of the room bore no furniture, and all the tapestries and paintings had been removed. Only the thick velvet curtains remained, and they had been drawn over the large windows lining one wall so that darkness resided in the corners that candlelight did not reach.

The same vampire who had read from the little black book motioned her toward a seat between two men she did not know. Angelica took her seat, her apprehension growing with each breath she took.

Alexander was seated across from her while Joanna, Kiril, James, and Margaret were scattered along either side.

After all ten seats were occupied, four more vampires remained in the room and the doors were closed, the sound reverberating through Angelica's head like a death toll.

Angelica.

Alexander's voice was in her mind and she realized with a start that she had allowed her barrier to slip! It seemed she did so every time she was distraught. Instead of being angry, however, she wondered why she had not done it before. How she had missed Alexander's voice.

Yes? she replied quickly.

No matter what happens, do not be afraid. I will not let anything happen to you. Do you believe me?

There was an urgency in Alexander's thoughts that told Angelica that whatever "this" was, it was beginning.

I believe you.

She knew that Alexander had restored his block and did the same herself as she listened to the two vampires that had begun singing in soft and melodic voices. Again there were no words, but merely an abundant amount of feeling in the notes that traveled the length of the room.

The little man who had read from the black book moved to the center of the circle, a large ornately decorated goblet in his hands. Angelica watched as he moved to James and offered the cup to his lips. The duke drank, and the vampire moved two seats to the left, once again offering the cup.

It took a moment for realization to sink, but when Angelica understood what it was that was being offered she felt full-fledged panic rolling in. She could not drink blood, she simply could not. She would certainly choke and then they would find her out and kill her, and there would be nothing Alexander could do about it.

Close to tears, she watched as the little blond man moved about the room. When the vampire to her left drank from the cup, Angelica held her breath, afraid of what she would do when the cup was held up to her lips. Would she gag from the mere smell of the stuff?

She opened her mouth, ready to protest as the man with the cup came closer, but shut it just as quickly as he passed her by. It was only then that Angelica realized the man had been skipping seats, offering the cup only to the males in the room.

Whatever the reason behind the ritual, Angelica had never felt more grateful in her life . . . other than the day when Alexander had given her the most precious gift she had ever received.

Looking at him now, she wondered how she managed, even now, to desire him the way she did. The vampire with the cup blocked her view temporarily and Angelica watched as Alexander drank from the cup. His eyes closed, then opened again, shocking her into biting her tongue. Where there had once been gray there was now red.

Angelica knew that if she glanced around the room, all the other vampire males would have similar red eyes, so she did not. She needed a cool head, and such a view would do nothing more than scare her senseless.

The last male vampire drank from the cup and the music changed, becoming slower, less sad . . . more sensual. Angelica wondered what would happen now, and if they were nearing the end of the ceremony. She hoped they were, because she did not know how much more of this her frazzled nerves could take.

Feeling a strong gaze, Angelica looked up to see Joanna looking straight at her as if she were trying to communicate. Raising her eyebrows slightly, Angelica tried to indicate that she did not understand. Joanna kept staring at her, and then she lifted her hands to the clasp of her cloak.

Time slowed as Angelica watched her friend undo the golden hook of her cloak and let the material fall off her shoulders to reveal her nude form.

Her eyes wide, Angelica looked around the room quickly and saw Margaret repeat the gesture. A small mark above her navel attracted Angelica's attention until it dawned on her that she was meant to follow their lead!

Oh God, oh God!

Her gaze traveled to Alexander. She could see that his eyes had returned to their normal state, though he was not looking at her.

She could not hesitate or they would notice her reluctance!

Just don't think. Don't think. She reached her fingers up to undo her clasp.

It is better than drinking blood, she kept telling herself as she parted the material, *they might have made me drink blood.*

Lowering the wrap slowly over the back of the chair, Angelica felt goose bumps appear over her arms and chest. No man had ever looked upon her naked, and now seven of them saw her at the same time.

Shame threatened to creep into her chest, but she held it off. She understood that the other women in the room were not in the least disturbed, and that between vampires, what was happening was not the least bit shameful.

Picking a spot above Alexander's shoulder, Angelica stared into nothingness, trying to clear her head and separate herself from her nudity. She did not allow herself to think about anything other than the music.

The vampire with the goblet returned to the center of the circle, this time carrying an ornate bowl and a thick paint-brush. He approached Margaret first, and dabbed the brush inside the bowl, then raised it to draw a short line on her forehead.

When it was her turn, Angelica cleared her mind and con-centrated on feeling anything but the warm blood across her forehead.

Within seconds, the round was complete and all the women had been painted. The music changed once more, retaining its sensual sway as the man left the circle. For a moment, there was complete stillness, and then Margaret stood, her body beautiful in its pregnant fullness. She moved across the room, unperturbed that all eyes were on her, and stopped only when she reached the duke's chair. There she kneeled, and waited until James leaned forward, bringing his forehead against her painted one. The paint that had yet to dry left an identical brown line on James's skin as he helped his wife stand and took her out of the room.

The woman that had been sitting to the left of Margaret stood next; her blond tresses falling just below her shoulders. She was a golden goddess, every curve and line perfect. An-gelica saw her hesitate for a moment before walking toward Alexander.

No, Angelica thought with sudden fear as it occurred to her that she too would have to stand and kneel before a vampire. If the blond-haired woman took Alexander out of the room, she would be alone. She could not . . . Alexander could not leave her!

Only when the woman walked past Alexander and knelt in front of the vampire beside him did Angelica breathe again.

Joanna went next, her red curls flowing behind her as she made her way across to Kiril and knelt. Angelica saw Joanna's nod as her friend left the room and knew it was her turn.

She stood on shaky feet and commanded her body to move. Male and female eyes watched her as she walked toward Alexander. Only his eyes were averted from her body as he sat rigidly in his chair.

She breathed slowly as she walked. She wanted to know what he was thinking; she wanted to pull the hair that was flowing down her back so that it might cover her breasts. She wanted to know if he found her pleasing. She was wishing everyone else away.

In the end, none of her prayers were answered, except the one that had her quickly crossing the circle and kneeling in front of Alexander without incident. When he leaned forward and his hands cupped either side of her face, she closed her eyes and let him pull her up to touch his forehead with hers.

Images of red eyes and sharp teeth filled her head, but she pushed them away. Alexander was the man who had saved her life, and he was doing it yet again at that very moment.

He lifted her up from her position on the ground and held her hand in one of his own. His eyes held hers as Angelica listened to the next female stand up from her seat. She had done it! They would not find her out.

Her feet moved to follow as Alexander led her out of the room. They did not speak until they entered the guest chamber that had been given to her earlier.

With no thought to the darkness inside the room, she flew to the wardrobe and picked out her nightgown, putting it on in record time. Alexander moved to the windows, not once looking in her direction.

Everything crashed in on her at once. The slayer, red eyes, blood . . . With her back to the wall, she let herself slip to the floor, hugging her legs tightly.

Her tears streamed down her cheeks in silence, slipping from beneath closed lids.

Alexander said nothing as he came to her and lifted her in his arms, carrying her to the large bed across the room. She moved her hands around his neck and clung as he sat on the bed.

"It is over now," he whispered softly, his hands stroking her hair, her back, and her arms. She only held on tighter. She needed the warmth he gave her; she needed him.

Taking deep breaths, she calmed herself. All was well. She was with Alexander. He would not allow her to be hurt.

Feeling more composed, Angelica turned to him.

"I . . ." Words failed her and emotions overwhelmed her once more. She did not know where to begin, had no idea what to say first.

Alexander stroked her hair.

"You are tired, you should get some rest."

Angelica knew it was not sleep that she needed. She needed him this night, right this minute, more than she had ever needed anyone.

"Perhaps it is foolish, but I do not feel afraid now," she said softly.

"You need not be afraid when I am around, Angelica. I have told you that before."

She considered as she touched the cloak that covered his chest.

"What if you had already been picked?" She would have had to kneel in front of a strange man. A strange vampire who would expect her to leave with him and do what?

At Alexander's silence, she asked, "Where are all those couples that left the room?"

Alexander's eyes bore into hers for a moment before he returned to looking out of the window. "They are reaffirming life."

Angelica had known, but she had not wanted to admit it to herself. "You would have left me in that room if another woman chose you first?"

He did not look at her, but she could feel the tension building in his body.

"It could not have happened."

"And why is that? That blond vampire looked unsure," Angelica said, too drained to inject much head into the words.

"No one would touch you. They knew you were mine."

His. He must have lied to them to keep her safe, but he did not know that it was not as big a lie as he might think.

"Your engagement will be undone." Her eyes flew to his face, but his eyes were averted. It was the first time he mentioned the engagement. What was he saying? It was no question . . . It could not be. This was what she had wanted him to say, was it not? Perhaps he had not lied when he told them she was his.

"They believe we are 'reaffirming life'?" she asked.

Alexander only nodded in response.

"It is a part of the ceremony?"

He nodded once more, though more slowly this time.

Angelica bit her lip as she considered her next words. There was no use denying that she wanted the man. She wanted his arms around her, holding her, she wanted his lips on hers as before . . . she wanted him to make it so that she did not have to think of anything at all. Not the slayer, not the ceremony, she wanted to think of nothing but him and the feelings he could evoke. She wanted him to make it so that she would have no choice but to be with him.

"You are defying your laws."

Alexander looked at her, the moonlight from the window lighting his face allowing her to see the surprise in his eyes.

"What are you saying?"

She did not know what had come over her, perhaps it was the fear she had experienced in the woods, or the tension downstairs, but she suddenly found courage in herself she had not known she possessed.

"It is the law that you have to attend the ceremony, and yet you have not completed the last task."

Alexander continued looking at her, his expression intense and serious.

"I will not stop." The roughly spoken words caused a tingle of excitement in Angelica. She did not want him to stop this time. She did not want him to stop, ever.

She leaned away from him, looking into his eyes.

I want you.

She slipped the buttons of her nightgown out of their holes as she sent him the thought. Inch by inch the cloth parted to reveal her soft flesh.

I want you to kiss me like you did before.

She let her hand travel down her middle, pulling the material farther apart, giving Alexander a tantalizing view of the swell of her breasts.

I want you to touch me like you did before.

Using both hands she pushed the gown off of her shoulders and down her arms until it pooled around her waist.

Alexander sat silently watching, as she waited before him in her naked glory.

Lie down.

She obeyed his command, and moved beside him on top of the soft satin sheets. The cold material felt good on her burning skin. She closed her eyes, waiting for his next words.

You are so beautiful.

His thoughts were clear. She shivered as he kneeled between her legs and ran his hands along them, his strong fingers grasping her small waist and pulling her toward him.

The kiss was long and hard and had her panting for air.

"Alexander," she tried to speak, but he cut her off, pushing her back down and turning her over before she could catch her breath.

Angelica trembled as she tried to listen for his next move.

His hands were there once more, on her hair, pushing the tresses away from her slim back. He kissed her nape and she shivered.

Alexander, please . . .

His fingertips ran down her spine and over her backside, removing her gown and prompting her to turn into his arms.

He was naked, she realized as her sensitive breasts brushed against his hard chest. He was so powerful, so strong, and so hard all over. Before she could look her fill, he was kissing her once more, leaning over her.

His lips were potent; they took her breath away and made it so she could not think.

I can't wait, Angelica. Part your legs. Open for me.

She followed his command thoughtlessly, her stomach clenching as his weight settled against her. The nervousness began once more.

"Look at me."

It took a moment for her to realize that Alexander had spoken, but when she did she looked up at his face. She could not tell what he was thinking, could not even begin to guess and it made her want to squirm.

"Open your mind to me, Angelica."

"What?" she asked confused.

"Come into mine," he said, his face softening as he watched understanding rush through her.

Angelica moved away from her quiet place and let herself go. She entered Alexander's mind just as he did hers and their thoughts mingled.

Feeling his desire, her nervousness left her and she moved her arms down her back. It was as if she was sensing both of their feelings, completely confusing but absolutely wonderful at once.

Do not hold back any longer.

I do not want you to be scared.

Can you not see that there is no fear?

I want you so.

Come.

He entered her slowly. Angelica bit her lower lip as the sensations overwhelmed her. He was hurting her, stretching her to accommodate his size, but she also felt the pure explosive pleasure of being sheathed within her own warmth.

Alexander!

Alexander could not help pushing deeper. He felt her pain, and knew that it was almost gone.

Her hands slipped around his waist and pulled him toward her, and he was lost.

The rhythmic movement that gained in speed as every second sped by had Angelica on the verge of screaming. She could not stop the pressure that was building inside her.

Alexander growled deep in his throat as he felt her explode beneath him. Her pleasure pushed him over the edge, and Angelica cried out yet again as his feelings washed over her.

As her heartbeat slowed down, Alexander rolled them so that she was tucked in the crook of his arm.

"Alexander?" Her voice sounded sluggish to her own ears, and she realized how tired she was.

"Hmm?"

"Thank you."

He shifted beneath her and held her even tighter.

"Angelica?"

"Hmm?"

"Come with me to Moscow."

"I will need a warmer coat."

Angelica thought she heard him laugh as she gave in to sleep.

Chapter 28

"Good morning, Herrings, is my brother in?"

Herrings's jaw went slack and the surprise in his eyes made Angelica realize that she might have made a mistake.

"Herrings, is something the matter?"

"Forgive me, Princess, I just was unaware that you had left the house. I must have gotten confused."

Angelica realized belatedly that Herrings, like her brother, was being made to think she still lived at the house. How on earth Alexander's men managed to do this every day, she had no idea.

Feeling slightly guilty, Angelica put herself out to ease. "Do not worry yourself. I just now walked out when I realized I needed to speak with Mikhail. He is in, is he not?"

"I am afraid Prince Belanov left earlier this morning to attend to some business. He should be back shortly."

"That is quite all right." Angelica was so happy this morning that she did not mind if she had to wait hours for her brother's return. Alexander had agreed to let her come home as long as Kiril waited right outside the door, which was where the trusted Kiril was even now.

The thought of Alexander had her insides going warm. He had made love to her again at dawn, before he left the house.

Come with me. His words from the night before played in her head again and made her want to dance with joy. True, it was not exactly a marriage proposal, but that would come soon enough now that he had shown her that he wanted to be with her.

"Herrings, please tell Mikhail I am waiting for him in the music room when he comes."

"Yes, Princess." Herrings bowed formally.

Angelica had just finished a beautiful sonata by Tchaikovsky when she heard the door open behind her.

"Mikhail, thank God, I was growing old waiting for you."

"It is me, dear." Lady Dewberry's voice came to her in a hushed tone.

"Lady Dewberry! I am so glad to see you. I thought you made your way to your country home without telling us when I did not see you all of this past week." She stood to take her aunt's arm and guide her to the nearest chair.

"No, dear, I have been feeling a little under the weather that is all." Her aunt sniffled a little as she took the seat Angelica offered.

"I am sorry to hear that, Aunt. Shall I ring for some tea?"

"No, no, that is quite all right, dear." Clearing her voice, she took a deep breath as if to steady herself. "I came here to tell you something you likely should have heard a long time ago."

The coldness with which her aunt spoke surprised Angelica. She had never before seen such a serious expression on the older woman's face.

"What is it, Aunt?"

A faraway look in her eyes, Lady Dewberry began to speak.

"I told you before that your mother spent two years in those dreadful highlands. What I did not say was that she married while she was there.

Graham was a fine-looking man with the charm of the devil and your mother was so young. She stood no chance against him, and within a year of her arrival they were married. Your grandfather was in the Americas at the time, blissfully unaware of the huge mistake his oldest daughter was making, but I knew. I was there at their wedding.

Your mother kept insisting that she was blissfully happy. Graham was the laird of a beautiful castle. I can still see your mother's face as she showed me the grand room I was to stay in. . . ."

Angelica tried not to fidget as her aunt stopped speaking. She had never heard this story before, could not believe it in all honesty, but an unexplainable feeling inside made her want to know more.

"I was right. All my feelings of misgiving turned out to be correct. He was crazed.

"At first we did not notice, your mother especially refused to see it, but I knew. I caught him sneaking out of the house in the middle of the night to run through the woods. I saw him . . . I kept warning your mother that he was bound to hurt her, but she would not believe me." Lady Dewberry's eyes burned as she looked into Angelicas. "She did not believe me."

Seeming to recover herself, her aunt continued in a calmer tone. "We were all lucky. Graham disappeared one day. When your mother finally lost hope, she decided to return to London with me. At the time I did not realize her true reasons for returning, but six months after she married Dimitri Belanov, I knew."

"Knew what?" Angelica burst out with the question. She could not believe what she was hearing.

"She returned for you, Angelica. She knew her only chance at making a swift marriage was in London and she did not want you to be born fatherless."

"What?" the word came out as a mere whisper.

"Oh, my dear." Lady Dewberry reached across the space between them and held Angelica's face between her hands. "My dear. You must be grateful that you turned out so wonderfully normal. We are so lucky, so lucky. If you only knew, your father . . . he was a monster!"

Angelica moved out of her aunt's hold and stood. Words kept rolling around in her mind, and she could not get them to stop. She could not make sense of anything!

Alexander, she thought desperately. He would know what to do . . . he would know what all of this meant.

"I need to go," she said as she moved quickly to the door, uncaring that she was being unforgivably rude.

"Where are you going? Angelica, wait . . ." Her aunt stood to come after her, but Angelica would not stop. She could not stop. She walked swiftly past a wide-eyed Herrings and found Kiril waiting near the gate.

"I need to go to Alexander." She did not wait for him to reply as she stepped into the carriage. Kiril followed her in.

"I cannot take you there, Princess, Alexander would—"

"Please!" The word came out as a near scream and had Kiril backing away from her. "Please, Kiril, just take me to him."

After another silent moment, Kiril leaned out of the window and gave the driver instructions she could not make out. As the carriage rolled forward, Angelica leaned back and closed her eyes.

It couldn't be. Her father was not her father. Graham . . . a Scottish laird was her father, and he was . . . he was a monster?

"What is she doing here?" The anger in Alexander's voice was palpable as he ignored Angelica to address Kiril. His first reaction at seeing her coming into the third-floor apartment near the docks was happiness. Her mere presence made him want to push all of the people out of the room and kiss her until she would not mind being taken on the floor.

And for that precise reason, she had to leave.

"I need to speak with you."

Kiril held up his hands and stepped back, so that Alexander had no choice but to look at her. Beautiful, she was so damn beautiful to him. Upon further inspection, however, he saw the telltale signs of worry.

"What happened?"

Angelica looked at the vampires milling around a large table laden with maps. "Is there somewhere we can speak privately?"

Alexander grabbed her arm and steered her to a small back room.

"Speak."

"I went to speak with my brother this morning, as I told you I would, but Mikhail was not there."

Barely containing his impatience, Alexander waited for her to continue.

"I was waiting for him, when Lady Dewberry came and she told me . . . she told me that my father is actually not my father!"

Confused, Alexander brought his thumb and forefinger up to the bridge of his nose and rubbed.

"Angelica, you are not making sense."

"My mother was pregnant from another man when she married Dimitri Belanov."

"I see." Alexander tried to understand why this news was upsetting her this much. Yes, that must have been a shock, but as far as he knew, Dimitri Belanov was dead, so nothing much would likely change. Unless she knew who her real father was and wanted to find him. "And your father, do you know who he is?"

"I only have a first name, but I do not know how I would go about finding out who he was as he is dead. Unless Lady Dewberry would tell me—"

"Angelica." His patience at its limit, he cut her off. He would have liked to have been more sensitive and caring, but he had to find Sergey and the slayer before they killed more innocents, and in Alexander's mind that took precedence over this situation. "Can we talk about this later?"

She looked shocked at his suggestion and he soon understood why.

"You do not care?"

"Of course, I care about you . . ."

"No, I mean you do not mind?"

Was she speaking a different language? She made absolutely no sense to him.

"Why would I mind, Angelica?"

Angelica looked relieved. She laughed a little as she shrugged. "Oh, I don't know. I suppose other men might worry if they did not know whose offspring they were planning to marry. After all, my father could have been crazy, or sick or . . ."

"Marry?" The word was out of his mouth before he could reconsider. The silence that descended in the room was his first warning that he had erred.

"Angelica, I do not know how I might have given you the impression that I wanted to get married," he began hesitantly. Damn his unthinking mouth! He had not wanted to broach this subject. Not now, not before he had had time to explain to her about his duties to his clan.

"You made love to me."

Alexander cringed at the disbelief in her tone.

"Yes, I wanted you, Angelica. I want you still."

"But only as your personal whore, is that it?" Her sarcasm was designed to cut, and it did so. Alexander had no idea how they had gotten to this point, but the hurt in her eyes made him want to reach out and hold her although he knew she would not let him. Not now, not when she was obviously so angry.

"Angelica, you know that is not true."

"Fool, I've been such a fool!" She paced away from him, then turned back. "Why did you ask me to come with you to Moscow? Are there not enough women in Russia to take care of your needs, Prince Kourakin?"

His own temper began to boil. Not wanting to say anything he would later regret, he closed his eyes and waited silently for the anger to pass.

The slamming of the door had his eyes snapping open. Angelica was gone. He took a step to follow her, but stopped himself. She was too emotional to be able to speak rationally. Kiril would take her to his house, and later, when he was done working, he would explain things to her. But for now, he had to go back inside and try to work out who had been giving information to Sergey. Someone definitely was, since there was no other way he could have avoided being found for this long.

Chapter 29

Sergey paced his receiving room in frustration. Lady Joanna had not come to him with information in more than twenty-four hours. He was beginning to think that she would not come again, and that meant that his time was running out!

"How could you have botched it up so miserably? I gave you one task, one simple task. You were just going to kill that boy, and it would have been enough to anger Alexander."

No response came from the corner of the room where a figure sat in shadow.

"The boy is too well protected now. We need to aim higher. That woman ruined our plans. According to our Lady Joanna, she is under the prince's protection and lives under his roof. She must be Alexander's woman, so she must die." Sergey looked at the vampire slayer and felt an intense hatred he was hard-pressed not to show.

"You cannot do this one on your own. I will bring the bitch to you. All you will need to do is kill her. Do you think you can handle that?"

A scraping sound filled the room as the slayer stood and picked up the dagger lying on the table between them; it was a yes.

Chapter 30

"What the hell was Nicholas Adler doing at Margaret's today?"

Angelica grabbed at the towel she had just dropped beside the large tub and wrapped it around her.

"How dare you come in here without as much as a knock?"

Alexander shot her a look that clearly said *it is nothing I have not seen before* and continued as if she had not spoken. "I asked you a question, Angelica."

"And I asked you one." Angelica was not in the mood to back down. She had just spent an hour having tea with Nicholas, feeling like a horrible fraud. The fact that she had to marry him did not relieve her mind at all. Standing in front of her, his gray eyes flashing anger, was the man she truly wanted. Somehow she would forget him and perhaps even learn to love Nicholas . . . perhaps.

Sighing audibly, Alexander pinched the bridge of his nose. "This is my house; I do as I want here. Now answer me, if you please."

"I invited Nicholas for tea; that is what he was doing there."

Although Alexander did not move, Angelica got the impression that he was holding himself back.

"Are you trying to drive me mad?" The quiet tone of the question should have warned her that Alexander's anger was at its boiling point, but Angelica ignored it.

"I fail to see what this has to do with you at all."

He took a step toward her, and to her utter shame Angelica stepped back. She was not afraid of him, she was afraid of herself. If Alexander touched her, she could very well break down and beg him to reconsider.

"Angelica, you are mine. When you take tea with other men, it does concern me!"

"I am not yours!" The half scream surprised them both, but Angelica forged on. "And the other man you speak of asked me to marry him and I accepted."

"That is it, isn't it, Angelica? You are going to him, because I cannot marry you!"

"You will not marry me! There is a difference, Alexander."

Raking his fingers through his hair, Alexander paced across the carpet.

"I cannot marry you, Angelica. Just listen to me." He stopped to indicate a small ottoman near her feet. "Just sit for a moment and listen to me."

Plopping down angrily, Angelica pulled the towel more firmly around her body and cursed her partial nudity. Why did they have to have such a conversation at this moment of all moments? Not having clothes on made her feel defenseless.

"You must have gathered that our race is dying out," Alexander began.

Angelica nodded.

"And we only become fertile when we reach our fifth century."

"Alexander, just say what you mean," Angelica said impatiently.

"Vampires and humans cannot procreate, Angelica. I have a duty to sire children, and I cannot have them with you. I have to marry a vampire."

His explanation silenced her. Vampires and humans could not make babies . . . she could never have Alexander's child. She would never be a mother, never hold her baby in her arms.

Angelica had always wanted children, but only faced with the possibility of never being able to have them, did she realize just how much.

And yet, yet, she wanted, no needed, Alexander far more. A life without children would be difficult, but a life without Alexander would be unbearable.

Her eyes were sad as she regarded the harassed man in front of her. She could see that he cared, it was right there in his face . . . and perhaps that hurt more than anything. He cared; he wanted her, but not enough. It just was not enough.

"I love you, Alexander," she said the words softly. "And I do not know if you love me. You have never said so, but if maybe you do, even if you do . . . you simply don't love me enough." His expression never changed, his eyes never wavered. It was as if he had not heard her and she could not bear it.

"Leave me please; I need to prepare for a ball and am running late as it is."

Alexander looked at her for a moment more, before he turned on his heel and left.

The room felt as though it had turned cold, Angelica noticed as she sat there unmoving on the ottoman. The mirror on the opposite side of the room revealed a face that might have belonged to someone else. It was the visage of someone without hope; a hollow someone.

Angelica walked toward it, the towel fisted at her breast.

"What are you doing?" The question bounced off the walls and came at her with a force that had her loosening her grip. Her eyes followed the white material as it fell down her body and pooled at her feet.

Tears blurred her vision and fell unheeding of her desire to be strong.

"Stop crying, you ninny. Pull yourself together, for God's sake." *If only tears would listen*, she thought as she pulled her hand roughly against her cheeks.

A dark dot on the mirror caught her eye and had Angelica reaching out to brush it away.

"What?" The dot moved as she reached out and had her looking down at her stomach. There, right above her belly button was a black mark.

"It can't be."

In a daze, Angelica crossed to the bedside table and picked up the thick black book. Heedless of her nakedness, she sat and turned pages until she found what she was looking for.

"And when the Vampire comes of age, and finds herself with child, she carries on her lower stomach the mark of our ancestors."

Angelica's eyes took in the drawing at the bottom of the page and closed her eyes.

There in front of her was a picture of a half moon with a circle inside, the same mark she now carried.

Running her finger over the stain, she rubbed. Slow at first, then faster.

"Come on . . . ," she mumbled as she pressed harder, leaving red blotches across her skin, but the offending mark would not come off.

Pregnant. The word played in her head over and over until she felt like laughing hysterically. The irony of it all was priceless. Alexander wouldn't marry her because he claimed that humans couldn't have vampire children and here she was . . . pregnant!

Now what was she supposed to do? She could hardly marry Nicholas in this condition. She was going to have to tell Mikhail about their finances.

What if he got sick? Damn it! She would not marry Alexander, not when he had refused her . . . it would kill her to be with him when she would always know that he had only wanted her because of the baby. But, what if Mikhail got sick? Perhaps she could marry Nicholas, anyway?

Her mother had been pregnant when she married her father; but no, she could not do that to Nicholas. At least her mother was pregnant with a normal child.

Oh God! Oh God! Oh God! She was going to give birth to a vampire!

Losing her balance, she fell to the ground and retched.

Chapter 31

Angelica avoided acquaintances as she walked around the ballroom, looking for Mikhail. She spotted Joanna with several of her friends, speaking animatedly. Not feeling up to smiling for strangers, she walked the opposite way toward a plant she had seen earlier.

It reminded her of the one she had hidden behind only a short while ago, though it felt like years had passed. It was behind that plant she had first laid eyes on Alexander. It was there that she met Nicholas.

How odd to think that her life had changed into what it was, because she had decided to hide behind a pair of gigantic leaves.

Angelica reached out to touch the thin bark of plant, noticing how fragile it was. Little spots, due most likely to some type of pest, littered several of the leaves, while yet others had curled as if kept too long in the sun. And yet the plant stood tall.

That was what life was about, was it not? Standing tall, even when things became heated or when others wore away at your restraint.

"Care to dance?"

She turned. Nicholas stood a few paces away, just as he had so long ago. Angelica did not feel ready to face him, to tell him that she could not be with him. But, he did not wait for an answer, coming to take her hand before she could formulate a denial.

Feeling defensive and edgy, Angelica realized that she could resort to sarcasm as she was wont to do, but decided against it. She did not need sarcasm or big leaves or moonlit rides across grassy fields any longer. Angelica Shelton Belanov was through hiding from the world. She would be a mother soon.

"How are you?" Nicholas asked as they began their dance.

"Fine, thank you," she replied smoothly. "And you?"

Nicholas held his silence, his eyes slipping from hers only to return a moment later. "Well, although I will be better when you tell me what the matter is."

"You are right, I do not feel well, Nicholas. There is something I have to tell you."

"What is it, love? What has you so upset?"

Did he have to be so sweet? Angelica suppressed the urge to run as he turned them smoothly about the ballroom.

She breathed slowly, and turned her face to look at his.

"I cannot marry you, Nicholas."

His step faltered, but he recovered quickly.

"Why?"

Angelica contemplated all the possible reasons she could tell him. She thought of plenty of excuses, but none of them would suffice. Nicholas had never been anything but wonderful to her and he deserved the truth.

"I am pregnant." Her body tensed, ready for Nicholas to leave her then and there and walk off. Or perhaps he would cause a scene, call her names and then leave. She would not be surprised, nor would she blame him. How had things gotten so out of hand?

"Are you going to marry him?"

The question surprised her. How did he manage to stay so calm? Was he not angry?

"No."

She felt his shoulder lift under her left hand and knew he was trying to calm himself.

"And you will not change your mind tomorrow?"

Angelica did not understand where he was going with his questions, but she did not refuse him answers. He deserved that, and so much more.

"Perhaps it is unfair to withhold his identity, but you deserve to know that he and I will never marry. He does not want me, Nicholas."

"You love him? No . . . don't answer that. I do not wish to know. We can work through this. Marry me, Angelica, now, today, and your child will be mine."

Tears gathered in Angelica's eyes as she shook her head in denial.

"I cannot, Nicholas. I cannot do that—"

Nicholas cut her off before she could finish, "Don't say you can't do that to me. If this is only about me, I will tell you,

Angelica, I love you. The worst thing you could do to me is leave me. This is not about me, so what is it about? Do you just not wish to marry me?"

If only he would get angry, Angelica thought desperately. His anger would be so much easier to deal with than the terrible sadness in his voice.

"I am sorry, Nicholas."

Nicholas stopped their movement as he walked them to the edge of the dance floor and kissed her hands. When he looked into her eyes, the expression on his face nearly broke Angelica's heart.

"You do love him." He looked away, toward the large double doors that opened up to the ballroom and spoke without looking at her. "I do not wish to leave you, but I have to. My heart hurts, Angelica. It hurts for your hurts and mine. I told you that I will accept you, child and all, but I do not want you to regret marrying me."

"Nicholas," she said softly as she pushed a lock of hair away from his eyes. "I don't know what to say."

"I am sorry, darling; I have put you in a position where there really is nothing you can say. If you change your mind, you know where to find me."

He bowed to her and walked away.

Angelica felt as though she had taken an ice-cold bath. Goose bumps formed on her arms and her hands shook.

"Angelica?"

Was she to get no peace this day? Pasting a fake smile on her face, Angelica turned to her brother.

"I have been looking all over for you," she said lightly, all the while fighting the rising bile. She had just broken the heart of a good man, a wonderful man. God, she wanted

to crawl under her covers and sleep. She could not marry
for money anymore. She was pregnant and now she had to
think of a way to tell Mikhail that they would be broke very
soon!

Mikhail's grin was carefree and had Angelica wishing she
could throw herself in her brother's arms and ask him to slay
all her dragons as he had once promised to do.

"Sorry, I didn't mean to keep you waiting. I'm glad that
you came with the duchess, though, because I got held up
at home."

"Really, what happened?" Eyeing the empty terrace, Angelica wondered how she could convince her brother to let
her get some air on her own. She wanted to be on her own so
badly, she was prepared to tell all sorts of lies to manage it.

"The oddest thing, really. Mr. Hoisington turned up just
as I was leaving, you remember him, don't you? He was our
father's solicitor."

Her heart in her mouth, Angelica held her breath.

"Well, he came, blabbering something about ships and
how I should be praising the Lord because they had been
found. I really have no idea what he was talking about, but
after I got the old man to calm down, he told me our ships
had returned and with so many goods that the enterprise has
made far above the amount that was predicted." Wiggling his
brows at his sister, Mikhail leered. "Now that we have all this
new loot, I suppose you are going to raid the jewelry stores."

"Mikhail, I need some air." The relief that Angelica felt
was overwhelming, turning her legs into jelly.

"Are you all right?" Mikhail turned serious as he took
her arm.

"Yes, yes. It is just too stuffy in here. The fresh air will do me good, I am sure."

They got to the balcony, which to Angelica's delight was still empty.

"Mikhail, I don't want to sound rude, but would you mind very much leaving me alone?"

Frowning, Mikhail looked out toward the dark gardens. "I don't think that is wise, Angelica."

"Please? I won't be long," she promised. "Just let me have two minutes to myself before I must join the gossiping women surrounding the duchess."

Mikhail nodded reluctantly, and walked back into the ballroom. "Don't be long."

"I will not." Angelica turned her back to the crowd inside and released a small sigh. Her emotions were so confused that she could hardly form a coherent thought.

Not wanting to be seen, she moved to the right corner of the terrace, a shadow falling over her face as she reached the railing. She was tired, so tired of all the parties and balls. Tired of the murderous plots and vampires and humans.

"Free." She said the word with reverence. She did not have to marry any longer. She did not have to dress up and dance any longer. She was free to go back to their country estate. There she could raise her baby and forget. Forget the pain she caused Nicholas, forget the intrigues . . . forget Alexander.

Leaning her arms on the vine-shaped balustrade she looked out toward the shadow-filled grounds. Being on the terrace alone was her act of defiance, her way of doing something wrong to rid herself of the pain she was feeling. Did that even make sense?

"Hello, Princess, let me introduce myself. My name is Sergey."

Angelica only had time to take a breath before she was dragged forward and over the railing.

"Where is she?"

Margaret turned at the urgency in the voice. "Alexander? When did you arrive, you mischievous man? It really is not—"

Alexander cut her off as his eyes scanned the ballroom. "Margaret, I really don't have time for pleasantries. I am looking for Angelica. Where is she?"

The duchess regarded him with interest. "She was dancing with Nicholas a little while ago, I am sure he will return her any minute now."

Frowning, Alexander scanned the dance floor. It had not taken him long to realize that he could not be without her, but his Angelica was always a step ahead. "What is she doing with him, anyhow?"

"He is her fiancé, what can be more normal than for her to dance with him?" Margaret too looked around the dance floor for the young woman she had come to view as a daughter.

"Not for long."

"What was that?" The duchess refocused her attention on the man beside her. Alexander had seemed angry to her a moment earlier, but now he looked his usual self: unemotional and in control.

"I said he will not be her fiancé for long."

Margaret frowned at the news. "Why ever not?"

"Because she is going to marry me."

"What?" If she had tried, Margaret could not have looked more surprised. "What do you mean?"

Margaret watched as Alexander made one last scan of the area and then turned toward her. What she saw had her taking a step forward before she could stop herself. Alexander Kourakin, the man who showed no emotions, the man who was always in control was smiling.

"I am going to ask her to marry me."

"What was that you said?" James questioned as he stepped up beside his wife.

"Alexander is going to ask our Angelica to marry him," Margaret spoke with disbelief.

James looked from his wife to his friend, then frowned. "You will have no offspring?"

"I cannot think straight when the woman is beside me, but I cannot think at all when she is gone. My first duty to my clan, ahead of producing offspring, is to be a good leader. Without her, I cannot be."

Laughter surrounded them as James clapped Alexander on the back. "Well, I'll be damned! You love her, don't you?"

It was Alexander's turn to look baffled.

Leaning to place a kiss on her husband's cheek, Margaret joined his laughter. "I believe he just realized it himself."

"Well, where is the girl?" James asked as he looked around him.

"She was dancing . . ."

A voice blasted through Alexander's head.

Alexander.

"She is here, I just heard her voice!" Alexander interrupted Margaret's explanation.

James looked around then at him. "She is nowhere in sight, Alexander. Do not worry. Kiril is likely with her, or Mikhail. She will probably come back in a moment."

"Duchess?" Mikhail Belanov approached them hesitantly.

"Well hello, Mikhail, is something the matter?" Margaret asked as she took in the concern on the young prince's face.

"Not exactly." Casting an apologetic glance toward the men Mikhail continued. "I just cannot seem to find my sister. She was on the terrace a few moments ago, said she wanted to get some air, but she has disappeared."

A sickening feeling settled in Alexander's stomach. There was something wrong, something . . .

Alexander.

Alexander ran.

Chapter 32

Alexander! Angelica screamed for him, over and over as the pain exploded at her throat.

Sergey pulled his teeth out of her soft skin and let her body fall to the ground. The bitch had fought harder than he expected and had managed to tear his favorite shirt.

"Spiteful little whore!"

Angelica moaned as he grabbed her from where she lay at his feet and tore at her dress. The material fell away to reveal a thin white shift, but she barely noticed. The hot pain from her throat was the only thing she could think about. She did not notice the cold, damp grass beneath her feet, or the distant sound of music. Random lights had been placed around the gardens, illuminating flowers and fountains, but she noticed none of them. All she knew was pain.

Cruel hands gripped the top of her shift. Angelica felt his sharp nails pierce her skin as he began to tear.

"What are you doing?"

The familiar voice had her blinking upward, trying to see behind Sergey's tall frame.

"Leaving her helpless, so there is no room for you to mess this up," Sergey said over his shoulder.

"Leave her, she will not get away."

To Angelica's surprise, Sergey's hands left her as he moved aside to address the figure shrouded in darkness.

"Quickly then, kill her and go back to the party. They will soon catch the scent of blood and come looking."

Angelica caught the glint of a sharp object as the slayer moved into a patch of light.

"W-w-why?" Blood still seeping from her throat, Angelica stared dizzily at the woman in the green ball gown.

"I prayed. I prayed that I would not have to do this one day, but you disappointed me, Angelica. I should have guessed you would turn out like your father: a monster!"

Sergey's departure barely registered as black dots formed in front of Angelica's eyes.

"I do not understand. Aunt Dewberry, please. I need a doctor. . . ."

Grotesque laughter surrounded her befuddled mind as Lady Dewberry knelt close to her ear.

"Your father did not disappear, Angelica. I killed him. I killed him because he was a vampire. And now I will kill you, because you are a monster too!"

Angelica watched the knife that her aunt raised high above her head and gave in to the darkness that beckoned her.

* * *

Alexander jumped from the side of the terrace and ran into the dark garden. The scent of blood was strong, though Sergey's trace was disappearing quickly. He tried not to recognize the sweet smell of Angelica's skin as he neared a particularly dark corner of the yard, but there was no avoiding it.

His mind went numb as he saw her body; sprawled on the grass, blood pouring from her neck.

"Angelica." His voice was hoarse with pain as he knelt by her side. Her eyes flittered open, and he could see that she was conscious, though barely. He recognized the sheen of pain in her eyes but could do nothing. Nothing!

"I will get you a doctor, sweetheart. You will be fine, don't worry."

"*Aaa* . . . ," Angelica made gurgling noises as she tried to speak.

"No, love, just rest now . . ." His words were cut off as a shriek was followed by a burst of pain in his chest. Alexander looked into Angelica's terror-filled eyes and then down to where the end of a long dagger showed through his chest.

"Die, you bastard!" Lady Dewberry's maniacal shriek echoed around the gardens and in Alexander's ears.

"A . . . Alex . . ." Tears streamed freely down her cheeks as Angelica reached for his face. Swinging his arm around his back, Alexander grabbed the hilt of the knife and dragged it out of his flesh.

"No!" Lady Dewberry came at him, intent on retrieving the knife so she could stab him until she was certain of his death. Alexander stayed put; the only part of his body that moved was his right hand.

The dagger found its mark in Lady Dewberry's heart. The slayer fell dead into a nearby bush.

"Alexander!" James was by his side, his eyes on Angelica's quiet form.

"She needs a doctor," Alexander got out. The path the knife had taken through his chest burned as it healed.

James felt Angelica's waning pulse as the others appeared. The blood on her neck had dried, but the knife wound near her heart looked irreparable.

"Angelica?" Joanna screamed as she threw herself down beside her friend. She saw the marks on her neck and stood shakily.

"I know where he is."

Alexander, James, and Margaret stared, but it was Kiril who spoke.

"Move."

The two of them disappeared into the night.

"James, the doctor!" Alexander said, his face tight with anguish, but James could only shake his head. It was too late.

"It is too late . . ."

Unwilling to listen, Alexander tore at his shirt quickly. Cradling her head in his lap, he pulled away the torn material of her shift and pressed the makeshift pad on the deep gash.

"Alexander?" Panting, Mikhail came running from the direction of the house. "What is going on? You ran like a crazed man and then . . . Angelica!"

Mikhail tried to push Alexander out of the way when he noticed his sister lying on the ground, but James held him back.

"Let go, man, or I swear I will kill you!"

Alexander turned pained eyes at the furious man. "I am trying to keep the blood from flowing! Now pull yourself together. If you have an attack and cause her more pain when she wakes up, I swear *I* will kill *you*!"

Face the color of ash, Mikhail stopped struggling and stepped out of James's grasp.

"Did you call for a doctor?" His voice was labored as he crouched beside her.

"The flow has eased, but she has lost too much blood; a doctor would not get here in time," Alexander said, his voice harsh with emotion. It was the first time he admitted to himself that she would likely die. Mikhail's rapid heartbeat rang in his head and had him grabbing the man by his collar. "Calm down!"

"Alexander, please!" Margaret came forward as Mikhail pushed his hands away.

"She will not die!" Grief clouding his mind, Mikhail slipped his arms under Angelica's body and began lifting her. Alexander stopped him with a hand on his shoulder.

"What the hell are you doing?"

"Taking her away from here, now let her go!"

"No," Alexander said as he tried to stand, but his body was taking longer to regenerate than he had anticipated. He needed blood.

"You are hurt!" Mikhail stammered as he saw the blood that covered his friend's chest.

Alexander made sure the hole was covered by his hand as he tried to lend strength to his voice.

"I am fine; a small scratch."

"A small scratch, indeed. You, Prince Kourakin, will die and very soon."

Alexander closed his eyes briefly as the voice he had not heard in over a century pulsed in his ears. Kiril and Joanna moved forward with the villain, their faces inscrutable.

"I challenge you, leader of the Eastern Clan!"

"No one will fight you, Sergey. You will be judged by the leaders!" Margaret roared her anger.

Sergey's laughter filled the ominous silence. "It is the law. A challenge to the leader cannot be ignored."

"Take your sister and get out of here," Alexander spoke softly. Mikhail stood uncomprehending as he stared at Sergey.

"You do not need to fight!" Margaret called to Alexander, but it was too late for that now. Sergey lunged for him. Expecting the impulsive move, Alexander stepped aside and swung Sergey by his arms so that the vampire landed several paces away.

"Now, Mikhail," Alexander said as he gave the man a shove. Sergey recovered swiftly and began to circle him.

"Come on then, leader. Let us see what you can do!" Sergey smiled at him with glee.

"Let me . . ." Mikhail attempted to speak, but was cut short by an angry growl.

"I said now!" Alexander shouted, his pointed teeth gleaming in the moonlight as he charged the smiling vampire.

Mikhail watched horrified as the men collided in midair, each one grasping the other with impossible strength. The teeth, the blood . . . they were in the air! Mikhail couldn't move, his eyes fixed on the two figures who fought to the death before him.

"Move out of the way, Mikhail!" It was Joanna's voice. He had not heard her approach, but now as he looked to his left he noticed several other figures in the dark: the duchess, the duke, that Kiril fellow who always hung around Alexander, and several others who seemed to have only just appeared. It was as if he had come out of a trance. He looked down at the figure of his listless sister, and tears filled his eyes.

"I . . ."

Isabelle laid a hand on his arm. "There will be time for explanations later, move back now."

Mikhail nodded, but as he attempted to readjust his sister in his arms, Kiril appeared from his right and took her from him. He did not know what was happening, he had no idea who these people were, but resisting them was not a choice, so he moved back.

Pain ripped through Alexander as his head cracked against a tree. Feeling the blood trickle from a gash on the side of his waist, he cursed.

Shaking his head, he moved toward Sergey once more. A large rock flew toward him and neatly missed his ear as he jumped to the side, rolling quickly back up to his feet.

"Alexander?" It was James's voice. Alexander knew his friends were around him, but he also knew they would not touch Sergey unless he asked them to.

He would not ask them to. This was personal, it had become that way the moment Sergey laid his hands on Angelica.

"Give yourself up!" he shouted at Sergey.

He was cut up and bleeding but none of that was important. He felt only anger as the image of Angelica's bleeding body clouded his mind. It made him numb to his wounds, it made him strong.

"Give myself up? To you, Alexander? Why would I do such a thing?" Sergey snarled, his eyes glowing bright red with an insane light. He was stronger than Alexander had anticipated, likely due to the wildness that came from drinking human blood.

Taking three quick steps, Alexander hurled himself into the air and came down on Sergey. Their hands clasped on each other's arms as their incisors grew. Alexander pushed hard, his muscles straining to get Sergey on the floor.

A powerful kick nearly threw him off balance, but he held on and brought his opponent down to his knees. Sergey grabbed his legs in an attempt to throw him off, but succeeded only in breaking several of his bones.

With a swift elbow in Sergey's ear, Alexander had him feeling disoriented, and taking advantage of the brief opening, he grabbed his neck.

"Alexander!"

Sergey's voice held fear, but Alexander was beyond pity, toughening his resolve as he squeezed the pliable skin under his hands.

"Please."

It was a desperate plea. Alexander's eyes were drawn to the crowd of vampires surrounding him. Seeing Angelica's listless body in Kiril's arms clinched his resolve.

"It is too late for please." With those last words, he sunk his teeth into Sergey's neck. Sergey's fingers clawed at his hands, but to no avail.

The blood filled his mouth and Alexander spat it out knowing the vampire blood would make him sick. He bit down again and felt the life fading from the man in his arms.

When Sergey's hands fell to his sides, Alexander let go, allowing the villain's body to fall listless to the floor.

James moved to Alexander's side while Margaret signaled one of her clan members to take Sergey's body. Alexander had not killed him; she had known he would not. One could not kill in a challenge, and just as she had guessed, her old friend was too bound by the laws of the vampire to ignore them even in the highest rage.

Sergey would be put on trial, and after being judged for breaking vampire law, he would be hanged.

"Alexander." James stopped. He did not know what else to say.

Spotting Kiril, Alexander moved to him without a word. He was healing quickly, but he felt torn inside.

"Is she . . ." He couldn't bring himself to say the words. Kiril held the woman in his arms to his prince, who took her tenderly.

The soft pulse he felt radiating from Angelica's body did nothing to lighten Alexander's heart. He stood, holding her body close as the others watched.

"Alexander," Margaret said softly from behind him. Alexander did not want to listen, he did not want to think; he only wanted to feel Angelica in his arms.

"Alexander . . ." The sad tone in Margaret's voice triggered a memory. Angelica's voice. He had heard her voice in the ballroom. She had called his name, in heartbreaking tones . . . how could it be? Such a connection was only possible between life mates . . . between vampires.

"What is that?" Margaret was pointing at Angelica's body. She moved closer and removed the last of the tattered pieces of material, leaving Angelica's body revealed to the night air.

"Alexander?"

James moved closer as Alexander looked at the mark above Angelica's navel.

"It can't be." Margaret shook her head as her hand traveled to her stomach.

"She was a virgin before me," Alexander whispered.

James cast a quick glance around the garden to make sure the others were keeping their distance. He too could not seem to believe his eyes. "What you are suggesting is . . . what are you saying?"

Alexander turned tortured eyes to Margaret. "She did not know who her real father was . . . is it possible? How could it be possible?"

Margaret froze as she tried to come to terms with what she was seeing. Everything she knew about vampires and humans told her the child could not possibly be Alexander's . . . but her woman's intuition said yes. "I do not know how it could be, but I believe it is true."

Alexander could not resist the hope that filled his heart. He did not hesitate as he called for Mikhail.

"I need your help."

Mikhail stepped forward and held himself still. He did not know who or what the man in front of him was, and he was trying his hardest to keep his heart from spiraling out of control, but none of that could stop him from approaching Alexander. The man held his sister in his arms.

"What can I do?"

"She needs blood." Alexander spoke without blinking. Joanna and Kiril looked at each other and several others stepped closer.

Mikhail's face reflected distrust and horror. Alexander understood the impulse, but had no time to waste.

"I would give her my own blood, but it will not heal her. You are the only human here, Mikhail. Without your blood she will die. Angelica will die." Looking at the woman in his arms he drew in a deep breath. "I do not want to force you, but I will."

"Alexander, what on earth are you doing?" James asked incredulously, worried that his friend may have lost his sanity.

Alexander ignored him, his eyes never leaving Mikhail's. A long moment passed before Mikhail nodded.

"How?"

Alexander crouched and laid Angelica's nude body softly on the ground. Motioning Mikhail beside him, he reached for the man's arm and tore the bottom of his sleeve.

"This may hurt a little," Alexander warned.

Mikhail looked at the man who was more a stranger to him now than ever before. He did not know what made him trust the man. Perhaps it was the concern he saw reflected in Alexander's eyes. Perhaps it was the love.

"Save her."

Alexander averted his face and let his incisors grow. Before Mikhail had a chance to feel fear at the sight of the two pointed teeth, the vampire bit into his wrist.

Mikhail's face lost all color as Alexander dragged his arm over Angelica's lips.

"Alexander, what are you doing?" James moved forward but Margaret put his arm out to stop him. "Margaret?"

"He has to try," Margaret said slowly. She could not believe that what Alexander was doing would work, but she knew that her friend had to exhaust every possibility before he would accept his love's death.

The air grew warm as the vampires gathered around the

three figures on the floor. The seconds ticked by, and as the darkness was chased away by the first rays of dawn, Mikhail's voice pierced the silence.

"The wounds!"

Joanna kneeled quickly beside Angelica and followed Mikhail's gaze. The marks on her neck had all but disappeared, and the cut above her heart was closing. But that meant . . .

"Alexander?" Margaret whispered reverently.

James watched Angelica's face. Where it had once been pale, it now looked healthy. Her brother on the other hand looked as if he was about to faint.

"Is she one of us?" Joanna asked at long last.

Alexander traced the ancient symbol of their race on his beloved's stomach and shed a tear.

"No, she is the Blessed."

Angelica opened her eyes.

Chapter 33

Angelica stood with one hand covering her rounded stomach and the other firmly grasping Alexander's hand. The past weeks had been the most difficult and wondrous of her life. After her near brush with death she had asked to return to Polchester Hall, and Alexander had not disappointed her. Her brother and Alexander accompanied her home.

Getting over the fact that her aunt had killed her father, and gotten very close to killing her, had not been easy. It took even longer for her to accept that she might be the Blessed, and in all honesty Angelica had resisted the idea until Margaret had convinced her that there was no other way that Alexander's baby was growing in her belly.

Are you all right?

Alexander's voice pulled her back to the present. She had still not gotten used to being able to speak to him in her mind. No matter where he was, she could communicate with him; he was truly her life mate.

Her love for Alexander made everything worthwhile, but

she could not help being afraid. She looked around her at the hundreds of unfamiliar faces. They were there to see her, to bear witness to the prophecy. It was unnerving to be a prophecy, unnerving to be standing on a platform of stone, surrounded by hundreds of vampires.

You have no reason to be afraid.

Angelica nodded. The wind blew, scattering her hair behind her and pushing the black cloak she wore more firmly against her stomach.

"Angelica?" Having finished his lengthy speech, James turned to her. He was asking her to step forward, to the edge of the large stone, so that she could be seen by all who had come to witness the spectacle. Angelica looked at the two other leaders who stood beside him. Isabelle gave her an encouraging smile while Ismail looked on with something akin to reverence.

Shall we, my love?

Alexander would not let go of her hand, she realized with some relief. With him by her side she could do anything.

She stepped forward, to the edge of the stone, and was met by complete silence. Looking down at the crowd she spotted Joanna and Kiril. Her friend had stood trial for aiding Sergey, but due to her part in apprehending him later her sentence was reduced to what Alexander described as "open prison." After the ceremony she was to be taken to a residence in Romania where she would have to stay in confinement for fifty years. Joanna had accepted the sentence without flinching. Her friend smiled at her now, but Angelica was too nervous to form a similar expression. It was as if everyone present was expecting her to say something or do something.

What am I supposed to do? She sent the thought frantically, hoping that Alexander would help her.

It is up to you, my love.

What do you mean? Alexander, help me, I do not know what to say!

Her frantic thoughts were met with silence. Angelica slid her hand out of Alexander's grasp. She would not be afraid, these were her people. Her father was one of them and her child . . . Her child would be one of them.

Closing her eyes against the sting of tears she slid her hands over her stomach and held tight. Her baby was one of them.

"Blessed!" a voice came from the crowd. Angelica opened her eyes slowly. The crowd was kneeling; one by one the vampires bent their knees and bowed their heads. Worried she had made a mistake, Angelica turned to Alexander and found him on his knees with the other leaders.

Alexander's eyes shown with pride as he looked up at her.

You are their hope, my love, and our child is the salvation of my race.

"Blessed." The word reverberated among the trees and far off into the distance, *"Blessed!"*

Angelica let the word travel over her skin as she tipped her head toward the sky.

The smile came slowly, then took over her face as she let her eyes close.

Does that mean you want to marry me?

Alexander suppressed a laugh with some difficulty.

You are in my mind, my love, can you not see the answer to your question?

biography

Hande Zapsu, who writes as Mina Hepsen, was born in Istanbul, Turkey. To her parents' surprise (and frequently misfortune) she began to speak at six months old. Soon she was telling stories of crazy monkeys who jumped on people from tall trees (some blame it on her horoscope signs: Leo with Scorpio rising). After spending the first ten years of her life in Germany (where she became addicted to pretzels and roasted chicken), Mina's parents moved her back to Istanbul (her father had made the transition from businessman to politician), and she studied there at an international school.

Ten years later Mina was wearing six layers of fleece, two scarves, a hat, mittens, and four pairs of socks on top of each other in Boston, Massachusetts. Four years after that (when she had grown truly comfortable with the idea of black ice and freak snowstorms) she graduated from Tufts University with a degree in political science and philosophy. Having had enough of the cold weather, she then moved to Miami, Florida, where she was a regular of Books & Books, a store that would open bright and early and make the best fresh lemonades and organic spinach soups.

A year after that, Mina felt it was time to move again, and so, after receiving a pop-up e-mail in her Hotmail account saying "Come to Edinburgh!" she decided "Why not?" and moved to Scotland. She spent the next year carting her stuff around various cafés in Old Town, writing a series of children's books, doing a master's degree in Creative Writing at the University of Edinburgh, and trying to convince her two younger sisters not to grow up.

Who knows where she is now . . .